DARKNESS VISIBLE

DARKNESS VISIBLE

A Lambert and Hook Mystery

J.M. Gregson

This first world edition published 2009
in Great Britain and in the USA by
SEVERN HOUSE PUBLISHERS LTD of
9–15 High Street, Sutton, Surrey, England, SM1 1DF.
Trade paperback edition published
in Great Britain and the USA 2010 by
SEVERN HOUSE PUBLISHERS LTD

British Library Cataloguing in Publication Data

Gregson, J. M.
  Darkness Visible.
  1. Lambert, John (Fictitious character) – Fiction. 2. Hook,
  Bert (Fictitious character) – Fiction. 3. Police – England –
  Gloucestershire – Fiction. 4. Extortion investigation –
  Fiction. 5. Detective and mystery stories.
  I. Title
  823.9'14-dc22

ISBN-13: 978-0-7278-6798-8   (cased)
ISBN-13: 978-1-84751-166-9   (trade paper)

All Severn House titles are printed on acid-free paper.

Typeset by Palimpsest Book Production Ltd.,
Grangemouth, Stirlingshire, Scotland.
Printed and bound in Great Britain by
MPG Books Ltd., Bodmin, Cornwall.

To John and Frances Milburn, who have supported me over many years with enthusiasm and a wealth of lively comment!

'No light, but rather darkness visible'
Milton, *Paradise Lost*, Book One

ONE

He preferred the winter. It suited his personality, as well as what he did. He told himself again that he should rejoice in the summer warmth. He ran his fingers over the thin flesh of his arms, feeling them warm, assured himself that June was a comfortable month. But the wish was skin-deep; his mind yearned for the winter dark.

The silhouette of Gloucester Cathedral rose above him against a summer sky which still held the last vestiges of light. At ten thirty on this balmy evening, you could see no detail save the massive outline, soaring away towards the deepening navy of the infinity above.

A neutral, pitiless infinity, Darren Chivers told himself contemptuously. Not that all-seeing, all-knowing heaven which had dominated the thoughts of those ignorant builders and the peasants who had flocked in to gaze at their handiwork. The cathedral was a vain leap, not towards heaven but towards an impersonal, indifferent infinity. He sneered again at the pretensions of those fourteenth-century men who had let their lives be dominated by stone and superstition.

Yet the cathedral made Darren uneasy, as it always did. A massive certainty had lain behind its building, a certainty which made his confident rejection of those ideas seem very puny. He turned his back determinedly upon this silhouette of the past. He listened to the noise of the city, to the sounds of voices raised in laughter and in argument, which were carried to him through the warm night. Then he padded away quickly towards the place he had to go, cursing again the summer and the warmth and the night which did not have the blackness of winter.

He needed darkness for what he had to do. Winter darkness. No one really wanted the cold and the rain, but he needed the dark to cloak his actions. 'Darkness visible': he remembered that phrase from his schooldays, which belonged now to another, more innocent, world. A world where he had been a bright boy, studying for A levels, knowing nothing of this different world awaiting him.

One of those dusty old poets – he couldn't remember which – had used that phrase. But he liked the idea, now that he was threatened by the garish hues of summer. Darkness which you could almost see and touch was what he needed. 'Darkness which may be felt.' A phrase in the Bible, which he now found so quaint.

The pub wasn't far from the cathedral. He threaded his way through the narrow streets towards the old docks. He liked the contrast between the respectable tourist parts of the ancient city and the spots where he now made his living. The cathedral and the old streets like Eastgate and Westgate were within half a mile of the spot where the gruesome Fred and Rose West had perpetrated their appalling murders. He liked that proximity; it seemed to afford a shield for his activities.

The pub was crowded, as Chivers had known it would be. He sat in one of the alcoves which were all that remained of the pub's original design. What had once been a labyrinth of small rooms had been converted long ago into one large bar, but these recesses still afforded a little of the privacy which had been automatic in the old building. It wasn't until he was sitting with a pint of lager in front of him that he realized that one of the three small light bulbs above his head had fused. He had automatically chosen the dimmest of even these less-illuminated spots.

Darren Chivers pulled out his copy of the *Gloucester Citizen* and scanned the headlines. Immigrant workers were providing easy copy again. The farmers in Herefordshire and Gloucestershire maintained that they needed them to harvest the strawberries and raspberries in the summer and apples, pears and plums in the autumn; the residents muttered darkly about housing problems and rising crime statistics.

He had not been there more than five minutes when a long-haired youth slid into the bench seat on the other side of the scarred table. He felt the new arrival's anxious eyes upon him, but he did not look up from the newspaper. The youth coughed, then asked urgently, 'Darren Chivers?'

Still he did not look up from his paper, with its half-page picture of polythene strawberry tunnels stretching away to infinity. 'We don't deal in names here.'

'I need to know. I don't want to try to deal with the wrong man, do I?'

Darren looked up, stared directly into the anxious, too-revealing face. It was a little older than he had thought: twenty, perhaps twenty-one. He was twenty-seven himself, but he felt immeasurably older than his gauche young questioner. 'Fair point. I'm the man you want. But forget that name. As soon as you leave here, I'm Gary Peters. Got it?'

'Gary Peters. Yes, I've got it. It's just that—'

'What do you want?'

The young man glanced automatically to each side of him, checking whether there were listeners. He shouldn't have done that. It was likely to draw curious eyes to what you were about. It was a mistake that wouldn't have shown, wouldn't have mattered, in darkness. 'What you got?'

Darren didn't check for listeners, didn't twist his head in that too-revealing movement his customer had made. But he was aware of everything around them. 'I've got most things. What you buying?'

'You got coke?'

'I've got good rocks. Quality rocks. Clean rocks. Not cheap, mind. But you'll find the quality warrants the price.'

'Horse?'

'Yeah, I've got horse.' He looked at the arms the man had folded on the table, wondering what puncture marks lay beneath the wool of the thin sweater. Thin but expensive, like the fawn chinos hidden under the table; this customer should be able to afford the new prices.

'Rohypnol?'

The sex drug, the scarcest and most highly priced of his wares. The one which would get a girl into bed with you, whatever she had thought she would do at the beginning of the evening. Or even a man, if that's the way your cookie crumbled.

Darren said with a small, sour, unemotional smile, 'Dirty bugger! Yes, I've got Rohypnol. It'll cost you, though.' He looked into the eager young face, thought contemptuously of the racing hormones which would drive this man into parting with his money.

'It shouldn't be that dear. It doesn't cost that much to produce.'

'Supply and demand, son. Short supply, high demand. You don't have to buy. No one's forcing you to buy.' He let a little mockery creep into his voice, knowing that this client couldn't afford to take offence. 'You can just carry on wanking.'

The youth tried to assert himself. 'Let's have some prices. Let's see what you have to offer, before we go any further.'

The man's hand slipped automatically to his pocket. Darren heard the rustle of notes.

'Easy, mate, easy. Not here. We don't deal here. Little pigs have big ears and big eyes.' His customer stared round again, looking for cops in plain clothes. You'd think he was deliberately trying to attract suspicion, thought Darren Chivers with a mental sigh.

'Where, then?'

He hadn't even pinned down prices. This was the kind of client you needed, the kind the bosses always pretended were queuing up for you: affluent, non-violent, amenable. There weren't many of them about nowadays. In another few months, even this one would be wilier and more difficult. Make hay while the sun shines, Darren told himself. Perhaps there's something to be said for the summer after all.

'There's a small yard at the back. Go though the door beyond the gents. Twelve minutes time – not before that. I don't want you hanging about out there and exciting the wrong sort of interest. Go back to the bar now. Don't look at me again. Talk to someone there, if you can. We mustn't be seen to go outside together.'

The young man checked his watch and Darren gave him a grimmer, more businesslike smile. He always gave a precise time, and never used a round figure. It seemed to impress the punters, that. He sipped his lager slowly, glancing occasionally at the pub clock, not at his wrist. Without moving his head as the younger man had done, he checked the people who sat at other tables, as far as the limited view from the alcove permitted. There was no one around who looked like an undercover drug squad man. Or woman – you had to be alive to every possibility these days.

Chivers was apparently reading the *Citizen* when the long-haired youth left the bar. Ninety seconds later, Darren finished the last of his drink, rose unhurriedly, folded his newspaper, and slid it under his anorak. He was the only one wearing such a garment on this warm evening. He'd considered abandoning it for the summer, so as to blend in with the crowd.

But he needed the four capacious pockets in the worn, baggy garment for the goods he was selling. He was glad to find a reason for its continued use. It felt to him like a uniform, offering the protection which other, more genuine and respectable, uniforms accorded to their wearers.

He put his glass back on the bar, nodded his assent to the barman's thanks, and went down the corridor to the gents' toilet. He'd sold in here, when he'd started, but he knew of two people who'd been arrested in such places. There always seemed to be a cubicle with a locked door. You never knew who was using the secrecy of such places, and he saw no need to take unnecessary chances. You needed caution and luck to survive in this game; if you were cautious enough, you made your own luck. That was what he'd told one of the new recruits yesterday. He smiled in the welcoming darkness. In this trade, you could be a veteran at twenty-seven.

The youth was where he'd told him to be. Ninety seconds can be a long time when you stand alone in darkness, waiting to conduct an illegal transaction. He was nervous, anxious to have this over with, as Darren had known he would be. There was a low brick wall here, the remnants of an outside privy which had never been completely removed. Chivers laid his samples out for inspection, as he had done many times before, flashing his tiny torch six inches above them to show the range and the quality. 'The coke's a hundred quid.'

The youth raised a tentative hand towards the rocks of cocaine, but Darren clamped a steely grip upon his wrist. 'You don't handle the goods, son. Not until you've paid for them. You've got eyes in your head, that's all you need.'

'They're not very big.'

'They're quality. You can cut them. Even cut them again, if you want to. Mix them with cheaper stuff, if you care to take the risk. That's up to you.' He switched off the white light of his torch.

'It's not much, for a hundred quid.'

'Price isn't for negotiation, son. Take it or leave it.' Darren knew that the man was going to take it.

'All right.' The hand moved again towards the white cubes, faintly visible in their paper on the top of the wall, now that their eyes were accustomed to the night.

Claw-like fingers fell again upon his wrist. 'Payment upfront, son.'

The rustle of paper, the welcome feel of notes in his palm. He flashed the torch again on what he held. He didn't like fifties; he always feared counterfeits, though he'd never been passed any. These two looked genuine enough. 'The Rohypnol's fifty a shot. Do you twice if you use it with discretion.' He gave a sinister chuckle at his humour, at the mention of discretion in such a context. Chivers had no idea whether what he said was true, but he fancied it wouldn't be tested. When the blood pounded and men wanted women they couldn't have, economy was the last thing on what was left of their minds. Another hundred pounds changed hands.

The long-haired man took a long, deliberate breath, trying to still the thumping he felt in his chest. Darren smelt the whisky on his breath, the chaser he must have given himself at the bar before he slid out into the darkness for this meeting. First time, he reckoned, for this lad. But worth cultivating as he seemed to have plenty to spend.

Chivers hadn't got much sales talk – he didn't need much, in this game, where people were anxious to buy. But he said, 'You'll find everything I push is good stuff. We only do the best.'

'If that's right, I'll be back.'

'You know where to find me. Gary Peters, not that other name you've now forgotten. I'm here most Thursdays.' He wouldn't give him other venues, other times. The less the man knew, the better. That was true of everyone in this trade. Chivers himself knew no one in the hierarchy above him except his own supplier, and didn't wish to. If you knew the names of the big boys and revealed them, wittingly or unwittingly, you'd be found in some derelict site with a bullet through the back of your head – or not found at all. Ignorance was not exactly bliss, but it afforded a measure of safety in a dangerous world.

The man hesitated, then repeated, 'If what you say is right and this is good stuff, I'll be back. Maybe with bigger orders. I have friends who use coke.'

Darren smiled an unseen, contemptuous smile in the darkness. The middle-class professional set who used coke for kicks on nights in. He could see this young fool snorting the white stuff after dinner parties in a few years' time. 'I can do as much as you want.' The man probably didn't realize the different court sentences which came to a user and a supplier, but it wasn't up to Darren to point out that he'd be carrying too much for his own use, that he'd be taking risks for other toffs in his circle. *More fool him, more profit for me.*

Chivers slipped away the heroin and the LSD he had not sold, tapping down the flaps on the anorak pockets. 'You leave now. You'll need to go out through the pub – there's no exit from here. I'll depart in my own good time.'

That old saw about the customer being always right had no application here. It was the seller who called the shots in this trade. He turned his client towards the door of the pub, gave him a tiny push in the back to set him in motion. The orange light of the aperture blazed briefly for a moment, unnaturally bright to eyes now accustomed to darkness. The raucous laughter of the group at the bar blared for a second, then was abruptly silenced as the door shut.

Chivers, senses acute as was appropriate for a creature of the night, listened for a moment to the sounds of the city as eleven o'clock approached. Car horns, car doors, engines roaring into life as feet pressed carelessly upon accelerator pedals. The sound of muted communal laughter and shouting was so distant that it seemed to him to come from a different world. He gave it two minutes, then moved soundlessly to the door which his client had slipped through a minute earlier. He opened it an inch, pressing his ear automatically to the gap to listen for any noise which might alert him to danger. Caution, as usual.

It was caution which saved him.

He did not catch the words of the challenge, but he heard the high, apprehensive response of the man whose two hundred pounds nestled in his pocket. Then the other voices in the pub fell silent and he heard the beginning of the words of arrest, the warning that the man did not need to say anything but anything he did say would be recorded and . . .

Darren Chivers didn't wait any longer. He was away over the wall at the back of the yard, using the foothold he had noted when he had surveyed his chosen dealing spot in daylight, dropping with simian agility into the deep shadow at the other side of it.

There was a police car on the double yellow lines outside

the pub entrance, as he had expected. Its siren was off, but its blue light blinked rhythmically, dazzlingly bright against the dimmer lights of the old street lighting. There was at least one copper inside the vehicle, probably two, but they were watching the front door of the pub, waiting to cover their colleagues if anyone tried to escape by that route.

There would be others by the exit from the car park, the rear exit from the pub, he was sure. He turned away from the police car, hugged the shadow of the wall as long as he could, a fox concealing himself from the hounds who had the odds on their side. He had to skirt that rear exit to get to his bike, but that was better than trying to pass the police car with its watchful occupants.

He crossed the road, feeling as if a searchlight had been turned upon him when he left the concealing shadow. He paused at the dimmest point between two lamps, by a terraced house with no lights. The pigs were there all right, standing silent as sentinels by the pillars at each side of the car park exit. People came out of the door of the pub as he watched; he counted four, five, six against the light from the bar behind them before the door shut. As they moved towards their cars, one at least of the police officers moved forward to challenge them and Darren saw his chance.

He did not run, but moved in a rapid half-walk, half-shuffle, hugging the front elevation of the old terraced houses, feeling the sleeve of his anorak actually catch the grime of the bricks as he fought for obscurity. He moved fifty, sixty yards, passed the car park, left the pub behind, felt the safety of the next corner and salvation almost within his reach.

It was then that a car moved out of the car park and on to the street behind him, its headlights picking him out like a fugitive in a spy film. That was only for a couple of seconds, and he thought at first that he had got away with it. Then a challenge came through the darkness, a harsh police voice commanding him to stop. Whistles, he thought he heard, among a confusion of noise. He saw curious civilian faces turning to focus upon him as the car passed him, then disappeared around the corner.

He was running now. Running as he had not done for years, his arms flailing in search of a rhythm he felt he had lost and could never regain. He rounded the corner, moved into the street which should have been his refuge. But there was pursuit now; younger and fitter legs than his were behind him. And he was panting, regretting the way he had let his fitness go, realizing just how much his present lifestyle had cost him.

His brain was still working. He knew this area well, probably better than his pursuers did. There was a labyrinth of alleys and narrow streets between here and the cathedral. He turned into the first of these, running between houses which seemed almost to meet over his head, then turned right again, away for the moment from the direction he wanted to take. The police voices behind him were alarmingly close, but there was confusion in them now. Questions were flung from one to the other about the whereabouts of their quarry.

He turned right again, into an alleyway too narrow for traffic, avoiding the streets and the lights which were so pitilessly exposing. He slowed to a swift trot, pacing himself to reach the spot he was aiming for, his thin face crafty as a tiring fox's, his pricked ears listening as he ran for the sounds of the hounds behind him.

Anxiety stretched the seconds, so that it seemed to take him a long time to reach the high, concealing walls of the cathedral close. People had claimed sanctuary here at one time, fled into the vast concealing cave of the cathedral itself. He didn't think that ploy would work now, and in any case all the stout doors had long since been locked for the night against intruders. But he stood for two long minutes in the alcove beside his bicycle, willing his breathing to slow, listening to the sounds of the police search diminishing into the darkness as it moved away towards the centre of the town.

He smiled as he turned on the lights on his bike. He was making himself strictly legal, a model citizen who would leave no carbon footprint behind him. He told himself sternly that he wasn't out of the wood yet, that the price of freedom was eternal vigilance. Some old Greek bloke had said that; Chivers bet he hadn't thought that a drug-pusher would be quoting him thousands of years later. He also bet those pigs in blue who thought they were so clever wouldn't know about the Greek bloke.

It took him another minute and a considerable effort of will to mount the bike and ride out on to the open streets. It felt as bright as noon as he turned on to the main road and the harsh orange neon blazed above him. But it was as he had promised himself it would be. Behind him, the police were stopping cars and moving into the noisy crowds of pedestrians who were leaving the city centre hostelries. But they hardly noticed the unthreatening progress of the cyclist who made his quiet, unhurried way along this more open thoroughfare. As he pedalled the two miles towards home and safety, he was more endangered by cars that passed too close to him when overtaking than by any police interference.

He hadn't realized how exhausted he was until he slumped into the armchair, too tired even to fill the kettle. He lay with his eyes shut for a full ten minutes, congratulating himself upon his escape. The old fox had outwitted the hunt, but it had been a damned close-run thing. The Duke of Wellington had said that about Waterloo. There wasn't one in ten of those frustrated coppers who would have known that. A slow, superior smile edged on to Darren's face. Relief pulsed round his veins.

The clever fox surely deserved some reward. He walked across to the kitchen drawer, moved the towel which was so carefully folded on top of the needles. He pulled up the sleeve of his shirt, ignored the existing scars, and found the vein with practised ease. Moments later, the heroin surged through his body, lifting his spirits and his energy. Darren Chivers had been too clever for the pigs again. Too clever by a long chalk.

It was a good two hours before he went to bed, still on a high of elation. Old Darren wasn't stupid, he told himself. Old Darren knew when it was time to lie low for a while, steer clear of the spots the pigs would be watching. Old Darren knew a thing or two too many for those stupid sods to catch him. This would be a time to play down his drug dealing. A time to keep a low profile, to do just enough to keep the bosses happy and the supply lines intact.

It was a good thing he was developing another line of business.

TWO

Friday morning, and the June sun was already pleasantly high and warm over the centre of the old city.

Michelle de Vries thought that Gloucester was at its best on mornings like this, when people poured into the streets and were ready to spend. She enjoyed strolling through these busy streets to her shop, which was in a cul-de-sac just outside the busy town centre. She had no need to hurry; her assistant would have been there for at least half an hour. There was rarely anything as vulgar as a crowd around her shop – designer clothes didn't deal in crowds. Many studied the carefully arranged window displays at Boutique Chantelle, but few were both bold and affluent enough to venture within. That was how it should be. Michelle had never aimed at the popular market and wouldn't have been sure how to handle it if it had been available to her.

There was no one studying her display at this early hour. She paused for a moment to weigh its effectiveness. The silk jersey top with its floaty lace trimmings oozed class. She nodded her approval. The more conventional two-piece suit at the other side of the window made up for its orthodox design by its cut and its striking sapphire-blue colour.

Michelle still wasn't quite sure about the effect upon her display of the two hats, which had ample space to themselves in the centre of the window. She had invited the milliner, whose business in the adjoining street had failed, to display her wares here for a trial period. The woman had grasped eagerly at this unexpected straw and agreed to pay a handsome percentage on all hat sales. As some of her models were priced at over a hundred pounds, this was a substantial windfall profit for Michelle.

She was not a hat person herself and didn't pretend to be an expert, but there had been other unexpected spin-offs from the millinery experiment. Not many women regularly wore hats nowadays, but they came in to buy them for special occasions. By far the commonest of these were weddings, and

Michelle found that, once they had ventured into the shop to buy a hat, women with money could be induced to look at other clothes. Three times during the spring she had sold complete wedding ensembles to mothers of brides who 'did not want to let things down on the day'.

Rather to her surprise at this early hour, there was a customer talking to her assistant when she entered the shop. A middle-aged lady, like most of her clients; even that adjective was a little flattering, since most were over sixty and many would need to live to a hundred and thirty or forty to be genuinely 'middle-aged' now. One of the ironies of clothes of this class was that the young women who would have looked stunning in them could generally not afford them. It was the women with widening hips and sagging busts who could afford the best.

Still, Mrs de Vries didn't waste sympathy on the young. Youth was its own compensation; you didn't need clever tailoring and expensive hairstyling when you were under thirty. The converse was also true; however much you spent on skin creams and outfits and coiffures, you couldn't keep the wrinkles and the thickening waists at bay. Fortunately, most women refused to recognize that, or there would be scant trade for shops like hers.

Michelle looked at the flustered face of her assistant, at the sour expression of the woman she was serving, and assessed the situation without hearing a word. 'I'll take over, Jean,' she said quietly.

'This is too tight!' said the woman petulantly, gazing into the full-length mirror, as if the garment and not her own lumpish body was to blame for that.

'You're right. That dress just isn't you, Mrs Armathwaite,' said Michelle de Vries decisively. 'I think it's a little too severe, if you want it for everyday wear.'

Never be afraid to disparage your wares. She'd found long ago that people with money rarely bought the first thing they tried on. If you disparaged it a little yourself, you got a reputation for honesty, so that they trusted you when you approved of the third or fourth thing they tried. There was no place for the hard sell at this elevated level of the trade. But you always blamed your clothes for the shortcomings, rather than make any mention of the imperfect contours beneath them.

Mrs Armathwaite had more money than she would ever be able to spend and if you expended a little time and diplomacy on her she would usually purchase something. She was looking for summer dresses. Michelle discouraged her from the striking large-flowered patterns which she seemed to favour. It was surprising how often the women who shopped here attempted clothes which they might have struggled to carry off thirty years ago. She spent a lot of her time encouraging hemlines to creep down over substantial knees and raising necklines to mask the wrinkles women refused to see. Everyone liked clothes which would flatter them, but 'flattering' was a word she had long since learned not to use.

It was a full twenty-five minutes later that Michelle said with enthusiasm, 'Now that really is you, don't you think?' Five minutes later, the sale was clinched, and Mrs Armathwaite left with a heart uplifted and a bank balance six hundred pounds lighter. Everyone needed little spending treats, Mrs de Vries reflected. There was no reason why you should be deprived of pleasure merely because you were affluent. If it cost the moneyed classes a little more to get their pleasures, that all helped to keep the wheels of commerce turning.

'You handle ladies like that so well,' said Jean admiringly when the door was safely shut upon Mrs Armathwaite. At thirty, she was fourteen years younger than her employer, and after two months still in awe of her.

'And you will, too. You can't hurry ladies like that. Be tactful and be patient and never expect them to buy the first thing you show them. Indeed, if you have something in mind you think will suit them, it often pays you to produce it after they've rejected a couple of their own choices. Skill comes with experience.' And if it doesn't, thought Michelle, you'll be looking for another job. I can't afford to employ anyone who lets trade slip through her fingers.

She glanced at her watch. It was almost ten o'clock. 'The accountant's pressing me for the documents he needs for our tax return. I'd better put them into some sort of order,' she said. She went into the storeroom behind the shop and shut the door firmly behind her.

Ten minutes later, the call she had been waiting for came. Michelle snatched at the receiver, trying to control her breathing as the caller announced his identity. Don't appear too eager, she told herself. For a successful businesswoman with a wealth of life experience behind her, she felt ridiculously like a teenager. She had a tremulous smile on her face, which turned into a frown of disappointment as she listened.

'No, I can't. Not tonight,' she said reluctantly.

'I'm sure you could if you really tried. You're an ingenious woman, you know.'

The smile was back, twitching her lips despite her efforts at control. 'And you're a persuasive old lecher, aren't you? All right, leave it with me. I'll be there.'

The man who had been arrested for buying drugs from Darren Chivers spent an uncomfortable night under lock and key.

There is nothing inhumane about conditions in the modern police cell, but he got very little sleep. The thin mattress on the narrow ledge of a bed gave him a lie which was much harder than his bed at home. The stainless-steel toilet bowl, three feet beyond the bed, was perfectly clean, but the stink of strong disinfectant reminded him of where he was whenever he awoke from an uneasy doze. His eyes opened on the crude graffiti some previous occupant had managed to inscribe upon the wall beside him. He wondered why the men who insisted on the most obscene drawings were always the worst artists. A drunk in an adjoining cell made raucous scatological protests throughout the night, whilst an anonymous voice of authority warned him equally stridently to shut up. By the time the early dawn thrust in through the small high, curtainless window at the end of his cell, Luke Hetherington was feeling very sorry for himself.

An officer in shirt sleeves brought him thick white toast and a mug of tea which was so strong and sweet that he struggled to drink it. The man stood over him for a moment, watching him drink, studying with apparent interest the ball-pen drawings beside the bed. 'You do these?' he asked.

'No. They were there when I got here.' Luke couldn't convey the artistic outrage he felt at the accusation.

'Bugger shouldn't have been left with a pen. They smuggle them in, you know.' He gathered up the crust of the toast and the half-empty mug of tea. 'They'll want to interview you presently, I expect.'

Luke wondered who the anonymous 'they' would turn out to be. The sergeant at the desk had taken his watch away with his other valuables and his belt and shoelaces before they had locked him up, so he had no idea of the time as the hours dragged by. He began to think they had forgotten him. A little more experience of these things would have told him that the CID were softening him up a little, leaving him to reflect upon his situation as the sun climbed higher in the summer sky and people outside moved freely around the city.

At ten o'clock, he was led upstairs to an interview room and told that he would be interviewed in two minutes. The sage green walls of this small cube of a room, the single fluorescent light high above his head, the three upright chairs and the small scratched table which were the only furniture, made this airless place seem even more claustrophobic than the cell where he had spent the night.

By the time Detective Inspector Rushton set the cassette recorder going and announced that he and Detective Sergeant Hook were conducting an interview beginning at 10.03, Luke Hetherington was sweating.

Rushton was thirty-two. He looked much older to Luke. The man beside him was in his early forties, but he looked to Luke as if he should be retired. He felt at a huge disadvantage in the presence of these two men, as if anything he said would be immediately overwhelmed by the sheer weight of their experience.

Rushton said formally, almost wearily, 'Do you want a brief, Mr Hetherington?'

'A lawyer? Do I need one?'

The DI shrugged his shoulders, allowing himself a small smile. 'Up to you. Open and shut case as far as we're concerned, but you're entitled to legal advice, if you want it.'

'I shan't bother then. I've not done anything too awful, have I?'

This time DI Rushton's smile was broader and more genuine. Such naivety made a welcome change from the streetwise thugs who called this a pigsty and dealt only in blasphemies and scatology. 'You're in trouble, Mr Hetherington. I wouldn't like you to have any illusions about that.'

Luke licked his lips and tried to sound far more confident than he felt. 'A little coke, for recreational use. It's not going to make the national press, is it?'

'A class A drug. Maximum sentence for possession is seven years. Maximum sentence for supplying to others, life. Were you intending to supply others, Mr Hetherington?'

Luke's mind reeled. Surely he couldn't be facing prison for this? 'No, I wasn't. Millions of people use coke. One in five at my age.'

Rushton nodded. 'Probably more than that, by now. That statistic is four years old, Mr Hetherington. Illegal drugs are now a ten billion pound industry in this country. Almost out of control. Almost, but not quite. Arrests aren't easy. That's why when we catch someone red-handed, we find magistrates and judges usually want to make an example of him.' He sat back a little on the upright chair and allowed himself a complacent smile.

'I don't think I'll go to prison, just for possession.' Luke tried hard to sound as if he believed himself. He wondered if it would be losing face to change his mind about that lawyer.

'Rohypnol will interest the magistrates. They don't like that drug at all. Lots of rape charges are connected with the use of Rohypnol.'

Hetherington said, 'I didn't intend to rape anyone. I just thought . . .' He stopped, unsure what he had thought, unsure of any words which would not make the situation worse as he saw the amusement in the inspector's eyes.

Bert Hook leaned forward. He looked concerned, avuncular, almost friendly. 'It's possible you might not get a custodial sentence, Luke, if this interview goes well. Have you a previous criminal record?'

'No. Nothing. Well, three points on my licence for a speeding fine.'

'That's not a criminal record.' Bert paused, pursed his lips, nodded slowly. 'I think the magistrates might be persuaded to take a lenient view, if there were other things in your favour. If we were able to point out that you had cooperated fully with the police, for instance.'

Luke Hetherington, with all the phrases from his contemporaries about not trusting the pigs racing across his mind, was immediately suspicious. 'What does that mean?'

'Nothing other than doing what every good citizen should do, Luke. Helping the police in the course of their inquiries. Giving assistance rather than being obstructive as we try to ensure that the law is upheld.'

'I'm not getting anyone else into your bloody cells!' Luke found that he enjoyed this first, belated flash of defiance.

Bert Hook smiled a jaded, experienced smile, as if this was just what he would have expected from a spirited but mistaken young man. 'You sound rather like one of the succession of young thugs we get in here, shouting, "I ain't no grass, copper!" Those silly sods always end up in trouble. I can understand why they do, in a way. They haven't your education, Luke. They haven't the sense to realize that when you're in a hole, you should stop digging and look for help.'

Hetherington stared at him suspiciously. He said sullenly, 'And who's going to help me? Not bloody coppers, for a start! All you lot want is convictions.'

Hook gave him a grin which was almost conspiratorial. 'You're right there, lad! We're given targets to meet, like every other poor bugger nowadays. But what we can do is help you to help yourself. Oh, we can take you to court and get a conviction easily enough. Leave you with a criminal record, which might or might not inhibit your career as an accountant. But what we really want is a conviction of one of the big boys. If you can help us to get that, we might be able to take a lenient view of your own lawbreaking.'

'What do you want of me?' Hope and suspicion fought for supremacy in the young, revealing face.

'The name of your supplier, for a start.'

'I don't know that.' The denial was automatic, but Hetherington was not a good liar.

'I think you do, Luke. One of your friends put you on to him, told you where you might meet him, didn't they?'

Luke knew little about the ramifications of the drug trade, but he knew enough to know that those who informed on their suppliers could be killed. He had had a lot of time to think about this in the cells, to remember what his dealer had told him to say. 'His name was Gary Peters.'

There weren't many jokes in this evil industry, but the police were on the wrong end of this one, dreamed up by some bright boy in the local branch of the trade. Every user who had been arrested in the last two months had given Gary Peters as the name of his dealer.

Chris Rushton said sharply, 'Don't piss us about, Mr Hetherington. DS Hook was giving you the chance to save yourself. If you choose not to do that, you will find that—'

'That's the only name I know. That's the man who sold me the drugs last night. I'm telling you what I can, trying to cooperate.'

They pressed him as hard as they could, but he was too scared or too ignorant to give them any more. Rushton eventually said, 'We'll decide on the nature of the charges against you in the next few days. If during those days you remember the names of people dealing in illegal drugs or any other item of information you think might be useful to us, it will be very much in your interest to contact this number immediately.'

The Crown Prosecution Service probably wouldn't want to take the case to court at all for possession in these quantities, though Rohypnol, the date-rape drug, might excite their interest. Rushton couldn't honestly see any great advantage in prosecution himself, beyond the minor one of chastening this naive young man and setting an example for others like him. Hetherington would get a fine and a rap over the knuckles from some magistrate conscious of overcrowded prisons and the accused's middle-class background. In his experience, JPs always thought public schoolboys were more capable of reform than any other offenders. He sent this one sourly back into the world outside.

That evening Luke Hetherington was full of bravado with his friends. His arrest had given him a fleeting status he had not enjoyed before. On his own when the raucous evening was over, he wondered what charges he would face and how he should conduct the next years of his life.

At the other end of the city, the man who had sold him the drugs was speculating about what Hetherington had told the police and how he might support himself with only minimum drug dealing in the weeks to come.

THREE

B y eleven o'clock on Friday morning, it was not just warm but hot in the centre of the old city of Gloucester. Traditional exam weather. The young people suffering the agonies of A levels and GCSEs unscrewed the caps on their bottles of water, cudgelled their minds, wished they had worked harder during the year, and wrote down things which would have made their teachers writhe.

The Severn, that great river which has witnessed so much of British history, ran slow and sluggish around the edge of the town. The ancient docks, now largely a tourist attraction, were thronged with visitors. Business was particularly brisk in the antiques centre, which had once been a warehouse for the exotic imports brought up the Severn estuary from around the world.

One building remained cool, even as the sun climbed towards its zenith and tee shirts and shorts dominated the dress of its visitors. Robert Beckford, verger at Gloucester Cathedral, looked up at the vast stone cliff of the building's eastern elevation and reminded himself again how lucky he was to have secured this job. The clergy who had interviewed him had avoided direct references to his army career, but he was sure that his active service in the Falklands and Iraq had helped him to get the appointment. Which was ironic, because he couldn't imagine any greater difference than that between the brief hell-on-earth he had endured in those strange sideshow wars and the quiet, unchanging peace of the cathedral and its close.

When he was interviewed, he hadn't known the differences between the various solemn-faced, anxious, well-meaning members of the cathedral chapter who had spoken with him. Now he understood most of the distinctions among deans and archdeacons and rectors and rural deans and humble vicars, though he didn't even try to fathom the recondite exchanges which seemed to take over as the doors closed firmly upon meetings of the cathedral chapter. The language might be a little different, the iron fists sheathed in a little more velvet, but Rob thought these lengthy meetings must contain many of the elements which took over when military brass hats closed the doors upon the rankers to plan the subtleties of military strategy.

The deliberations of the chapter were interesting but largely irrelevant to Robert Beckford. The really important thing was that he had landed on his feet here. He loved the solemn vastness of the cathedral. He loved the voices of the choristers at choral evensong, loved the quiet services in the Lady Chapel and in the other small chapels which fringed the main body of the building. He also loved the other extreme of the solemn services, where many clergy moved in a slow-motion ballet upon the ancient high altar and the bishop glided among them like some benevolent despot, presiding over the participation of clergy, choir and congregation in the ramifications of ancient rituals. It reminded him incongruously of the parade square on formal military occasions, where men stood like statues until propelled into action by orders bellowed from deep within the torsos of officers and sergeant majors.

Robert Beckford imitated his old sergeant major now, telling the day's first party of schoolchildren to stop running and move in an orderly fashion among the massive circular pillars. He gave them his most forbidding frown and tightened his lips beneath his neatly trimmed moustache to still them into silence. Then he relented, as he usually did with children, and gave the wide-eyed boys a whispered introduction to the tomb of the murdered king, Edward II, who had lain here since 1330.

Robert went and stood for a moment beside the empty choir, looking north-east and enjoying the light pouring through the multicoloured stained glass on to the deserted benches. He congratulated himself once again on being here, on having this humble but wonderful job amidst the stones which had seen more of devotion and love, anger and treachery, violence and blood, than any individual could ever encompass. He said as much to Gwen, his wife, after he had walked the eighty yards to his cosy house in the cathedral close for his morning coffee.

Gwen thought one of a wife's functions was to keep her man's feet on the ground. 'You're an old sentimentalist at heart, Rob Beckford. You choose not to see the worst parts of modern life.'

'I'm not ignoring what goes on. I know the trouble the police have to deal with in Gloucester on some nights. I just think we're lucky to have found a place like this. A place where we can ignore the worst features of life in the twenty-first century.' He looked out with satisfaction on the tiny weedless garden at the back of the house, where the petunias and antirrhinums he had planted last month were already providing cheerful colour.

'All right, Rob! We've fallen on our feet here. You don't need to tell me that, after years in married quarters in some pretty Godforsaken places. But you've earned it. You don't need to be apologetic about it. And in particular, you don't need to tell me every day how lucky we are! Once a week will be quite enough in future, thank you. Now be off with you, before you put this job you like so much in jeopardy by skiving!'

The old military word. Rob liked that in Gwen. She never pretended to be anything other than exactly what she was. He surprised her with a brief kiss on the forehead before he went obediently back to the cathedral.

Gwen washed the coffee cups and put them on the drainer, then changed her blouse for a lighter one and went joyfully out into the town. The city, she should say, but to Gwen it had all the cosiness of an old market town, with the added benefit of some of the bigger stores. She had spent much of her married life making the best of limited company in married quarters and limited shopping in strange and isolated spots. And all the time she had had to remind herself that she must not put down roots, must not become too attached to people or to places, because she and Rob might be moved on to a different part of the world with only a week or two's notice. Or worse still, he might have to go off without her, as he had done to the Falklands, when jingoism had taken over the nation and she had waited among its noisy trumpetings for news that her man was still alive.

Despite her cheerful mocking of her husband, Gwen Beckford also congratulated herself on her good fortune, as she moved unhurriedly among the amply stocked shops and exchanged cheerful greetings with tradesmen who knew her.

She loved the combination of old and new in Gloucester, loved the fact that she could be among the most modern shops and yet in an ancient city with venerable buildings. There were still individual shops here, like the new Boutique Chantelle. Gwen loved looking at the gowns and the hats in the window, though she would never have dreamed of venturing inside. And whenever she chose, she could walk away from the throngs outside the windows of Debenhams or Next and be back after a few minutes of unhurried walking in the neat stone house with mullioned windows, with the frenzied modern world shut firmly out.

Back in the cathedral, her husband was encountering problems. Robert Beckford had worked in his army days for a widely differing range of personalities, priding himself on the fact that he could work with anyone, whether directing them or being directed by them. Miss Edwina Clarkson, the newly appointed civilian administrator of the cathedral's commercial activities, was testing this claim and giving him difficulties. He had so far failed to establish any satisfactory working relationship with her. As he strode back to his duties, she was waiting for him beside the stall which sold postcards, pamphlets and books about the cathedral's history.

'And where have you been hiding yourself, Mr Beckford?'

'I haven't been hiding at all, Ms Clarkson. I've been for my morning coffee. As permitted by the terms of my employment here.'

'It's Miss Clarkson, please. I don't hold with this modern feminist nonsense. "Miss" has been good enough for centuries, so it's certainly good enough for me.' Her lips tightened primly as she prepared to attack. 'Any more than I approve of shop stewards in cathedrals.'

'There are no shop stewards here, Miss Clarkson. I've never even been asked to join a union in the three years I've been here. And I've never felt the need for one.' Not until now, he thought. He found himself standing to attention and staring straight ahead of him, as he had learned to do as a young soldier when criticized on the parade ground.

'And where did you choose to go for this prolonged coffee break, Mr Beckford?'

'It wasn't prolonged, Miss Clarkson. I have never counted the minutes, just as I never watch the clock at the end of the

day if there is work to be done here, but as I understand it, I
am entitled to a twenty minute break. I have been away for
no more than that. I took my coffee with my wife at home.'

Edwina Clarkson sniffed. She had a formidable sniff. Even
Rob Beckford conceded that – credit where credit was due.
'I should prefer you to take your coffee break here in future.
It's bad for the morale of our younger workers if their
colleagues are seen to be enjoying special privileges.'

She spoke as if she were deploying a workforce of a hundred,
rather than the two full-timers and four part-timers over whom
she held jurisdiction. Rob tried to lighten the atmosphere a
little. 'Have you tasted the cathedral coffee, Miss Clarkson?
My Gwen does a much nicer cup, and a nice line in ginger
snaps. You're very welcome to drop in whenever—'

'I would prefer no insubordination, Mr Beckford, if you
don't mind. You will take your coffee break within the precincts
in future.'

She turned and strutted away. He watched her formidable
backside rotating towards the transept and wondered how
many petty tyrants had strutted beneath this high roof over
the centuries. Much more cruel ones than Miss Clarkson, no
doubt, and until the last few years exclusively male. Rob
Beckford, who had spent a military career in a male-dominated
world, tried hard to persuade himself that a male administrator might have been just as pompous and just as petty as
Miss Edwina Clarkson.

He gave two boys in the latest school party a little help
with the list of tasks on their worksheet, then went and sat in
the empty Lady Chapel for a couple of minutes to calm his
mind and forget Miss Clarkson. He liked the Lady Chapel,
which seemed to him a smaller and more intimate version of
the choir, where he had stood for a moment before his coffee.
These were the moments when he wished he had the serene
religious faith he saw in so many of the clergy and the congre-
gations who attended services in the cathedral. He felt
immensely lucky to have this holy place to himself for a few
minutes, but also immensely inadequate in that he could not
summon that unclouded, automatic belief which had informed
the thousands of people who had sat in this place in centuries
past. He willed himself to pray, his mind flicking automatically
back into the unthinking words of worship he had learned as

a child. 'Our Father, which art in heaven, hallowed be thy name . . .'

Robert Beckford was halfway through the paternoster when he became conscious that he was not alone. Someone had slipped into the pew behind him; he had heard no noise, yet he was aware of a presence. He kept his eyes closed and continued his silent prayer. This could not be Edwina Clarkson or she would have spoken by now, chiding him harshly for his presence here and his lack of activity. This could only be some member of the public, who probably wanted to be as quiet as he did in this sacred, peaceful place. He would conclude his prayer, then go out and sweep the cloisters.

The voice behind him came in a hoarse whisper, which seemed to Rob far too loud. 'I need money, soldier boy.'

He didn't turn to confront the speaker. He did not want to see the thin, crafty face, so out of place here, so unwelcome as it shattered the composure he had been recovering. Rob kept his eyes closed; to open them as he spoke would have been a desecration of the chapel, a mocking of the sacred icons on the walls and in the windows. 'You said you wouldn't come again. You said the payment in April was the final one.'

'Unforeseen circumstances, soldier boy. Things beyond my control.'

People like this always came back for more. Everyone said that. But you didn't have a choice. You paid because you had to, because the alternative was unthinkable. 'I don't have money.' Still his eyes were shut. Still he would not turn shoulders rigid with tension to face this tormentor.

'You'll find it. You don't have a choice, do you?'

'I do. I could let you do your worst.'

'But you won't. The stakes are too high for you to do that, soldier boy.'

It was ridiculous, a man of fifty being taunted by a creature like this, who was half his age and no physical match for him. Rob wanted to whirl on the man, to take him by surprise and wring his miserable throat. He wondered if anyone had ever died in the Lady Chapel before, whether perhaps in the gory medieval conflicts which had rent the area some power-mad cleric had slit the throat of some overambitious priest here.

Robert Beckford said, 'I'll need time!' and knew in that moment that he was lost, that he had agreed to pay.

'You can have a week. Five hundred. Final demand, so long as it's delivered on time.'

'How do I know that?'

'You don't. You're dependent on my good will. On the respect I have for our fighting forces.' A coarse, guttural, scarcely human clicking, which might have been amusement at his own humour.

'When and where?'

'Don't you worry about that, verger. I'll be back in my own good time. I'll give you a week, seeing as how I'm so fond of you.'

'I can't carry money about with me and just wait for you like that.'

But the voice was gone, as silently and anonymously as it had arrived. When Robert Beckford finally brought himself to turn, the chapel was as deserted as it had been when he had tried to pray.

'It will get better as the months pass.'

'Time, the great healer, you mean.' The corners of the widow's mouth turned down a little, as if to show her contempt for the cliché.

Karen Lynch took a deep breath and pressed on resolutely. 'I suppose I do, yes. The pain grows a little less sharp with each passing day, Barbara.' It was the first time she had used the bereaved woman's forename. 'I don't mean that it will ever go away completely. The sense of loss will remain with you as long as you live, whatever you do with the rest of your life. That's natural and as it should be. But the raw pain, the feeling that life is completely pointless, will gradually disappear.'

'Lost many husbands yourself, have you?' The tear-swollen eyes beneath the grey hair looked directly at her with this barb.

'Not yet. I've been lucky. But I've lost other people who were close to me. We all have.'

'Of course we have, I'm sorry, Karen.' The older woman took the plunge and called her by her first name; she had always been Mrs Lynch, the vicar's wife, before, and thus always in her husband's shadow. In doing this, Barbara Lawrence acknowledged that she welcomed the use of her own forename by the woman who had come to comfort her.

How subtle are the unwritten rules of English society, how baffling any foreigner would find the social interplay in this odd race!

'I'll get us a cup of tea, shall I?' said Karen, and bustled away into the kitchen, her crippled leg giving her that irregular dot-and-carry-one action but scarcely slowing her movement.

Barbara would rather have made the tea herself, but she let Karen do it, sensing that her visitor would be more at ease if she was allowed some physical action. The seventy-year-old, stricken with grief, thinking of the needs of the strong young woman who had come here to comfort her, Barbara thought ruefully.

'There's some shortbread in the cupboard near the kettle,' she called.

They were more at ease with each other when Karen came back, carrying the tray before her as carefully as a dutiful child.

Barbara said without thinking, 'Have you always been a cripple, dear?' and then wondered immediately if she had been incredibly rude.

Karen smiled. 'That's what everyone called it when I was a child. By the time I was twenty, it had become 'handicapped'. Now that I'm thirty-four, I'm 'disabled' and there are all kinds of provisions for us. Except that I don't use them, because I never really think of myself as either handicapped or disabled. I grew up with a gammy leg, you see. Learned to cope when I was a kid. Learned that the best way of dealing with it was to pretend that it didn't exist, as far as possible.'

'I'm sorry. It's personal. I shouldn't have asked you that.'

'Your grief's personal too, isn't it? And yet some interfering busybody comes into your house and tries to tell you how to run your life!'

'I'm glad you're here. Glad to find someone like you trying to help me.' Barbara Lawrence found to her surprise that she meant every word of that.

Karen grinned at her. 'Even someone with a gammy leg? I was born with my right foot turned sharply inwards and my right leg a bit crooked. Nowadays I think they'd operate in infancy, but they weren't as clever or as confident in those days. But when you've never known life to be any different, you don't even think about it. I'm told that people who've been blind from birth cope with that much more easily than people who have had full sight and lost it.' She firmly thrust aside her memories of being the last one selected when they were picking teams for childhood games, of maintaining a glassy smile while others were taken on to the dance floor at teenage discos.

Barbara was pleased to find her visitor talking so freely, delighted that they had found a subject other than her own suffering and her grief for Brian. She said abruptly, her words surprising herself as much as her listener, 'I'm going to mourn him, you know. I'm not ashamed of my grief!'

'Nor should you be!' Karen's response was instant and vigorous. 'Brian was a good man. He deserves your grief. And so do you. It's a necessary process. Not always pleasant, but something we have to go through. It can be a dark tunnel sometimes – usually at around four o'clock in the morning – but eventually you'll see the light at the other end.'

'So long as it isn't the front light of a bloody great train coming to splatter me!' said Barbara, and found herself enjoying the first genuine laugh she had allowed herself since the death two weeks ago.

'Have you been out much yet?'

'Not at all. Well, just to the corner shop for bread and milk.'

'You must venture out, you know, now that the funeral's over.'

'I do know that, yes. I'm going to go to church on Sunday. Perhaps I'll get back to the WI next week.'

'You'll probably find that people seem to be avoiding you at first. You should be prepared for that. They don't mean to be unfriendly – they just don't know what to say. Death is still a bit of a taboo subject, you know. Then, at a later stage, you'll find that people never mention Brian, for fear of upsetting you.'

'I've heard that before, now that you mention it. I've probably done it myself, with other people. Well, I'll be happy enough not to talk about Brian at present. I'd be frightened of breaking down myself, you see.' And immediately Barbara did just that. She had to take a determined bite at the short-bread she had hitherto neglected, attempting to disguise her emotion.

'No one will expect you to be the life and soul of the party, but people will be feeling for you. You should remember that they're being sympathetic, even though they might not know quite how to show it.' Karen wondered why she seemed to be able to rustle up no more than the routine clichés of consolation. Perhaps they had become clichés because they were undoubtedly true.

Barbara Lawrence didn't seem to mind. She declared herself much cheered by the end of the visit and seemed delighted when Karen offered to call again in a week. After she had gone, Barbara reflected on how much easier it was to talk to the vicar's wife than to the vicar himself. Peter Lynch was never unkind; he was popular in the parish and had increased church attendances. By all accounts, he was good with the young people, and he certainly preached a good sermon in the modern, ecumenical way. But he didn't quite have the common touch. Mrs Lynch was far better at appreciating just how you felt and just what you were going through.

As she nursed the old Fiesta back towards the vicarage, Karen Lynch was nothing like so confident of her empathy skills. She thought her visit had gone fairly well, after an unpromising start. She could certainly see the value of such visits. People like Barbara Lawrence could easily descend into isolation and despair without the tactful support of the church and its congregation.

Tactful: that was a word Karen had never had to consider until she had met Peter and taken up vicarage life. Sometimes the unquestioning rectitude of the people and the homes she visited could seem almost claustrophobic, because of that very different life she had led in the years before Peter. He knew about it, of course. She didn't have secrets from Peter. But even Peter didn't know the worst of it, the sordid details she herself tried unsuccessfully to forget.

It was clearer than ever to her that no one else here should know about her past.

'Anything of interest in the criminal world?'

Anne Jackson knew that Chris Rushton wouldn't tell her if there was, that the details of any juicy case would remain confidential until it came to court. He was a stickler for playing things by the book. But that was one of the things she found unexpectedly likeable in Detective Inspector Rushton. In a world where people cheated routinely and integrity was almost a dirty word, you could rely on Chris to be absolutely honest and to operate within the rules. Almost stuffily honest at times, but that was part of the package. And Anne had liked the package so much that she had recently become engaged to Chris.

Sure enough, he now said a little starchily, 'There's nothing of great interest at the station at the moment. A few routine domestic beatings. Though I'm not sure one should ever describe them as "routine".' He looked at her anxiously, as if fearing her reaction. Chris was a handsome, dark-haired man of thirty-two, whose erectness made him look a little taller than he was. Like many a policeman of his age and rank, he was divorced. He had got over the loss of his wife, but not that of his five-year-old daughter, Kirstie, to whom he had access only every other weekend.

At work, he was supremely confident of his abilities, though he recognized that his chief, Chief Superintendent John Lambert, was a subtler judge of people and a better interviewer than he was. Lambert, despite his massive local reputation, was in Chris's view something of a dinosaur. He was content to leave DI Rushton in charge of the coordination of serious crime investigations in the CID section at the station. Lambert preferred to be out and about, assessing suspects for himself, sniffing out the key elements in any puzzle. A chief superintendent who did not direct from behind a desk was almost unique in the modern police service, but Lambert was indulged because of his veteran status and his impressive results. His working methods suited Chris Rushton, who was excited by the possibilities of modern technology and enjoyed the challenge of bringing together and cross-referencing the plethora of information brought in by the big teams in complex cases.

In his private life, Chris was much less assertive. His divorce had knocked his confidence and accentuated his natural diffidence. He had scarcely been able to believe that Anne Jackson, a young primary school teacher, whom he had met in the course of a murder investigation, found him attractive. She was almost ten years younger than him and now they were engaged; there were mornings when Chris still had to pinch himself to believe that it was true.

Anne stretched herself luxuriously on his sofa, deciding not to pursue the latest gloomy prognostications for the economy in *The Times*. 'You wouldn't believe how exhausting thirty eight-year-old children can be over a day.'

'I would. I know how wrung out one innocent five-year-old can leave me at the weekend. I don't know how you manage it.' Chris still marvelled at the qualities of his amazing new fiancée. Correspondingly, one of the things which pleased Anne was that through all the awful things he saw in his working life and through the vicissitudes of marriage and divorce, her man had retained a certain pleasing naivety. She was slightly surprised to find that she thought of him now as 'her man'.

'There are compensations. You see an amazing amount of development in an eight-year-old, over a year. It's good to feel you've contributed something positive to that process.'

He stirred the rice as it came to the boil in the pan, set the timer on the cooker for eleven minutes. 'Thanks for picking up the food on your way here.' He could still be cautiously polite at times, carefully thanking her for what others would just have accepted as part of being a couple.

'I saw that man in the supermarket, the one you were watching in the pub last week.'

'Which one was that?'

'The one you said was a drug dealer.'

'The one I said we suspected,' he corrected her pedantically. Facts were important to him. It was one of the things on which he and John Lambert agreed. His chief could be a positive Gradgrind about facts, insisting all the time on information before speculation. 'It's drug squad business really, but they're anxious to trap the big boys, not the small fry.' Then he added apologetically, 'I wasn't really watching him, you know. He just happened to be in the pub at the same time as us.'

'So you studied his every move, as long as he was there.' She was laughing at him, her bright blue eyes sparkling with mischief, the corners of her wide mouth crinkling as they resisted open amusement. 'If you hadn't given him so much attention last week, I might not have noticed him today.'

'Proper little detective, aren't you, Anne Jackson?' He left the stove and the small, neat kitchen of his flat and walked over to stand behind her. He ran his fingers though her hair, savouring the look of her, the scent of her, the feel of her.

She wriggled a little, then reached up and took his hand. 'He was behaving a little oddly, I thought.'

'He might well have been. Darren Chivers was a drug user himself. Still is, for all I know.' A pause, then came the question he had not meant to ask. 'How do you mean, oddly?'

'Well, I wasn't really watching him, but he seemed to be wandering up and down the aisles without buying very much. And he was still in the car park when I came out, reading a copy of the *Citizen*, or pretending to. I thought perhaps he was waiting for someone.'

'You seem to have noticed quite a lot, for someone who wasn't really watching him.' He enjoyed teasing her; it was a pleasure which had been denied to him in the last few years. Then suddenly, she stood up and turned to face him, and they were in each other's arms.

FOUR

The view was certainly spectacular. From the restaurant at the top of the Post Office Tower on a June evening, you could see the whole of London and much more. It was, Mark Rogers reminded himself, one of the definite advantages of being a British Telecom executive. For security reasons in a vicious modern world, this supreme view of the capital and its environs was now confined entirely to those attending BT corporate shindigs.

Rogers was on official duty here, entertaining important customers. It wasn't arduous and his role meant that the excellent food, as well as the visual delights, were entirely free. For an ambitious thirty-seven-year-old, who had risen quickly in the firm and planned to go further, evenings like this were tangible recognition of his progress and his status. He smiled willingly at an observation from the lady on his left, checked surreptitiously on the perfection of the knot in his tie, and transferred his attention to the supermarket chief on his right.

You had to direct your conversational efforts at the people

immediately beside you and the man or woman immediately opposite you. You could join in any more general exchanges if they stemmed from someone else, but you should not initiate them yourself. There was no official instruction to that effect. It was merely a common-sense procedure which Mark Rogers had devised for himself and tested satisfactorily on previous occasions. Common sense was a surprisingly effective aid in climbing the promotional ladder. If you used it shrewdly, it could even give you a reputation for insight and intelligence.

It really was a magnificent view. Mark agreed heartily with the supermarket director on that, then pointed out the splendid isolation of this tower, contrasting the view with the skyscraper-dominated skyline of New York. Though there was now inevitably a proliferation of high-rise building in London, there were no other very tall buildings to obstruct the immediate view in this area of the city. Mark managed to imply that it was the foresight and architectural genius of British Telecom which had secured this advantage over viewpoints in that other metropolis across the pond.

The circular restaurant, entirely surrounded by windows at eye level, rotated every twenty-two minutes, so that any building of interest missed on a first viewing could be seen again as it returned to the vision of these fortunate eyes. Mark pointed out the Senate House of London University, which had once dominated the landscape, but now looked almost insignificant below them. It turned out that the supermarket mogul had attended that august institution, whereas twenty years later Mark had read Business Studies at Reading. Neither of them had enjoyed what they agreed were the dubious joys of a public school. And so one of those little bonds was established between them which help to grease the wheels on such evenings.

Mark pointed out to the friendly lady on his left that the first lights were coming on now in the building known as the Erotic Gherkin and in the towers of Canary Wharf beyond it, proving that the view from here was not only supreme, but constantly changing. It was an hour now since people had first entered this room and gasped at the panorama below them. Most of them had walked to the windows, looked down at the vertigo-triggering streets so far below them, and moved hastily to the seats at the tables and the longer views. Mark had stood for a moment studying a minor traffic accident hundreds of feet below, where a van which looked like a Dinky toy was resting against the boot of a Jaguar and tiny matchstick figures were engaged in a noiseless pantomime of argument. Having established that heights were no problem for him, he had turned back to the guests with the understanding, unruffled smile of the experienced host.

The food was good and the wine plentiful. As he wasn't driving home that night, he did not need to count the units. He drank enough to encourage those around him to indulge themselves, noting surreptitiously how much his immediate neighbours were consuming. He had no plans to exploit the knowledge, but information was never wasted. If there was a teetotaler adjacent to you, you would be a little more careful with your own drinking; if someone was overindulging, you might be able to encourage the occasional useful verbal indiscretion.

No one was overindulging. Perhaps they were as watchful as he was. More likely they just wanted to enjoy the rare opportunity to see such vistas bathed in the soft sunlight of a June evening. The lady he was talking to was the wife of an eminent BT client. No need to be careful here, on the face of it, but wives usually reported back to husbands in the privacy of late-night bedrooms. This wife was a pleasant, intelligent lady in her mid-fifties, with a liking for music and literature; she was looking forward to another freebie at Glyndebourne next month. As the vista to the north-east moved gradually into view, Mark pointed out the white stone and green glass of the new NHS hospital, then the older listed buildings of the London University Medical School, in their distinctive St Andrews cross shape.

'George Orwell died in Room sixty-five of that building, on January the twenty-first, 1950,' he told his neighbour.

The lady was impressed; he heard her passing on the gist of the information to her neighbour on the other side a few minutes later. Mark had never really understood *Animal Farm* and *1984* when he read them at school, but it was useful to have a good memory for facts, however you acquired them. He finished his burgundy as the waiters began to serve the dessert.

The American opposite him had wanted to see the London

Eye, and Mark Rogers dutifully drew his attention to it as it
moved back into view. 'Originally the Millennium Wheel,' he
offered usefully, 'but it became the London Eye by popular
usage.' Americans were usually impressed by democracy, so
long as it didn't interfere too much with government.

'They tell me you get a great view from up there,' said the
American.

It was exactly what Mark had wanted him to say. 'An excellent view indeed. It doesn't compare with this one, of course,
which is much more extensive and rotates every twenty-two
minutes, but it's the best one most people are allowed to see.
This one is only available to a privileged few, I'm afraid.'

'I guess so. Sure is a shame, that.' But the man didn't sound
very regretful to be thus privileged.

Dusk fell pleasantly over the scene as the coffee and mints
arrived. Mark pointed out the now illuminated neo-Gothic face
of the St Pancras hotel and the roof of the newly restored
station. Mark's American visitor was much taken by the vast
arched-glass roof of the new terminal for the Eurotunnel trains,
whilst his female neighbour received the information that a
compelling statue of John Betjeman, the late poet laureate,
was a centrepiece of the station.

It was, all in all, a pleasant and successful evening, Mark
Rogers decided as he followed the BT guests into the lift and
descended to ground level. He even enjoyed the cooler air
outside as he strolled the two hundred yards to the hotel where
he was to spend the night. He had booked in and unpacked
his overnight bag earlier, so he had nothing to do now but
unwind, undress and retire for the night.

It was twenty past eleven. Samantha wouldn't be asleep
yet. She was probably reading her usual chapter of her novel
before switching off the bedside light. She answered as soon
as the phone rang. 'Just thought I'd report in for the night.
Try to convince you I wasn't with a London tart.' Mark lay
back naked on the top of the bed, enjoying a little coolness
on this warm city night.

'How'd it go?'

She even sounded genuinely interested as she made the
routine wifely enquiry, he thought fondly. 'Well enough, I
think. Good food and a wonderful summer evening helped.
And I didn't have anyone like that Boadicea who wanted to

clean up television that I got last time. But I'm glad it's over.
You can't relax when you're conscious that you're really on
duty.' It didn't do to make these junketings sound too attractive, when you were speaking to a wife coping with two lively
kids on her own.

'See you tomorrow, then.'

'I'm looking forward to it already!' Then, as an apologetic
afterthought, he asked, 'Did anyone from work ring?' It was
always best to be prepared, if there were problems.

'No one from work. Some odd bloke who didn't give his
name rang this evening.'

'What time?'

'About eight o'clock, I think. I was trying to get the kids
to think about bed at the time. He wouldn't give me his name.'

'What did he want?'

'He wouldn't say. He said that it was about money. That
you'd know who it was and he'd be in touch again shortly.
Who was it, Mark? He sounded an odd sort of bloke.'

'No idea, love. Might even have been a wrong number, if
he wouldn't say who he was and what he wanted.'

But as he put the phone down, Mark Rogers' face would
have told any unseen observer that this was no wrong number
call.

'This is harassment.'

The old whine, coming right at the beginning of today's
exchanges. That was good, DI Rushton told himself. It showed
that the subject was scared and defenceless. 'No harassment,
Mr Chivers. You are here on a voluntary basis, helping the
police with their inquiries, just as all good citizens should.'

Darren Chivers, this creature of the night, this man who
operated best and was most at home in semi-darkness, instinctively avoided the bright sun of midday. There was no sun
here, but the harsh fluorescent light above his head seemed
to him like a stage spotlight, seeking him out pitilessly and
illuminating every movement of his shifty face.

He picked out one of Rushton's words and tried to force
contempt into his repetition of it. 'Voluntary! That's a fucking
joke, that is, and we all know it!'

But in the pitiless, all-revealing box of the interview room,
he couldn't bring off the degree of scorn he wanted.

Detective Sergeant Hook gave him a grim smile. 'We're playing it by the book, Darren. We could have seen you in your den, maybe opened a few drawers, done a little search of the place, if we weren't being careful about the rules.'

'You can't do that without a search warrant.' But if they did it, what defence would he have to offer? A brief might make something of it, but courts weren't sympathetic to people like Darren Chivers.

Chris Rushton didn't trouble to disguise his contempt. Anyone involved in flooding the streets with crack and heroin excited his detestation, even small-time pushers like this man. 'We could get a search warrant easily enough, if we wanted one, Chivers. We might do just that if you don't cooperate with us today.'

'I am cooperating, aren't I? Joining the pigs in their sty is cooperating.' Darren tried to scrape up a little confidence to bolster his hostility.

'We've pulled in four users in the last month who say their supplier is Gary Peters. Your little joke, I suppose. But an expensive joke. It's led us to you. It's why you're here now.'

He allowed himself a crafty, self-satisfied smile, in spite of his vulnerability. 'You should be out there looking for this sod Peters, instead of harassing innocent citizens like me.'

'We know that Gary Peters is you, Chivers. It probably seemed a clever idea to you when you thought of it, a little joke at our expense. But it's the reason that you're sitting here now. Obstructing the police in the course of their inquiries, when a wiser man would be trying to get himself off the hook.'

'I ain't obstructing no one.' The denial came automatically. Darren had no idea whether or not it was justified.

'What were you doing in the supermarket car park on Friday?'

He tried not to be thrown by this sudden switch. 'Going about my lawful business, I expect. Even people like me have to eat, you know.' He had been following a possible victim for his other trade, but they couldn't possibly know that.

'Behaving suspiciously, I was told.'

'You were told wrong, then, weren't you?'

Bert Hook gave him a grim smile. 'Not much sign of assistance from you yet, is there, Darren? Not much sign yet of the information which would stop us throwing the book at you.' He leaned forward until his face was within two feet of the thin, apprehensive features on the other side of the small, square table. 'You can help yourself if you've got the sense to do it, Darren. We're not really that interested in putting small fry like you behind bars. But we need names. Names of your suppliers.'

'I can't do that.'

'Can't or won't?'

'I can't. I don't know who supplies me.' He added too late, 'Who used to supply me, I mean. I'm not doing drugs any more. I'm not using and I'm not supplying.' His lips set in a thin line, as if showing determination would make it true.

Bert Hook glanced down at the thin, wasted arms, then up into the scared, crafty face, saying nothing for a moment. Chivers dropped his folded arms back to his sides, as if he feared the burly man might seize his wrists and roll back the sleeves of his shirt to reveal the evidence of needle damage on the skin below. 'You and we both know you're concealing information, Darren. The best thing you can do is stop dealing from this moment and never start again, but I don't think that's going to happen. Do you?'

'I've already stopped.' Chivers leaned forward, at once sly and pathetic, truculent and vulnerable. 'I can take advice, even from coppers, when it suits me! I don't deal any more. So you're wasting your time this morning. And mine too.' He jutted his thin chin at them in a pitiful attempt at aggression.

It was Chris Rushton who finished the interview. 'I don't believe you when you say you can tell us nothing, Chivers. I don't for a minute believe you're going to stop dealing. Well, we shall be watching and waiting. We'll have you, and when we do, we'll hang you out to dry. Your failure to cooperate today has been noted.'

The two officers sat together in the interview room for a moment after Chivers had scurried from the room and the station like a fleeing rodent. 'How much do you think he does know?' asked Rushton.

Hook shook his head disconsolately, feeling the flatness which always followed an unproductive interview. 'Maybe the name of his immediate supplier. Maybe not even that. He's small fry – a user who's turned dealer to feed the habit. The drug squad aren't interested in people like him. They want people higher up the chain – the people who supply him and the tier beyond that.'

They nodded their agreement, then mentally shook their heads at the hopelessness of the task. The real barons of this multibillion pound industry, the people who supervised the importation of huge quantities of illegal drugs, were often not even UK residents. It was relatively easy to apprehend people like Darren Chivers, even to secure custodial sentences for them after repeated offences. But that solved nothing. There was a constant stream of men and women ready to replace him as small-time dealers, eager to seize their share of this lucrative but vicious trade, until they in turn were arrested.

Back in the privacy of his den, Darren Chivers tried to bolster his confidence. He had told them nothing. The pigs had come to the trough and found it empty. He had been too clever for them. But they'd be watching him now, so he'd better remain clever. He'd be careful. He wouldn't deal in the coming weeks – certainly not in his usual sites.

He'd better play up his other source of income, for a while longer yet. But that had its dangers too. The room was stifling, in the middle of the June day. He reached up over the sink and banged open the window whose hinges were stiff from lack of use. No cooling breeze came in from the still, sun-filled day outside. He resented the brightness, longed once again for the night which was his natural métier. 'Darkness visible', that's what he needed; he liked that phrase.

He was a natural loner, content with his own company, he told himself. But with the busy world outside bustling forward in the heat of the day, Darren Chivers felt a hopeless isolation dropping around his thin shoulders.

FIVE

It was a large, high-roomed stone house, set in what had once been extremely large grounds. It must have been very grand in its Victorian heyday. The modern extensions had still left acres of space around the buildings and many of the residents were sitting in the gardens on this sunny June day, which was made only more pleasant by the soft southerly breeze.

Superintendent John Lambert made his way slowly towards the main building from the visitors' car park, wondering exactly what he was going to say to his old chief. Early-stage Alzheimer's, the manager had told him when he rang. Too early yet to be certain how effective the new drug they were trying was going to be. Mr North was one of their friendliest residents – they didn't call them patients, and she'd be glad if he'd bear that in mind when he came to visit. No, she hadn't realized that Mr North had once been a chief inspector in the police. It would be on his file, of course, but they treated everyone the same here. She had found it worked out best when residents regarded their time at Westcott Manor as a fresh start.

Jack North wasn't one of the people enjoying the gardens. The young woman in a nurse's uniform in the reception area told Lambert that he was in his room, that he might find him 'a bit vague' today. She seemed to look at Lambert rather curiously, as if wondering why he was here, but that might have been his imagination. Perhaps they didn't get many visitors other than relatives. Or maybe he was exciting interest by his own awkwardness. John Lambert had never been a good hospital visitor and, though he reminded himself again that this was not a hospital, he found himself already ill at ease here.

He scarcely recognized his old chief when he saw him. North was sitting in an armchair, looking down at his hands. His thin white hair was neatly combed, but the alert eyes Lambert remembered had sunk into his head. They were watery, pale, diminished, almost the unseeing eyes of a blind man. They looked up at Lambert as he shut the door behind him, but there was no recognition in them.

'It's been a long time, Jack,' said Lambert. He was wondering already if he should have come here.

He sat down in a chair opposite the man who had once controlled his destiny, who had shaped his career when he was a detective sergeant hacking his way through the CID jungle. North was looking at him still, registering now a little curiosity, a puzzlement that might turn into panic if his damaged brain was not given something to fasten on. 'We used to work together,' said Lambert desperately. 'I'm John Lambert. You were good to me, Jack. Showed me the ropes, prevented me from putting my foot in it. I had a lot to learn, then, I can tell you.' He laughed, a rattling, artificial sound, trying to soothe this tense, diminished creature, to induce relaxation by a shared hilarity in a dim, half-remembered comradeship.

'John Lambert.' The slack mouth repeated the name carefully, like a dutiful child trying to please.

'You were a big man in those days, Jack' There was no reaction from the lined grey face. 'You were a bit of a bastard at times, if I'm honest!' Lambert wondered if he should have used that familiar police word in this place. He heard himself laughing again, a hollow, mirthless sound.

'A bit of a bastard.' For the first time, he had a reaction. North seemed pleased, though it was a muted, uncertain pleasure. 'I was a bit of a bastard.' He smiled, then said with a sudden, startling clarity, 'You could be a bastard in those days, you know. You can't now. You have to be person – no, pol . . .' His voice trailed away and he lifted both hands to his face in frustration.

'Politically correct. That's right, Jack. That's what you have to be nowadays, politically correct.'

Jack North nodded, seven, eight, ten times. 'I was a copper.'

'You were, Jack. You were a good copper, too. One of the best.'

'One of the best.' The brow furrowed, the brain tried to take in the idea and build on it, but wasn't able to do so. 'One of the best. Was I?'

'You were, Jack. Taught me a few things, I can tell you.' A few things to do and a few things not to do, thought Lambert. Jack North had been as straight as a die himself, but he'd sometimes taken short cuts you could never risk nowadays. 'You had a big team, Jack, in the old days.' He wished he had more experience of this, wished he had asked Mrs North for a little more guidance when he had acceded to her request to come here.

Amy North was a tiny, bright-eyed woman, with head and hand movements as quick as a sparrow's in pursuit of food. She was a little wizened now, but mentally as sharp as she

had been twenty years ago. That had made Lambert less
prepared for the frailty he was desperately trying to deal with
now. Amy came here every day. Perhaps she didn't realize
just how far her husband had degenerated. More likely, she
didn't wish to acknowledge the decline in the man she loved,
even to herself. Lambert was diverted for a moment by a surge
of admiration for the courage of that tiny, uncomplaining
woman, who should have been enjoying a serene old age after
a blameless life.

'You were a good detective, John.'

Lambert was startled from his reverie by the words, by the
pleasure in the old face opposite him at a sudden opening of
a door to a room in the past.

'You didn't let things go, John. You got Bruce Nixon.'

A name Lambert had almost forgotten himself. A man who
had been in prison for repeated burglaries when they'd pinned
a murder on him. A man the police machine had earmarked
as a petty criminal and as a result almost overlooked as a
potential killer. A man who had helped Lambert to make
Inspector when the Promotion Board considered him a few
months later. 'You supported me on Nixon, Jack. We got him
together.'

Bruce Nixon. The eyes had brightened a little as North
recalled the name, but apparently the memory did not extend
beyond that, for he was looking at Lambert as if he were a
stranger once more. He said uncertainly, 'Mother's dead. Did
your sister tell you that?' He had lost his bearings again,
thought now that this visitor was his brother.

Lambert said gently, 'I worked with you, Jack. I'm not your
brother. We were detectives together, not so long ago.'

'Detectives, yes. I remember that.' There was a long pause
and then he said, 'Was I any good?'

'Yes, Jack, you were very good.' But was North trying to
exorcize some ghost, some moral breach which gnawed at his
conscience, some wisp of guilt which troubled him still, in
this moving coma where thoughts surfaced and then sank
again without completing themselves?

Lambert looked out of the window at the gardens and the
people sitting and strolling in them. The world outside seemed
to him to be moving on, whilst he was trapped in this limbo
where ideas came and went but nothing moved forwards.

The young woman who had directed him here brought in a tray with a pot of tea and biscuits and spoke kindly to Jack North, who nodded back at her with a small, secret smile.

'She's a good girl,' he said to Lambert as if she had already left the room. 'Amy isn't able to do as much as she could, you see. I make allowances for her, but she doesn't do as much as she should. What do you think about it?'

'I think Amy's very good to you, Jack. You need looking after and she brought you to this nice place so that you could have the care you need. She comes and sees you every day.' Lambert walked across to the chest of drawers and picked up a picture of Jack and Amy North on their wedding day, thinking how recent it must seem to Amy and this shell of her husband, how impossible it would have been for the smiling, vigorous man and the small laughing woman in the brilliant white dress to foresee that it would end like this.

John Lambert was falsely bright over the tea. He tried another couple of conversational sallies which went down very short cul-de-sacs, and then took his leave. He took his time deliberately to walk through the grounds, smiling and greeting those of the residents who acknowledged him, feeling that his transition to the real world needed to be gradual rather than sudden if it was to be successful.

That night, Amy North rang him to ask about his visit. 'He was pretty vague, to be honest,' said Lambert.

'He's better some days than others,' said Amy North, determinedly cheerful. 'He remembered you'd been, so that's good, isn't it?'

After midnight, there were few people around here. It would be foolish to challenge those who were, unless you had the power and authority of a large organization like the police service behind you.

Darren Chivers had no such support so he trod warily. He wanted no contact other than the single one he had come here to make. He was careful to avoid the police patrol car which slid past him as he remained deep in the shadow of a high warehouse wall, and equally careful to avoid any less legal and more sinister agency operating in this part of the city. He remained motionless until the sound of the slowly moving vehicle died away and the silence of the night was his again.

Despite his alertness to any activity around him, Chivers felt much more at ease here than in the blazing light of a June midday. In his dark blue jeans and trademark navy anorak, he felt he could merge into the shadows, become a part of this black, inanimate landscape, whenever he chose. A kind of chameleon, he thought, capable not of changing colour but of avoiding all colour, to disguise the fact of his existence. Of merging into that darkness visible which was his natural element.

Darren was used to being patient. Waiting was a fact of life for him, one of the tools of his existence. The ability to endure long periods without motion whilst still remaining intensely alert was a necessary skill for a drug-dealer. The ability was also useful when he followed this other trade of his, this lucrative activity which had at first seemed very dangerous, but which at present was less so than pushing heroin and coke.

Earlier in the evening, he had seen his supplier and explained why he proposed to keep a low profile for a month or two, until the fuzz got bored and moved on to other more active possibilities. It had been a rough interview, but the man had seen sense eventually, accepting with a surly reluctance that it was in the interest of himself and his masters that Chivers should steer clear of trouble. Arrests helped no one.

It was after midnight now, and the silence here was almost tangible. Even the thin sliver of the new moon was not visible if you kept on the right side of buildings. Half a mile away, someone dropped a piece of some sort of metal on to concrete. The sound rang as clear as if it had been within a hundred yards, startling the man who slid like a feral cat through the shadows of high buildings, stilling for a while the yowling of real cats which had been the only previous nocturnal sound in the area. He moved away from the docks and the unmoving mirror of water below the quays; in the streets which ran away to the south of the tourist area of dock museums and antique warehouses, it was even darker.

The street lighting was sporadic here. There were no houses, and the businesses which operated behind high walls and locked gates were expected to provide their own security, which might or might not include security lights. Strangers would have been quickly lost, but Darren Chivers knew exactly where he was going, just as he knew exactly what he planned to do.

That did not mean that he was not excited, even fearful. More fearful about this than about any other of the contacts he proposed to make in the pursuit of this other branch of his income. He had not planned to contact this man again. For once, the blackmailer's old assurance that this would be the final demand had been genuine, because Dan Steele scared him. But needs must, when the devil drove. Or rather the police; this was all the fault of the pigs, really, for closing in on his drug dealing. Darren Chivers slipped into the warped logic of the habitual criminal.

The double gates were high between the pillars of brick. And of course they were securely locked. Darren didn't even bother to check that. But he did look up and down the dark street on either side of the gates, checking that he was alone here. It was the instinctive caution of the hunted man. But the quarry was about to turn predator. Chivers settled into the deep shadow of the wall beside the gate and waited for his moment. He was good at waiting, he told himself again. Somewhere on his left, a hundred yards away at the next small opening in the wall, there was a scuffling, a small, investigative scratching, which would have been inaudible in anything other than this profoundest of silences. A rat, probably. Darren didn't mind that thought. Rats were creatures that made the most of anything they could find in the darkness, like him.

Ten minutes passed. The man should be here by now, unless he had changed his routine. They did that sometimes, security men. It didn't do to be too predictable, when there might be violent people around. Darren wasn't violent. His danger was far more subtle than that. He soothed himself with that thought as he waited, with the collar of his anorak turned up even on this still, warm night.

Another ten minutes. Then he heard movements in the distance, which translated themselves into the sound of footsteps as they drew nearer. Darren inched his head to the edge of the gates, resting his forehead on the cool metal, waiting to check that this was the right man before he made his move.

The footsteps seemed as loud as the tramp of a marching army as they drew nearer. He could see little but a dim presence beyond the bright circle of light thrown by the torch's beam. Then the feet caught an empty tin can flung over the gates by some anonymous reveller, and the muttered curse told Darren that this was indeed his quarry.

Chivers waited until the man was in the very centre of the gap between the two gate-pillars, then said, 'Job going well, is it, Mr Steele?'

There was a startled gasp from the dark shape behind the torch. Then the light flashed full upon Darren's face, white and pitiless, causing him to blink and recoil. But this exposure did not matter, he told himself. The man already knew who he was, so that the light gave him no advantage. He could do him no harm with the strong iron gates between them, despite his superior strength and the pick handle he carried.

Darren forced confidence, even contempt, into his voice. 'I'm going to need a little more, Mr Steele. It's unfortunate, but there it is. Unforeseen circumstances, cost of living, and all that.'

'You're getting nothing else from me, Chivers. Get your miserable skin out of here before I call the police.'

'You won't do that, Mr Steele. We both know that you won't do that. You'll meet my modest demand, and then see no more of me. A thousand, that's all. A small price to be rid of me for ever.'

'I've heard that before!' The hatred and frustration poured through the metal bars of the gates, causing Darren to step back another pace. 'You'll get no more out of me. I should never have dealt with scum like you in the first place.'

'You'll pay. You can't afford not to pay.'

'I'll see you at the bottom of the Severn first!'

Darren Chivers resisted the temptation to glance over his shoulder towards the quiet depths of the great river. He could hear Steele's harsh breath, the anger thrusting itself into that uneven, rasping sound. Even with his eyes accustomed to the darkness, he could not make out the features of his adversary's face. With the vestigial lighting of the empty factory behind him, Daniel Steele was no more than a black hulk. A very large hulk, with a weapon in his hands. Darren was glad of the heavy metal gate between himself and the pickaxe handle. 'You won't do that, Dan Steele. You know that if anything happens to me, the evidence is waiting to be discovered. You wouldn't want that, so you won't harm me.'

'Go to hell!'

'You'll pay, because you have to. I'll give you a week, but no more. Your credit's good, so I'll take a cheque, if you like. Made out to Darren Chivers Esquire. I know it won't bounce, because you've too much at stake for that.' He did not want to meet this man, did not want to encounter face to face the frustrated violence which might overflow into physical action.

'If I ever get my hands on your miserable throat, you won't last sixty seconds, scum!'

But with that final wild threat, he was acknowledging that he was going to pay, thought Darren. He managed a parting taunt. 'You have a week, Steele. But earlier payment will oblige!' Then he forced himself to turn his back and slip away into the warm, concealing night.

SIX

Michelle de Vries was feeling guilty. Her husband was a good man. She should not be cheating on him. But she couldn't help herself.

Even as she framed that thought, she thought how tawdry and second-hand it was. The excuse which weak and sensual women had given to themselves over the centuries, which should be fiercely rejected by a modern woman. Of course she could help herself. Of course she had a will of her own. She was making her own decisions, not a victim of some sexual spell which she could not control.

Gerald de Vries was a good man. He did not deserve what she was doing to him. She certainly could not deceive herself with that old evasion that he deserved all he got because he had invited it. He was not a rich wimp. He would not tolerate what she was doing if he somehow got to know about it. That should have been all the more reason to give it up.

Instead, she found herself making the resolution that Gerald must certainly not find out about her affair.

'How did things go at Boutique Chantelle today?' he asked her now.

'All right. I made a useful sale to a very rich old lady. I

think she'll recommend me to other rich old ladies. These things pass around among what we used to call the county set.'

'But can you exist on the county set alone?'

'No. You're right, as usual. We need the nouveaux riches as well. If it wasn't for people with more money than sense, there wouldn't be enough trade for shops like mine. But don't spread that thought around!' She grinned at him, enjoying behaving as a working equal with this man who had made more money that she could ever hope to make from her modest enterprise.

'Is your turnover increasing? Is the extra member of staff you took on paying for herself?' He was treating her as a serious businesswoman. He had put money into her enterprise. He could afford to treat it as an expensive hobby, to indulge this whim of his wife's to run a high-class fashion outlet and if necessary simply write off the money involved, but he wasn't doing that. Perhaps it was instinctive in a man like him to want to see his investment justified. Either way, his interest was genuine. He was certainly not patronizing Michelle.

She said, 'Sales are up on last year, and I think it was a good move to bring the hats into the shop, as you suggested. Our busiest three months are coming up, so it's a little early in the financial year for me to speculate, but I'm optimistic. As for Jean, I'm not sure about her yet. I can definitely justify an assistant, but she may not be the woman for the job. You can't rush my customers into purchases. But she's only part-time. Either she'll prove a quick learner, or she'll have to go.'

Gerald glanced at her approvingly. He hadn't expected this strain of hard-headed ruthlessness in his wife when he'd set her up in the shop. He took a sip of his burgundy, paused to savour it for a moment, and then asked unexpectedly, 'Are you enjoying Boutique Chantelle?'

'I am, yes. I'm enjoying meeting the challenge. Enjoying generating new business – there wasn't a shop selling clothes of my quality in the city before we took the lease. Enjoying showing my clever old husband that he isn't the only one who can make a success of a business.' She reached across the table and stroked the back of his hand for a moment. The feel of it brought the treacherous thought that it was older, more sinewy, and much less strong than that of her lover.

'We can get more help in the house, you know, if you need it. Someone to help with the meals.'

'There's no need, at the moment, honestly. We already have someone in to clean and I hardly do anything in the garden nowadays, except give directions to Ted. I feel quite a slut about the place.'

'But you're my slut! And long may it remain so, I say!' Gerald gripped the hand she had been trying to withdraw, held it between both of his.

She thought for a moment that he was going to lift it to his lips and kiss her fingers.

She said abruptly, 'I have to go out again this evening, I'm afraid, darling. Pressure of business, you see. The price of expansion.'

A little sigh, a little hurt creeping into the brown eyes. Perhaps a glimmer of the suspicion always likely to beset a man sixteen years older than his wife, but she couldn't be sure of that. Michelle said, 'Penalty of success, I'm afraid. I have to visit a lady who wants to be measured up and advised on clothes in the privacy of her own home. Rather a grand lady, as a matter of fact.'

'Too grand to come into the shop?'

'Too rich to be compelled to, if she doesn't fancy it. I think she might want to come in, after I've presented her with a taster of what we have to offer tonight. Obviously I can't show her the full range in her own home, can I?'

She smiled at him mischievously on that last thought, and he grinned back and said delightedly, 'We'll make a tycoon of you yet, Michelle de Vries!'

It had been once a week at first. She should keep it to that, if she wasn't going to risk Gerald being suspicious. But whatever resolutions she made, Guy seemed able to make her dismiss them. She felt quite guilty as she reversed out of the drive and waved to Gerald's face at the front window. But within a mile, excited anticipation had taken over from guilt.

Bert Hook arrived early to pick up his sons from cricket practice. He was hoping to see them in action, to check on their progress in the game he loved, but of course he wouldn't admit any such fatherly weakness to the boys.

Jack Hook wasn't quite fifteen, yet, but he had already had the odd game in the first team and was practising with them in their net. He had already had his twelve minutes' batting practice and was now bowling his occasional off-breaks to the man taking his turn at the batting crease. Bert felt he could watch him for a few minutes without putting him off. Jack was an out-and-out batsman who had no pretensions to be a bowler.

With the smell of newly mown grass and the sound of bat on ball, Bert felt that old mixture of pleasure and pain which besets the retired sportsman, a yearning for things past. He had been a doughty performer for many years for Herefordshire in the various Minor Counties' competitions, a pace bowler who had made some of the best batsman in the country hop about a bit. There had even been offers of trial contracts with Worcestershire and Gloucestershire in his youth, but the former Barnardo's boy had not dared to jettison the career in the police service which had been presented to him as a wonderful opportunity.

Now, with cricket balls whizzing around the practice field and the familiar cricket banter in his ears, his fingers itched to caress the seam of the ball again, whilst his shoulders twitched in remembrance of the thousands of balls they had delivered over the years. Nostalgia was a wonderful thing. You never bowled a bad ball in the selective memory which took over in retirement. Don't be so damned silly, Detective Sergeant Bert Hook told himself firmly. Stand back and watch the next generation take over.

In the junior net, his younger son Luke was just beginning his allocation of time for batting practice. He was concentrating far too hard to notice his father, so that Bert was able to sidle round behind the net without being spotted. One of the people bowling was a lad of eighteen anxious to make his mark in the first team, who was plainly going to make no concessions to the new batsman's youth. He was a bowler of brisk but erratic pace. Bert winced mentally as a short ball rose spitefully and flashed past Luke's nose. Then he swelled with fatherly pride as the lad got right behind the next ball and played it calmly down, his left elbow high above the handle of the bat. Nothing wrong with the lad's courage, then. It took guts to stand in line and play a ball coming at you at that pace. Bert stared at the ground, hoping that his parental satisfaction was not too obvious to any bystander.

'Your boys are coming on well, Bert. It must be something in the genes!'

Bert Hook started, then turned with a smile. He had been so intent on the actions of his younger son that the club captain, an old cricketing friend of his, had arrived undetected at his side. 'I don't know about that, Keith. I was a bowler, sweating buckets on hot days. These two seem to have the sense to be batsmen!' He tried to keep the pride out of his voice, but didn't succeed.

'Jack's in the first team tomorrow. Perhaps batting at five. Or do you think that's too high for him at his age?'

'Your call, not mine, Keith. Whatever is best for the team. Are you still opening the batting?'

The man who was only a couple of years younger than Bert shook his head. 'Times change, Bert. Our current openers are called Singh and Patel. Both have lived here all their lives – they might have darker skins than the rest of us, but they have strong local accents. Fortunately, they also have those steely wrists we associate with the subcontinent.'

'I watched one of them batting when I arrived. Silky. I wouldn't like to bowl to him.'

'I bet you could still make him hurry his shots.' Keith looked at his old friend and allowed his face to crease into a slow, mischievous smile. 'Why don't you trundle a few down, Bert? Give yourself a bit of exercise.'

A woman would have had the sense to refuse graciously but firmly. But Bert Hook said diffidently, 'I'd make a fool of myself, Keith. And I've only got my trainers on.'

Within two minutes, he had a ball in his hand and was windmilling his arms to flex his creaking shoulders. He cautiously marked out a run-up considerably abbreviated from that of his palmy days. Hook noticed with a chagrin he could not register publicly that the tail-end batsman had been replaced by one of the dark-skinned specialist batsmen his friend had mentioned. His once rhythmical run was laboured. His first ball was short enough to be dispatched comfortably off the back foot. His second was the leg-stump half-volley which all bowlers seek to avoid. The batsman showed his class as he leant on it comfortably, sending it along the ground for what would probably have been a leg-side boundary. Bert kicked the turf disgustedly and lamented the pretensions of middle age.

He dug the next one in just short of a length and was pleased to see the batsman surprised by the pace as the ball rose chest high; he fended it off in the air for what might have been a catch at short leg. There was a nod from the batsman, a little clap from behind the net. Bert realized to his dismay that spectators had gathered in the twilight to witness the humbling of the old warhorse.

His next ball pitched on a length and left the bat, the away swinger he had found it most difficult to bowl in his heyday. The batsman, still mindful of the previous rising ball, was a little slow into his forward defence and his thin edge would undoubtedly have been a catch to the wicket-keeper. He nodded a sporting acknowledgement to the panting bowler, who could not resist a grin of modest delight in response.

He would go for the in-swinger next, the one the commentators now called by that mystical name of 'reverse swing'. It had always been his natural delivery. To his secret surprise and delight, he pitched it exactly where he wanted to, found the tiny gap between bat and pad, and deftly removed the batsman's middle stump. This time there was combined and enthusiastic applause from behind the net, as the batsman acknowledged his defeat and ruefully replaced the stump.

Bert had enough sense to give up while he was ahead. 'The light's going now,' he said sympathetically to the batsman. He tried to disguise how heavily he was breathing as he picked up his sweater from the end of his run and went over to collect his boys from the appreciative group behind the net.

Hook was a genuinely modest man, so that he was glad to get away from the extravagant praise for his tiny renaissance. But he was only human. He lingered a little while in the attached garage as the boys scampered into the house, so that he could hear what they said to his wife.

'Our dad got Billy Singh out twice,' said Luke excitedly, anxious to be the first to deliver the news.

'He's the opening bat for the first team,' explained Jack to his mother. 'He's not really Billy, but we call him that.'

'He got fifty-seven last Saturday,' said Luke. 'But Dad had

him on a plate. Knocked his middle stump out with a break-back.'

'More of an off-cutter, really,' corrected his elder brother magisterially. 'Dad must have been pretty good in his day.'

Eleanor Hook knew enough of teenagers to realize that this was the height of praise. 'He was very good indeed,' she said stoutly, 'and now it's high time that you boys were off to bed.'

'You'll be a hero with the boys for at least a weekend,' she said to Bert as they sat in comfortable married relaxation, with the boys in bed and mugs of tea in hand. 'Of course, to my mind, it's just more evidence of the Peter Pan which seems to lurk in all men.'

'You're probably right. You usually are, in these things,' said Bert Hook dutifully. But even his most determined efforts could not quite remove the smile from his face as he sipped his tea.

As Bert Hook relaxed after his unaccustomed effort, Michelle de Vries was preparing to leave the house of her lover. She too was pleasantly exhausted, but from physical efforts of a totally different sort.

'I'll see you on Tuesday as usual.' Guy Dawson had the enigmatic smile he always seemed to reserve for the moment when they parted. It might have been satisfied recollection of their uninhibited abandonment in bed over the last two hours. It might have been anticipation of another meeting in four days' time. It might even have been the satisfaction of sex without commitment, of having a woman so under his spell that she abandoned all inhibitions in his bed and came to him whenever he called her. But Michelle didn't want to consider that possibility.

He kissed her briefly in the hall before he opened the door for her to leave. She held him firmly, feeling the firmness of his back muscles under her fingers, opening her lips and searching for his tongue with hers, insisting without words that this was real affection, not the token endearment of parting. She was more breathless than she wanted to be when she stepped back from him – like a silly teenager in the grip of her first passion, she told herself angrily.

To counteract this thought, she said, 'We'll have to be careful about our meetings. I don't want Gerald to get suspicious.

I thought he raised his eyebrows about tonight. That might be just my imagination, but I think we should watch it.'

'Cool it a little, you mean. All right.'

He had acquiesced a little too readily. She would have liked a little argument, or at least some expression of regret. She said, 'I don't mean cool it, no. I could never cool it, with you, Guy!'

But the teasing words fell oddly from her lips, although entirely sincere. You shouldn't play the coquette, she reflected wryly, when you were a married woman of forty-four and your lover was a single man of thirty-seven. She wanted Guy to take her in his arms again, to tell her that whatever meetings they could arrange were as precious to him as they were to her. Instead, he ran his fingers briefly over her forehead and through her hair, then opened the door upon the warm summer night.

'See you Tuesday, then,' he whispered conspiratorially.

Before she had reached the gate, the door had closed upon that composed smile and she was on her own in the warm, scented darkness.

Michelle made her way back to her car, which was parked discreetly under a tree a hundred and fifty yards away. Thoughts tumbled one upon another in her troubled, racing mind. What was this going to do to her relationship with Gerald, the husband whom she both loved and needed? She had never intended it to get as serious as this when Guy Dawson had advanced the theory that a little fling would do no one any harm. It was much more than a little fling now for her, but what was it for Guy? Was she any more than a convenient and responsive body, a passing phase in his sexual life? He assured her that she was more than that whenever she raised the subject, but she would have liked a little more evidence of his feelings. But she felt that she couldn't pursue the matter without becoming a clingy female, and no man liked that.

Michelle de Vries was far too preoccupied with her feelings to notice the slight figure who noted her departure from the house of Guy Dawson, who slipped from shadow to shadow to follow her at a discreet distance as she made her way to her car, who made a note of its number as she drove away.

Darren Chivers, creature of the night, had more material for his records.

SEVEN

Anne Jackson did not suffer from that Monday morning gloom her colleagues and the wider world found so debilitating.

She paid lip service to the idea, of course, nodding gloomily along with her peers about the prospect of the resumption of work after the joys of the weekend, but she enjoyed her work and secretly relished it. She liked children, so that the prospect of a day with her thirty energetic charges filled her with eager anticipation rather than the panic which the idea might have compelled in less accomplished young women.

Anne had already been in her classroom for half an hour, preparing materials for the day's work. At a quarter to nine, she was sufficiently on top of things to venture out into the sunshine and watch the children coming into school. Many of them lived sufficiently close to the quiet suburban school to walk here unaccompanied by an adult. Those who came with parents mostly left them at the gates and scampered happily into the buildings without a backward glance. A good sign that. Happy children made effective learners.

Anne walked down the short drive, returning the greetings of the children who spoke to her, smiling at the parents she knew. Her interest had been attracted by one figure outside the gates, but she did not wish to draw attention either to this man or to her own concern with him.

Anne Jackson did not subscribe to the present media-driven obsession with paedophiles; she thought it unfortunate that parents should be as fearful as most of them were of sexual or other interference with their children. The apprehension inevitably communicated itself to their offspring, who, in the worst cases, were sometimes terrified of people who only wished them well. Nevertheless, when Anne saw a man behaving in a manner she thought was odd, if not suspicious, she was certainly not about to ignore it.

The slight figure was presumably trying to be unobtrusive. The irony was that both his dress and his manner seemed designed to excite suspicion, especially at this time, in an area thronged with children. The man hurried from the shadow beneath one huge chestnut tree to the shadow beneath the next, then paused for a moment to get his bearings, as if confident that he could not be seen there. On this June morning, when the sun was already high, bright summer dresses and tee shirts dominated the dress among adults. This man was wearing a shabby navy anorak which was zipped up to his throat.

Anne Jackson thought she recognized that anorak. When the man within it turned his thin face to glance instinctively back over his shoulder, she was certain that she did.

This was the man she had seen in the supermarket car park ten days ago, the man her fiancé Chris Rushton had earlier been watching in the pub. A man with a criminal record. Not as a paedophile, thankfully, but as a drug dealer. There was much talk nowadays of drugs being dealt at the school gates in city schools; there had even been an instance of it in Cheltenham, that bastion of conservatism and traditional values, last year. Warnings had gone out to all the schools in the locality, with directions as to the action to be taken if teachers suspected their pupils were being offered illegal substances as they left the premises.

Surely drugs weren't revealing their ugly presence at the gates of a quiet primary school? But whatever the man's purpose was, it seemed to her relief that he had no concern with children. He was level with the entrance to the school now, but on the other side of the road. He made no attempt to turn towards the gates and completely ignored the chattering children who passed within a foot or two of him as he moved on.

Forty yards beyond this point, he stopped in front of a house and looked towards the street lamp adjacent to it and the houses on either side, apparently confirming to himself that this was the house he wanted. Then he produced a stub of pencil and a small pad and made a brief note. Anne presumed he was recording the number and name of the house, for he seemed to take his information from the gatepost in front of it.

Then he turned on his heel, and with the same curious, slightly stooping gait, moved swiftly back whence he had

come. No paedophile this, and, on this occasion at least, no
drug-dealer either.

From within the school grounds, Anne Jackson watched
curiously as he moved like a fugitive from tree to tree, checking
that no one was following him along the pavement. Before
he reached the corner where he would have disappeared from
her view, he pulled a bicycle from beneath the last tree,
mounted it, and rode swiftly away.

Ten hours later, on the same sunlit Monday, Mark Rogers
was feeling very weary. The evening in the restaurant at the
top of the Post Office Tower now seemed a lot more than six
days behind him. The meeting with his boss in Bristol had
gone on for a long time, and some harsh questions had been
asked.

There had been eight of them in the meeting. Some of the
others had received much rougher treatment than he had. He
consoled himself with that thought now that he was at last
alone. But there were harsh times ahead, everyone had agreed.
In the recession which was coming, the weak would go to the
wall and even the strong would need all their wits to survive.
Bonuses this year would be slim or non-existent; the main
aim would be to keep your job.

Work was going to be quite demanding enough, without
this extra thing he had hanging over him.

Like any great city in the summer heat, Bristol was hot and
dusty. The stale, diesel-tainted air tasted like ashes on Mark
Rogers' tongue as he made his way slowly to the multi-storey
car park to collect his vehicle. Arriving in early afternoon, he
had been forced to drive up to the top floor to find a space,
and there was a good signal from there for his mobile phone.

He rang Samantha. 'I'm going to be late, love, I'm afraid.
We've given ourselves a break, but the meeting is set to go
on for another hour yet.'

'OK. Thanks for ringing. I'll get the kids to bed, tell them
Daddy's working late. We'll have a quiche and a drink in front
of the telly whenever you get here. Allow you to unwind after
a long day.'

'Give them a kiss from me. Tell them I'll do the stories
tomorrow night.'

It made him feel worse that she was so unquestioning and

so accommodating. He didn't like lying to his wife and had done very little of it over the years. But he needed time to deal with this other thing which he couldn't tell her about, which he couldn't tell anyone about. He felt immensely tired and depressed. He had to make a conscious effort to start the Mercedes and turn it towards the long downward spiral which would bring him to the street.

At least the length of the meeting meant that the rush hour had cleared from the city. It was a glorious evening, and the sun was not in his eyes as he drove northwards towards Gloucester on the M5. He found himself driving more and more slowly as he turned off the motorway and moved towards the centre of the city and this appointment he did not want to keep.

He allowed himself a pint of bitter, found that it was surprisingly well kept in such a sleazy pub. The man wasn't there yet, but Mark was a little earlier than the time arranged, since he had thought originally that he would have been coming here from home after his evening meal. He felt automatically at the bank notes in the inside pocket of his jacket, then wondered if he should have done so. Might it be a gesture which gave too much information to the denizens of a seedy place like this?

But there weren't many people in the pub at this hour, which fell between those of the after-work drinkers and the more serious clientele of the later evening. He was sitting unobserved on the bench seat in the alcove, as the man had directed him to do. It irked him to be accepting direction from a man like this, to be at the mercy of such a creature. He was more than ever determined to do something about the situation. People like this never went away, though they perpetually promised to do so.

His pint was almost finished, though he had scarcely realized that he was drinking. What he did realize now was how much he had needed it, how much he had needed to wash away the ashes of a depressing day. A depressing day which had the most distressing part of all still to come. He wanted another drink, but he wasn't going to risk one; he needed his wits at their sharpest, with this evil still to be dealt with.

As he contemplated the dregs of his beer, the man slid in beside him, setting his thin thigh against that of his victim,

coming so close that Mark could see his broken teeth and smell
the staleness of his breath. As usual, Chivers had arrived without
his advent being noticed, as if he was an evil that had materialized from the air. Mark eased himself instinctively away from
him, but he knew that there was no escape from the hold this
fellow had over him.

'You got the money?' asked Darren Chivers.

'I've got it, yes.'

Chivers glanced automatically to each side of the alcove,
though he had checked that they would be unobserved before
he had ventured into it. 'Hand it over, then.'

Mark Rogers handed over the notes in the paper bag which
had once contained his child's asthma prescription from the
chemist's. 'This has to be the last.'

Darren Chivers flipped open the corner of the paper bag,
assessed the contents, flicked the corners of the twenty-pound
notes expertly between thumb and fingers. 'A thousand? That's
what we agreed.'

'There's a thousand in cash. More than I can afford. I don't
know how I'll explain the withdrawal to my wife, if she looks
at the bank statement.'

'Your problem, mate, not mine. You'll think of something.
You could even confess, but I wouldn't advise it. Women can't
keep secrets, especially ones that need to be kept, like this.'

'There'll be no more. I'm going to be pushed to keep my
job at BT, the way things are going.' Mark knew immediately
that he should not have said that.

'Have no chance at all, would you, if they knew what I
know? But they don't, and you'll need to make sure it stays
that way.'

Mark Rogers wanted to put strong hands round the thin
throat, to still those taunting, mobile lips for ever. 'I told you,
I can't give you any more. It will be the worse for you if you
try.'

'The worse for me if I try.' Chivers repeated the phrase as
if he needed to weigh it carefully. 'That sounds like a threat,
to me, Mr Rogers. You're in no position to make threats. I
call the shots here!' Darren Chivers delivered this last phrase
with real relish. He had never in his life been in a position to
call the shots, but he was now calling them with powerful
people, people like this, who would have curled their lips in

scorn without the information he possessed. He was finding more satisfaction in this second trade of his than mere money.

Mark pushed his hands deep into his pockets. They were itching to inflict serious damage on this squalid tormentor, but this was neither the place nor the time for action. For the moment Chivers called the shots, as he had just been reminded. He repeated firmly, 'There won't be any more. Not from me. I'm going to be pushed to survive and support my family in the next year.'

'You can make economies, if necessary.' Darren found himself enjoying taunting this man, who would not have given him the time of day without the hold he had. 'I find people can always make economies, when the wolf is at the door.' He smiled a vulpine smile, enjoying the image.

'I'm warning you. If you drive me too far, you'll regret it.'

But it was an empty threat, and both of them knew it.

Chivers said, 'Another threat, mate. Better be careful, I'd say. Just in case you get any silly ideas, all my information is filed at home. If anything dire was to happen to me, the police would search the place and turn up all sorts of interesting information.'

'I've a wife and two innocent kids. They've done you no harm. It's them you're hurting.'

'I'll bear that in mind, mate. But times are hard for me as well as you. We all have to live, mate.'

Mark Rogers wanted to tell Chivers that he wasn't his mate. That he'd rather smash his miserable face to pulp than sit here bandying words with him. Instead, he rose and left without a word or a backward glance, banging his empty pint glass on the bar as he went, a gesture designed to relieve his frustration and mark his re-entry to the normal world beyond the blackmailer's restrictive net.

Darren Chivers sipped his half of bitter, enjoying the feeling of being in the wider world but not part of it, an observer who noted the foolish actions of people in that world and made use of them. After all, it was only just that people should pay for their sins, wasn't it?

There was no need to deal tonight. This other branch of his business had been more lucrative than he had dared to hope. And he was in charge of it, not at the mercy of those anonymous drug barons who would snuff you out like a flickering candle if you stepped out of line. He bought himself another beer, nodding cheerfully to the plain-clothes policeman who might have persecuted him if he had been dealing.

By the time he left the pub, it was almost dark. He put up the collar of his anorak, unlocked the chain on his bike, and rode home happily.

Karen Lynch usually enjoyed Tuesdays. It was Peter's unofficial day off. Vicars were never really off duty, but when you worked at weekends you had to arrange a little time for yourself during the week. Karen had encouraged him to set aside Tuesday as his rest day and insisted that as far as possible he arranged his commitments for other days of the week.

Sometimes they even managed little outings. Last week they had walked undisturbed on the chalk grasslands of Minchinhampton Common. Next week she was determined that they would have a day at the seaside, probably at Weston-Super-Mare or Burnham-On-Sea, if they could persuade the old Ford to run that far. Pleasures didn't have to be expensive, but it was important to get away from the parish occasionally, if you were not to get stale.

This Tuesday wasn't free for them to use. Peter had a clergy meeting at the Cathedral, later in the morning, and she had work planned for herself during the day. But she had made her husband a rare cooked breakfast, then insisted that he took a leisurely half hour over it and talked to her. They tried politics, then talked a little about the second day of the tennis championships at Wimbledon. Inevitably they came back to their own immediate concerns, the parish matters they had been trying to eschew.

Karen said thoughtfully, 'I think I'll go to see Barbara Lawrence again this morning. She's gradually getting accustomed to life on her own, but she and Brian were obviously very close. She came to church on Sunday and she says she's ventured out to her local shop a couple of times, but that's all. I think she might let me take her into town today.'

Peter stood up, came round the table and stood behind her, raising his hands to stroke her shoulders, enjoying feeling her muscles relax under his touch. 'You're good with people like Mrs Lawrence. Far better than I could ever be.'

'I have the time to be patient. And elderly people like

Barbara are always a little in awe of their vicar. Even when he's an old soft pot like you.' She raised her hand to stroke his larger one as it rested on her shoulder, then twisted her head to smile up at him.

'It's not just patience. You get on to people's wavelengths, the way I never do. You communicate with them, and then they trust you and tell you what's worrying them. I've watched you at work.'

'Voyeur! You make it sound cold and scientific. There are no tactics to it. I just do what seems to work at the time.'

'It may be a natural talent, but don't tell me you haven't worked hard to develop it!' He caressed the back of her neck for a moment, then the top of her spine. Then he dropped his hands back to his sides and sighed. 'You've seen a lot more of life than I have, Karen.'

She rose abruptly and turned to face him. 'Let's not go there, Peter. Believe me, you shouldn't envy me that! You don't want to see the things I have seen, and I don't want you to make me remember them.'

'You make me feel inadequate, when I see how you get through to people.'

'And you make me feel proud, when I see your sermons making a whole congregation of very different people think about their lives. One-to-one contact is OK, but a major part of your job is communicating with people en masse. I see you doing that every week. Sometimes you even inspire people, and that's the most difficult thing of all!'

He grinned down into her earnest face, which was so anxious to convince him of his worth. 'You're at it again, Karen Lynch! Getting straight through to someone's psyche and massaging it for him. In this case, it's your husband!'

She grinned at him. 'Piss off, vicar!' She put her arms round his shoulders and kissed him firmly and with some relish. 'You said when you proposed to me that the modern parish church needed to be run by a partnership. That's what we are – a partnership. We complement each other's skills and muddle through to make the whole thing work. And now get about your business, please!'

She gathered the dishes noisily together and did not look at him again as she took them into the kitchen. The Reverend Peter Lynch watched her move with the pronounced limp which she never complained about. He marvelled once again at his good luck in wedlock.

Robert Beckford used the excuse of a dental appointment to leave Gloucester Cathedral that morning.

Edwina Clarkson was preoccupied with the clergy meeting arranged for later in the morning. Although the gathering was not directly concerned with her work as civilian administrator of the cathedral's commercial activities, she always felt on show when there were clergy around in numbers. She grumbled a little about the inconvenience of Beckford's absence, but made no further protest.

He had insisted on meeting Darren Chivers during daylight and away from the cathedral. The blackmailer came in his usual dress of worn blue jeans and navy anorak, but he did not look at ease. Perhaps he did not like the number of people in the city-centre coffee bar; more likely it was the brightly lit interior and the sunny day outside which upset this creature of the night.

Beckford slid the banknotes across the table to him in their crisp white envelope. 'Count them!'

Chivers glanced at the edges of the notes, then pocketed them swiftly, his eyes glancing slyly from left to right to check that the transaction had not been observed. 'I don't need to do that, do I? Not with a pillar of rectitude who works in the Cathedral. Besides, you've too much at stake to try to con me.'

'It's the last you're getting.'

'I hope that's true. But you're not in a position to call the shots, are you, soldier boy?'

'I'm not a soldier and I'm certainly not a boy. There's no more. I haven't got it and I wouldn't give it to you if I had.'

'I don't think those good people who employ you at the Cathedral would like to hear about your past, do you?' Darren enjoyed offering the taunt. He felt in a position of power, a situation he had never enjoyed before in his chequered life.

'Just don't push it, Chivers. You can drive people too far, you know. You'll regret it if you do that with me!'

Rob Beckford put his large hands on the table and levered himself up, looking all the while at the thin face opposite him, as if it was important to him to commit every detail of it to his memory. He did not speak again, but turned and strode swiftly out of the busy coffee bar.

Darren Chivers gave him a couple of minutes to get clear, fingering his latest takings lovingly in the pocket of his anorak. Another threat, the third in the last few days. He didn't see how any of his victims could risk harming him. But this other branch of his activities might be more dangerous than he had thought. Not as dangerous as drug-dealing, of course, where you could disappear without trace at the whim of some man you had never seen.

Nevertheless, perhaps he should think of some means of protecting himself.

EIGHT

On that same Tuesday afternoon, Karen Lynch visited the hostel again. She did not really relish going there, but it seemed that she could be useful. And she needed to work with people like this, as some sort of reparation for her past.

She passed quickly through the red-light area, which was very quiet at three o'clock on a bright afternoon, with scarcely a person to be seen. The building she was aiming for had three storeys, so that it towered above the terraced housing around it. Its series of square, plain windows were clean, but not all of them had curtains; plastic and paper litter was scattered over the derelict gardens to the front and side of this huge and grimy brick cube.

The man in charge fitted these surroundings. Father George Ryan wore a dog collar – when you worked with addicts some badge of authority was essential – but looked otherwise as if he might have been brought in to clear the drains. He had his sleeves rolled up and his shirt was stained with what looked like human vomit. The Roman Catholic priest greeted Karen warmly, then went on vigorously cleaning the floor with long mop and bucket.

Father Ryan's work here was aided by a charity. It is a charity which is perpetually short of funds; cancer research

or sick animals being far more appealing vehicles for dona-
tions and legacies.

There were some very sick human animals dependent on
St Mary's Hostel. Father Ryan did not talk much of success;
he had of necessity familiarized himself with failure. He did
not allow the people who used this centre to bring stolen prop-
erty on to the premises, but he knew well enough that the
addicts who had a haven here had to find the means of feeding
their habits. They roamed the city like birds of prey, seeking
the currency to purchase the deadly ammunition which would
pulse though their veins and blow their heads away from
reality.

By five or six o'clock on most days, the majority of the
young people who used the hostel were tooting heroin, snorting
or injecting the substance which would lead many of them to
early graves. By early evening, they would be back in the
hostel with bruised skin, dilated eyes and clammy hands. Their
young lives were shattered by utter dependency on the
substances which crippled their intelligence, replacing logic
and reason with derangement and illusion.

Those who were in the building rather than out on the streets
at this time were some of the successes of the hostel. Father
Ryan's exhausted face lit up when he saw Karen Lynch. 'Lisa's
around somewhere,' he said. 'Have a word with her, if you
can. You did wonders with her last time. She's scared. But
she seems to listen to you. She's even quoted you to me.'

'I muddle along as best I can. Like you, I don't think there
are any rules to help us. My only advantage is that I've been
there, done that. Sometimes it helps you to get through.'

'She's supposed to be going to the rehabilitation unit
tomorrow. I don't want her to run away from it.'

'I'll go and find her.'

Lisa was a heroin addict who had turned like so many to
prostitution to pay for her habit. Karen had discovered her
on the streets sniffing glue and brought her here. Today she
found her sitting on a chair in the kitchen, shaking from
head to foot, her breath degenerating from time to time into
a mirthless giggle which seemed scarcely human. Karen
stroked her hair, wrapped both arms round her for a moment,
feeling the bones beneath the thin flesh and the damaged
skin. Then she boiled the kettle, made two mugs of tea, set them

on the table and wrapped the sinewy fingers of the younger woman round the beaker in front of her, feeling how cold they were despite the warm day, hugging her again in an attempt to stop the trembling in the damaged body. She had still not spoken a word, preferring tactile reassurance as a prelude to any spoken contact.

It was the addict, not her mentor, who spoke first. Staring at the steam rising from the mug between her hands, she said, 'Fuck off and leave me! I'm not going. I can't do it.'

'You can do it, Lisa. You're going to do it.'

'I can't. I'm too far gone. For fuck's sake, piss off.'

Strange phrasing for a cry for help, thought Karen. Because this was what this was. There had been no vehemence, no hatred, in the woman's commands. Whatever she said, she did not want to be left in isolation with her devil. 'You can do it, Lisa. If I did it, you can!'

Karen tried to force conviction into the words. She knew the statistics as well as anyone. When addicts reached this stage, you had only a one in five chance of reclaiming them.

'It's too strong for me. Look at me, Karen! I haven't the energy to fight it. Not if it means what you said it would!'

Perhaps she shouldn't have been as honest about what the rehabilitation course involved, about the sickness and the pain and the endless, degrading diarrhoea. Most of the medics and counsellors preferred to get addicts on the course at any price, then let them find out the harsh truths for themselves. But she had made contact and established trust with this brutalized girl-woman by her absolute honesty and she wasn't going to jeopardize that trust now. 'You've got more fight than most, Lisa. You'll need it, but you've got it. And if you fight, lots of other people will help you. You won't be battling on your own. Everyone in that unit will be desperate for you to succeed.'

'Not as desperate as me.'

It was the first acknowledgement that she was going to take the course after all. Karen wondered if Lisa recognized that, in her present state of terror. She gave her another hug, pressing her harder, clasping the shoulder blades, so sharp, so pathetically close to each other. 'That's the spirit, girl! You need to be desperate, to go through with it.'

'Tell me about it again.' Lisa spoke quietly, earnestly, like a trusting child.

She didn't need the details. Not again. No point in upsetting her and myself with the details, thought Karen. 'The first days are the worst. There'll be times when you think you can't carry on, when the hell of the cure seems much worse than the hell of the addiction itself. But you'll come through it, because you're Lisa and you've got the will, and because other people will be helping you, however cruel they may seem to you at the time.'

'I'll tell them to fuck off and leave me! Call them everything under the sun.'

'You won't use any words they haven't heard before. You won't shock them. They'll take every "fuck" and every "cunt" as evidence of your progress.' Karen wondered how long it was since she had last uttered those words, what Barbara Lawrence and the other good ladies of the parish would think if they could hear her now.

'I've done bad things, Karen.'

'And I probably did worse, in my time, Lisa. When you're hooked on horse, you don't care what you do. Inhuman things, things that turn everybody away from you, except for a few good men like Father Ryan.'

'And a few good women like you.'

Karen Lynch shook her head. 'I've been through it, Lisa. Been through as much as you and worse. I know how lucky I was to come out of it – incredibly lucky. I'm just trying to help one or two others to survive and come back to real life, the way I did.'

'Is that what it is? Real life?'

'Believe me, it is, Lisa. You've lived the nightmare. Now you've got the chance to get back from it. For God's sake don't chuck it away!'

'I won't let you down.'

'Never mind me, you daft sod! Don't let yourself down. You're the one that's going to fight the battle. It will be a bloody awful battle, particularly in the first week. But the victory will be worth all the pain, believe me.'

The damaged young frame was rent with a new and more wracking bout of shivering. 'I need a fix.'

Karen nodded. 'I know you do. You needed one when I came, but you've been a good girl. Tomorrow you've got to be an even better one.'

'Will you come and see me?' She flung a hand up to her mouth as her teeth began to chatter.

'Of course I will, as soon as they let me in. They usually don't allow any visitors for a few days, because they have to control the process. But they know what they're doing. You'll have to trust them, even when you're calling them all these names you've got ready for them.'

She smiled at her, but Lisa was beyond teasing now. Karen gave her a last vigorous, prolonged hug and left. She looked in on Father Ryan, who was extracting sheets from the washing machine with one of his voluntary helpers. 'If she won't go in the morning, don't let them manhandle her. Give me a ring. I can be here in ten minutes if I use the car.'

Karen Lynch felt exhausted as she went out into the bright sunlight, grateful for the walk through the streets in the soft, restorative breeze. Her leg always felt worse when she was tired. In her fatigue, she made no attempt to disguise her limp, as she did in her parish activities. Visiting people like Lisa was far more exhausting than visiting the sick in hospital. You felt that what you said and did was crucially important, that you could send a damaged mind and a damaged body spiralling towards ruin if you used the wrong words or gave the wrong reaction.

So preoccupied was she with her own thoughts that she neither saw nor heard the man who hurried along behind her, even when he moved to within a few paces of her. He left it thus for a hundred yards or so, then moved up to her shoulder and spoke, almost in her ear. 'You've done well for yourself, Karen Burton. Very well, for a prossie and a junkie.'

She stopped so abruptly that he almost lost his balance beside her. 'What do you want?'

'Just a little chat. A little chat about your old life. And your new one. Bit of a contrast there.'

She looked with rising horror at the wolfish smile, at the sly malice in the sharp blue eyes. She knew this face, though it was thinner and paler than she remembered it. A user, her experienced eye told her; maybe not yet an addict. It took a second or two longer for the name to come back to her. 'I'm Karen Lynch now. And you're Darren Chivers.'

He raised his hands and brought them together in silent, mocking applause. 'Very good, that. Very well remembered. You sold me my first drugs. Five years ago.'

She had no idea now whether that was right. 'In that case, I apologize to you. I was selling to feed the habit. I wasn't responsible for my actions, by that time.'

He went on as if she had not responded. 'You introduced me to the habit. Provided me with my first supplier, when I decided to deal.'

'I doubt if that's true, but I apologize again.' She glanced down at the thin arm which his anorak concealed. There would be needle marks on the flesh there, probably the damage to the vein which repeated injections produced. 'You can be rid of it, you know. If you take rehabilitation now, before you're really hooked, it will be much easier. I can give you an address and a phone number, if you want it.' She glanced instinctively back towards the now invisible hostel where Lisa was preparing to fight her demons.

'I don't want your addresses or your telephone numbers. I'm a user, not an addict.'

The old protest, the old self-deception, she had heard in so many, including herself. 'Don't kid yourself, Darren. Get out while you still can.'

But now the voice which had been wheedling was suddenly full of malice. He took a long, shuddering breath, enjoying the fear on her face. 'I want money, Karen Burton.'

She startled herself with a sudden laugh. It made her realize how near she was to hysteria. 'You've come to the wrong place, then. I haven't got money, Darren. I'm a vicar's wife now. We can't even work out how we're going to support children, if they come along.' She regretted saying that immediately because it allowed him a glimpse of that precious, intimate life with Peter, the life she certainly did not wish to share with this strange and menacing figure from her past.

His smile became a snarl. 'You'll find the money! People always do, when they have enough at stake.'

'I won't, because I can't. There just isn't money available.'

'You will, because there's no alternative, Mrs Lynch. Née Karen Burton. Addict, prostitute and drug dealer. I'm sure your husband's superiors and the elders of his parish would be pleased to hear a full account of your former life. A very full, well-documented account.'

Karen tried to keep calm. There must be a method of dealing with this. It was just that she couldn't see one at the moment.

She realized with this spectre of her past leering beside her that this was what she had always feared, the reason why she had resisted Peter's marriage proposal for so long. In the environment in which he worked, her past would always be a threat, a nightmare waiting to burst into lurid reality. It was easy for the people she lived among now to preach tolerance, easy for them to believe that they practised it. But the revelation of this other Karen as the vicar's wife would make her a target for at best prurient curiosity, at worst revulsion and rejection. It would ruin Peter's ministry, which had made such a promising beginning.

'How do you expect me to raise money for you?'

'You'll find a way. I'm not asking for millions. A paltry five hundred pounds will get you off the hook.'

For the moment. People like this always came back for more. 'You might as well say five thousand.'

'Oh, you'll find a way, Karen Burton. I find people can always find a way. I'll give you a week. I'm not an unreasonable man.'

'You're a dealer. You don't need to make money like this.'

'Oh, encouraging me to deal now, are you? Makes you a hypocrite that, wouldn't you say, in view of the work you're doing at St Mary's?'

That gloating face was going to figure in her dreams in the nights to come, growing ever larger, leering down at her like an outsize billboard poster for a horror film. He knew about her visits to the hostel, had learned God knew what else about her life. But it was what he knew about the life that was gone, the life which belonged to that other Karen, which she could not escape.

She said dully, 'I can help you, Darren. You're right, you must stop dealing and stop using. I can help you to do that, help you to get a proper job. You were a bright lad, in the old days. You could have gone to university – you still could. You can do everything I've done and more, if you want to.'

'But I don't want to, you see. I've got this interesting new business which I'm developing. You're going to be part of that, Karen Burton. So you will be helping me after all, won't you?'

He gave her that awful, insidious smile again, driving all thought, all reasoned argument out of her mind. She repeated the logic of the situation dully, knowing now that it was going to have no effect.

'You've come to the wrong person, Darren. We're struggling to make ends meet as it is. How do you think I'm going to raise money like this?'

Darren Chivers felt a sudden, startling shaft of pity for this woman who had hauled herself out of addiction and into respectability. He had been enjoying the feeling of power over another person which his knowledge gave him. But this one had been worse than himself, much worse, and yet she had beaten all the odds.

Then envy thrust aside the pity. He could never do what she had done; never climb back into respectability like her. What did she think she was doing, this jumped-up junkie? What right had this whited sepulchre to lord it over Darren Chivers, to remind him through her work at the hostel of the lives he had ruined by his dealing? He had a hold over her, for all her present airs and graces, and he was going to use that hold.

'You've got a week, Jezebel! Bring me the money by then, or let the world see what you really are!'

NINE

Detective Inspector Rushton studied Anne Jackson across his breakfast table and thoroughly approved of what he saw. Not many women looked good in a towelling robe, but Anne did. Her face was flushed from the warmth of the shower, her dark gold hair tumbled pleasingly around her ears. There was an enticing suggestion of cleavage where the robe fell away from her throat.

'We should think about a date for our marriage,' he said. Normally, when he was interviewing suspects, he measured everything he was going to say before he spoke. Now the words had emerged as the thought was formed, surprising him as well as her.

'No hurry, is there?' said Anne with a smile. 'We're both busy people.'

'Perhaps that's why we should get on with it. There'll always be that excuse for putting it off. And it's all right for you, but I'm not getting any younger.'

'And I am?'

'You know what I mean. I want to wed you before I'm ready for the scrap heap.'

'You didn't seem ready for it last night. Well, not when we started, anyway. If you were eventually exhausted, I take some credit for that.'

The difference of almost ten years in their ages was a perpetual source of worry for him and teasing for her. Chris tried to tease her back, because he enjoyed her joking about sex; his first wife had never done that. 'I was thinking of enrolling at a gym, to keep up with a twenty-three-year-old. But now I find you're giving me all the exercise I can take! And I don't want to be an old man when we have our children.' As usual, he had quickly become serious, voicing his worries about their future when he had meant to keep it light.

Her brow furrowed into the little frown he found so winning. 'I'm a career girl, don't forget. I want to make some impact before you confine me to the nursery.'

'Marriage doesn't mean the end of a career, does it? Make you an even better teacher, having kids of your own.'

'Perhaps.' She thought of a method of diverting the flow of the breakfast conversation. 'I saw that man again on Monday morning. The one you said was a drug dealer.'

'The one you saw last week in the supermarket car park. Darren Chivers.'

She was pleased that he remembered her previous mention of the man; sometimes she thought Chris was merely polite about her references to his work. 'That's the one. He was hanging about at the school gates.'

'What time was this?'

'Just before nine. The road was quite busy with children and parents. I had difficulty following his movements, with all the cars stopping and starting outside the gates.'

'He wasn't trying to deal, was he?' Chris was suddenly professionally alert.

'No, he certainly wasn't doing that.'

'He hasn't any record as a paedophile.'

'And he still hasn't. I confess that's what worried me at

first, but whatever he was interested in on Monday morning, it wasn't children.'

'So what was he doing?'

'I can't tell you that. I haven't worked it out for myself. He seemed to be looking for a house. When he found it, he made a written note of something – possibly the name and the number. Then he went back to his bike and rode away.'

'You should be CID!' said Chris Rushton happily.

As recession began to bite and men like Mark Rogers at BT fought for their livelihoods, the clothes sections of the big supermarkets were busier than ever. Customers here sought value for money in what they put on their backs as well as into their bellies. With less money in their purses, the young mothers of Britain sought cheap clothes for themselves and their offspring.

Haute couture is not ruled by the demands of the rag trade. Nevertheless, Wednesday morning was quiet in Michelle de Vries's shop. Trade was so slack at Boutique Chantelle that she was glad her assistant was not working today. She studied the window display she always designed herself and made a couple of minor adjustments. Then she settled down to complete the details of her tax return for the accountant, and tried not to think too often of Guy Dawson.

The man slid into the shop as if apologetic for his own arrival; even the bell on the door seemed to have a more muted ring as he opened the door the minimum distance to permit the access of his slight frame. He was not at all the sort of customer Michelle wanted to attract. He wore threadbare jeans and the sleeves of his anorak were pulled down over his wrists, reaching to the palms of his hands. But you never knew who had money these days, Michelle told herself firmly. This might be an eccentric millionaire. If it wasn't, she would send him on his way quickly. It wasn't good for business having a specimen like this on the premises.

'Was it something for the wife, sir?' You always began like that, even if you were certain it was something for a mistress; you mustn't embarrass the clientele, if they had come here to spend.

'No.'

'We do an excellent range, but our clothes are rather

exclusive. I think I can guarantee that the lady won't find anyone else wearing one of our dresses.'

'I'm not here to buy.'

It was as she had expected. And the more she saw of this interloper, the less she liked him. She'd have him on his way quickly, before he could discourage more promising patrons from coming in. Michelle hardened her voice. 'Then you shouldn't be here at all. I've no idea what you're trying to sell, but I can tell you here and now that I'm not interested.'

'I'm not selling anything either.' He looked her full in the face for the first time. She saw lank hair, sallow skin, irregular teeth, eyes which flashed dark and menacing as he stepped forward to the counter and they caught the light.

She took a step to her right, feeling for the under-counter alarm button which Gerald had insisted on when he knew that she would sometimes be alone in the shop. This man was no taller than she was, and very slight; she would back herself to overpower him, if it came to a fight. But he might have a knife, or even a gun, if he had come for the contents of her till. He wouldn't get much at this hour of the day; there was only her float money in there. She wondered if that would annoy him and make him violent. She tried to sound calm, controlled, confident. 'There is nothing for you here. You should leave now, please.'

'I'm not leaving. But I needn't be here very long, if you see sense. I haven't come for your money, not now. I'm not interested in what you have in the till, Mrs de Vries.'

He knew her name. It wasn't displayed anywhere on the outside of the shop. How had he got hold of her name? She mustn't panic; he could have got it quite easily, in any number of ways. He could know some of the other traders in the street, he could have picked it up from the fulsome article about her in the *Citizen* when she began this new enterprise. She said firmly, 'You had better state your business or leave.'

He gave her an unpleasant smile. He had grown more at ease as she had become more nervous. 'Very well. I think that's an excellent idea, Mrs de Vries. I'm sure Mr de Vries would as well. I'm not sure about Mr Guy Dawson, though.'

'What do you know about Mr Dawson?'

'Not a lot. But quite enough for my purposes, Mrs de Vries. I know that you have been regularly visiting his house on

Tuesday evenings. I know that you were also there on Friday
last, when you left at ten thirty-two precisely and walked to
your car, which was parked discreetly as usual, some distance
from his gate.'

Michelle put her hands on the counter. Her head swam and
she felt she was about to collapse, but she wouldn't give this
creature the satisfaction of seeing her reaching for a seat.
When she spoke, it was in a croak which seemed to come
from someone else, 'You're a private detective.'

'Nothing so sinister or so threatening, Mrs de Vries. Your
marriage is not at risk, if you behave sensibly.'

She sensed now where this was going. 'I've done nothing
against the law of the land.'

'I'm sure you haven't, Mrs de Vries. You're a pillar of
respectability in many respects, I'm sure. But adultery is still
the easiest way to a divorce, even in this enlightened and
promiscuous age of ours. And I don't think you want a divorce,
Mrs de Vries.'

'And what do I have to do to avoid one?'

'You have to stuff my mouth with gold, Mrs de Vries. Know
who said that, do you?'

'I don't know and I don't—'

'Aneurin Bevan, Mrs de Vries. That's what he did to the
consultants, to establish the National Health Service in 1948.
I saw that on the television last night. Always willing to learn,
you see. And you can see now that I've learned interesting
things about you.'

'You want money from me.'

'You put it in a nutshell, Mrs de Vries. I do, yes.'

'How much?'

'Let's say two thousand. As a one-off payment, mind. Pay
up quietly and you need never see me again.' Darren Chivers
glanced meaningfully round the shop. 'I'm sure you'd like
that.'

'How do I know that you mean that?'

She hadn't argued about the sum; perhaps he should have
asked for even more. 'You don't, my love. You'll have to rely
on my word. I won't say as an officer and a gentleman, because
I've never been either of those.' He was enjoying the feeling
of power. This proud woman who had begun by treating him
like something she had trodden in was now beginning to

squirm. 'Two grand will see me permanently out of your life. You can afford it. Or your husband can. Get the money from him.'

'And how exactly do I do that?'

'I haven't a clue, my love. Your problem, not mine. But you'll find a way. A woman who can meet a lover every week for months without her husband knowing anything about it will find a way.'

'When?' She knew with that word she had accepted his demand, but she couldn't at the moment see any other way out of this.

'I'll give you a week. I'm a reasonable man, you see.'

He expected her to argue, but she didn't. She said dully, 'Be here at this time or a little earlier. I don't want my customers to see you coming in here.'

'Or your husband, eh? Well, neither of us wants that, do we? But just in case you get any funny ideas about double-crossing me, I should tell you that all my information will be recorded in a letter clearly addressed to Mr Gerald de Vries I have in my flat. The only method of preserving your little secret will be to pay me off. I think you've got a bargain, really.'

'I could pay this sum directly into your bank account.'

'You could, but I don't care to give you that information. I look forward to seeing you next week. It will be a pleasure to do business with you, Mrs de Vries. I shall recommend your clothes to my friends, but I don't think you should hold your breath.'

With that parting jibe, he was gone. The bell seemed to ring more loudly and reverberate longer with his departure than it had with his entry.

Darren Chivers was still doing enough drugs to keep his hand in and satisfy his supplier. Later that day, he waited outside the back entrance of one of the city's major solicitors' offices for the last occupant to leave. He passed four hundred pounds' worth of cocaine rocks across, with no debate about price and a minimum of fuss, and made an agreement to see the young man at the same time next week with double the amount.

He liked dealing with the professional classes, and lawyers

were the best of all. They had money and they had a lot at stake. They dealt quickly and efficiently. They could no more risk being caught than he could. Many of them used the drugs for what they called 'social purposes' and took them as readily after dinner parties as the previous generation had taken brandies. That was all right by Darren, if it brought in the money as easily and with as little risk as it did.

A successful day, all in all. He allowed himself a small spliff of cannabis to celebrate. Pot didn't seem to have the effect it once had, but he would ride on his success and make it do. The de Vries woman was going to dish up, and the drugs transaction had been as easy as they came.

He almost wished he hadn't tackled that Karen Lynch the previous day now. A small part of his brain which he did not wish to hear told him that she was a cripple, that she had come up the hard way and was making a go of it. Another, more heeded, part told him that five hundred quid was hardly worth the effort she was going to cost him. But she shouldn't have ideas above her station, should she? So what if it was difficult for her? The jumped-up bitch deserved to have it difficult.

There was still light in the west at nine thirty when he rode his bike to the pub by the docks, but the sun had set and the cars had their headlights on. It was past the longest day now, and the nights would be drawing in. By the end of August, it would be dark at eight o'clock and his natural element would be returning. 'Darkness visible.' He liked that. He remembered that it was Milton now. He could have gone to university if he'd wanted to, as Karen Lynch had said. He might start dealing more vigorously again in the winter. Or he might continue to expand his other interest. It seemed easier and safer to get money this way, and he had a natural talent for acquiring information which people did not want him to have.

He sipped his lager and listened to the gossip in the pub. It was surprising what you picked up in pubs. You saw things and heard things which you could follow up, document more fully at your leisure. No smoke without fire, they said; and if he sniffed the smoke, Darren Chivers could usually find the fire.

He chatted to two girls who were on the game. Women like

this found him an odd creature, but unthreatening. Most of them thought he was queer; that was why they found him so unthreatening and easy to chat to. Chivers was not in fact homosexual so much as asexual. He had liked girls at school, but never had much success with them. Rather than be repeatedly rebuffed, he had chosen to go his own way, enjoying the occasional romp when it was offered, usually by women seeking the next fix, but otherwise keeping his own counsel and avoiding sexual entanglements.

He recognized a drug squad detective, no doubt angling for bigger fish than him. Darren was delighted to go up and speak to him, happy that his pockets held nothing illicit; he enjoyed posing as a reformed character to this taciturn agent of the law. He bought himself another half, telling a barman who was not interested that he could not risk being charged with being drunk in charge of a bicycle.

It was quite dark as he left the pub and went through the car park at the back to the alley where he had left his bike. The two men were plainly bent on violence, but he saw them too late.

It was the darkness he thought of as his friend which concealed them. They came at him with what he thought were baseball bats, but which might have been iron bars. Darren did not waste time shouting or pleading, but dropped his bike and ran for it.

Even as he fell, he knew that it was hopeless. They were stronger and quicker than he was. Within ten yards they had him, within twelve he was down. The first blow caught his shoulder, bringing a yelp of pain from him as he fell. Then they set about his body, as he pulled up his knees and clasped his arms over his head in a hopeless, foetal crouch. There was only one blow to his head, but so many to his ribs and his back that he thought they were going to kill him.

The pain was in his trunk, in his heart, in his brain, pulsing faster with every blow. But he was still conscious when they told him this was just a warning, that blackmailers deserved much worse, and would get much worse, if they didn't see sense and give up. Then the blood ran into his mouth. His last thought as he lost consciousness was that it would soon be over.

TEN

Chief Superintendent Lambert was restless. There wasn't enough serious crime on his patch at present. That was a cause for public celebration and congratulations to the police service. But Lambert needed things which would demand his concentration and stretch his mind. He hated being behind a desk all day, and the rest of his team became uneasy if he was confined within the CID section.

DI Rushton reported to him on the events of the night of Wednesday June 25th. 'Bit of the fracas in the city centre just before midnight. Too much booze consumed as usual. Drunken young men showing off in front of drunken young women.'

'Usual yobs and tarts trouble.'

Rushton grinned. 'I was phrasing it for the magistrates, sir. Don't visit the locker room for an hour or so. PC Jones has been washing the puke off his uniform. I understand DC Pheasant has quite a lot of blood on hers, but fortunately it's not her own blood. Three arrests for carrying offensive weapons – all of them knives. None of them used, thanks to prompt action by our lads and lasses, and none of the arrests have previous. They'll get away with cautions.'

They sighed a little over the tedious repetitions of such petty disturbances, over the lack of imagination of modern youth. Then Chris Rushton said, 'There was one rather more professional piece of violence last night. A drug dealer received a pretty severe beating behind the Wagon and Horses. A man called Darren Chivers. Bert Hook and I interviewed him last week. A slippery, experienced, small-time operator. We got nothing useful out of him, but that may have been because he had nothing to give us. The drug squad say he's just a small-time dealer who may not even know the name of his supplier and certainly won't know the identity of any of the big boys. Bert and I thought at least we'd scared him off, that he wouldn't be doing much dealing in the immediate future because he knew he was going to be watched.'

'How badly was he damaged?'

Rushton looked at his computer screen. 'Possible broken ribs – he was being taken to X-ray an hour or so ago. The damage was done with our old friend the blunt instrument. Or instruments – we don't know yet whether more than one person was involved in the attack. Multiple bruising. A single blow to the back of the head which has been stitched up. Probable concussion, but no serious cranial damage.'

'Any idea who did it?'

'No. And he wasn't found until at least an hour after it happened. So we're not likely to find out who attacked him, unless he has an idea himself and is prepared to volunteer it to us.'

'Both of which are unlikely, from what we know of him. Unusual assault, for a small-time dealer, wouldn't you say?'

'I hadn't really thought about it. But you're right, John. If dealers aren't selling the amount they should, they're usually just dropped. If they know more than they should and are likely to reveal it, they're quietly liquidated. This looks more like a warning off. Whoever did it had Chivers down and at their mercy. They could have finished him off, if they'd wanted to.'

'I think we should get someone down to the hospital to see what Chivers himself thinks about it. Unless he has some idea who might have roughed him up, we've very little chance of finding them, as you say.'

'Bert Hook's seen him before. I can't go myself. The CPS have me on standby for a court appearance. They feel the woman's not going to plead guilty after all.'

'I'll go to the hospital with Bert. We'll see whether a beating has made your slippery Mr Chivers any more talkative.'

Lambert tried not to look too pleased at the prospect of escape from his office.

Daniel Steele was exhausted. He was only 48, but night work took its toll. He had done plenty of night shifts during his early days in the police force, but he had been young then. Everything had been a new experience as a young, uniformed copper. Those days belonged to another and very different world.

But you never seemed to sleep as well during the day; even though this was now his regular rest pattern, his body never seemed to adjust to it. He felt very middle-aged nowadays after a night on security work at Graftons. Well, you are middle-aged and a little more, he told himself firmly. You're a grandfather, for God's sake, have been for a while now. Just accept that and get on with enjoying the rest of your life.

It wasn't that the work was taxing. It was routine stuff, much of it not very different from the old night watchman's role. You still made patrols round the extensive perimeter of the factory and the warehouse, as you might have done half a century earlier. You kept an eye on the CCTV cameras, but that made the job safer, if anything. He had a direct line to the police station and the system required him to use it at the first sign of real trouble. Money for old rope, really. And he'd just been given a rise and put in charge of overall security at the works, on the grounds of his 'experience and integrity'. Bit ironic, that, if they only knew. But they didn't. Only he and bloody Darren Chivers knew.

He found himself nodding sleepily over his breakfast toast, then roused himself at his wife's excited call and went into the living room to witness his granddaughter's first faltering steps and his wife's delighted encouragement of them. Her face was full of simple, innocent delight as she held the child against her and said over her head to her spouse, 'She's only here for the morning, Dan. I'll take her to the park in a while, so that you can get to sleep.'

It was a good life, Steele told himself firmly. A life which could only be shattered if he lost his job. He wondered how much chance there was of that, how real Darren Chivers's threat to his livelihood was. He waited until his wife departed with her charge to the park and then picked up the phone. 'I'm just trying to trace an old colleague of mine. We were very friendly when we worked together, but I moved away when I left the police and we've lost touch.'

The young woman was suspicious until he gave his name and former rank. Then she relaxed and gave him the information he wanted. 'Chief Inspector North retired ten years ago. I can give you his address.' She rustled through paper. Not everything was computerized as efficiently as at Graftons, Dan thought with amusement. His informant sounded more hesitant when she came back to the phone. 'I'm afraid Mr North isn't – he hasn't been very well. He's at Westcott

House now, not at home. I've spoken to his wife and apparently he has mild dementia. She thought a visit would be all right, if you're an old colleague, but you should be prepared for the fact that he'll be very vague. He might not even recognize you.'

'Thank you. I'll bear that in mind.'

Daniel Steele stared at the phone absently for a few seconds with a widening smile. The one man who might speak out about him was almost out of it. There was only Darren Chivers to deal with now.

'We're here to help you. But we need you to help us.' Lambert delivered the routine formula to the battered man in the bed.

Darren Chivers weighed them up with the suspicion he always accorded the police. 'Chief Superintendent, you said. Why's the top brass concerning itself with the likes of me?'

'We take violence seriously, whoever the victim is. We don't want it on our streets.'

'Going through the motions are you? Trying to pretend that thieves and toms matter just as much as teachers and doctors?'

'They do when they're victims. It doesn't matter what your background is. If you've taken the kind of beating you took last night, we want to arrest the people who did it and put them behind bars.'

Chivers regarded the long, lined face balefully. 'You're a bit old for a copper, aren't you, mate?'

DS Hook took over hastily. 'Chief Superintendent Lambert has been given a Home Office extension on account of his very high success rate with serious crimes. The fact that he's here talking to you is evidence of how seriously we're taking last night's assault on you.'

Chivers transferred his attention to DS Hook's weather-beaten features. 'Don't give me that. You were giving me the third degree last week. You and that Rushton bloke. Accusing me of dealing drugs.'

'Hardly third degree, Darren. You came to the station voluntarily to assist us with our inquiries.'

Chivers sneered at him, his mouth twisting into a smile of contempt, his crooked teeth flashing yellow at them for a moment. When I feel no physical danger, I do sneering rather

well, he thought. 'And we all know what would have happened
if I hadn't come voluntarily, don't we?'

Hook smiled, acknowledging the games which men like
this man and himself had sometimes to play. 'You're a known
drug dealer, Darren. You've had a conviction for it in the past.
You've a record and you're a possible source of information.
You can't blame us for trying to discover the identity of people
higher up the chain than you.'

'Except that I'm not dealing now, am I? I've taken the
advice of pigs like you and decided to go straight. Fat lot of
good it's done me.'

Bert Hook regarded him steadily for a moment, then leant
forward and pulled back the sheet which covered him. Chivers
winced with the pain and started automatically away from the
large hands of the DS. The visitors looked at the bandaged
ribs, at the already livid bruises on the pathetically thin torso.

Chivers snatched back the sheet and covered himself. 'What
the fuck do you think you're doing, fuzz?'

Hook smiled at him. 'Examining the damage, Darren.
Confirming for ourselves that the photos in glorious techni-
colour will make the right impression in court. Those bruises
should be at their most vivid and colourful in a couple of
days, wouldn't you think, sir?'

Lambert smiled. 'I would indeed, DS Hook. The medical
staff here do excellent prints, but perhaps we should send one
of our police photographers down to make the most of these
wounds.'

'You're not having any pictures of me, coppers. Bloody
perverts!' Darren shook his head and tried another sneer, which
was less effective than his first effort.

Bert Hook hastened into explanation. 'Very necessary for
a Crown Court, Darren. That's where a GBH case will go,
you see. Juries are always impressed by photographs of the
effects of violence. Be an excellent back-up for your evidence,
photos will. Being as you're a known criminal with a history
of drug-dealing, we'll need back-up, you see.'

'I'm not bringing charges.'

Hook remained determinedly bright in the face of his
victim's sullen refusal. 'We can look after the charges, Darren.
You'll just be a star witness in a big court. You'll enjoy that.'
He leaned forward with concern, like one of the medics who

had tended the injuries beneath the sheet. 'Now, who was it that bashed you about in this shameful manner?'

'I don't bloody know, do I?'

'You must have some idea.'

'I bloody don't. You said I was a dealer, so it could be some heavies connected with the drugs trade, I suppose. Not that I'm admitting to any dealing, mind.'

Just when he had got used to abusing Hook, John Lambert came quietly back into the exchanges. 'Doesn't look like a drugs beating to us, Mr Chivers. Looks like a warning-off to us.'

'Well, you know more than I do then, copper.'

'We do actually, Mr Chivers. We know that the big boys in the drugs industry are ruthless. But they rarely need this sort of violence. They either dispense with people's services or see them off altogether, if they know too much. They don't often do warning assaults. This looks to us like a warning from a different source altogether.'

'It's a fucking mystery, then, innit?'

Lambert regarded him for a moment with steady, unemotional distaste. 'Give us the details of the attack.'

'Not much I can tell you. The bastards came at me in the dark and—'

'So there were more than one involved?'

'Two big buggers. They had baseball bats. Least, that's what I think they were hitting me with. I 'ad my 'ands over my 'ead pretty quick, I can tell you.'

Hook nodded slowly and said quietly, 'Who were they, Darren?'

'I don't bloody know, do I?'

'You may well have some ideas. People who suffer attacks like this usually have a shrewd notion where they come from.'

'Well, you're out of luck today. I don't have any bloody notion at all.'

'Don't you want them caught?'

Chivers paused for a moment. You had to be careful what you said to pigs. They'd turn it against you if they could. 'Course I do. I'd like to have the bastards on the floor in front of me and give them a good kicking. But that's not going to happen, is it? Dozy buggers like you won't catch them.'

'We might, if we get some cooperation from you. I know

you had your hands over your head, and you curled yourself up on the ground, but isn't there any detail of either of them you can recall?'

'No. It was dark and I didn't see them. All I can remember is these fucking baseball bats or bars hitting me.'

'Did they speak?'

He thought of that last harsh warning to lay off the blackmail. He couldn't tell them about that. 'I can't remember anything they said. One of them did shout something at me. I think he had a Brummie accent.'

'And what did he say? Do you recall his words?'

'No, I fucking don't! I had my arms over my ears and my hands over my face. I thought the bastards were going to kill me!'

Hook nodded, looking thoughtfully at the thin, battered body beneath the sheet. 'But they didn't kill you, did they, Darren? They could easily have finished you off, but they didn't. Why do you think that was?'

'I don't fucking know, do I? You tell me, copper.'

'I think you do know, Darren. This has all the hallmarks of a warning beating. You think and I think that these were professional hit men, hired by someone to warn you off, to tell you that there was worse in store if you didn't back off from something you were doing.'

'Don't tell me what I bloody think, copper. I've told you what I can. Just bloody leave me in peace, will you?'

The nursing sister's face at the door of the room told them that they were going to have to do just that, any minute now.

Hook said, 'A warning beating, Darren. What have you been up to? What were these nasty buggers warning you about, and who sent them after you?'

'I don't bloody know, do I? If you're so fucking clever, you can work it out for yourself. Just leave me alone to get better, will you?'

He turned away from them in the bed. The pain it caused him was real enough, but his groan was highly theatrical.

Mark Rogers was reading Winnie the Pooh to his seven-year old-daughter. Even ten years ago, he would never have seen himself doing this. A night on the booze with the boys had been much more in his line then. He had been a reluctant father; it had only been at Samantha's insistence that he had agreed to parenthood in his late twenties. Left to himself, he would have gone on postponing conception indefinitely.

Now, at thirty-seven, he could not imagine life without his children. Indeed, it had been Samantha's firm decision that they should stop at two, and even so there were occasions when, after a bottle of wine, he tried to convince her of the rewards of larger families. He was a doting and indulgent father. Samantha maintained cheerfully that it was as well his work at BT kept him as busy as it did, because it was only that which prevented the children being ruined.

Mark and his daughter laughed again over the wonderful Shepard illustrations of Pooh Bear stuck in the entrance to Rabbit's burrow. Then he resumed the familiar text. '"I thought at the time," said Rabbit, "that one of us was eating too much,"' Ellie joined in with him, '"and I knew it wasn't me."' Father and daughter dissolved into laughter together at the familiar text and the joke they had been waiting for.

It wasn't until she stopped joining in that Mark realized that Ellie was fast asleep. She looked just like one of the sentimental Mabel Lucy Atwell drawings he had always derided, with a contented smile on her smooth round face and a forehead which was totally unlined. He bent down and touched her brow softly with his lips, then went and looked in on his son, who was eighteen months older than Ellie. Samantha was in the last stages of his story; the boy waved a tired hand at his father, then resumed his concentration upon the tale.

Mark Rogers poured a glass of cool white wine for his wife, then took his own glass and sat down on the sofa in the living room. He felt a pleasant lassitude creeping over him as he picked up the copy of the *Citizen* he had bought on the outskirts of Gloucester on his way home.

It was a small paragraph at the bottom of an inside page which told him that a twenty-seven-year-old Gloucester resident, Darren Chivers, had been assaulted and severely beaten on his way home. He was receiving treatment in the city hospital, but it was understood that his injuries were not life-threatening.

Mark was looking thoughtfully at the sports section when his wife came into the room and sank down beside him with her wine.

ELEVEN

Darren Chivers was out of hospital in two days. He didn't want to stay there any longer than he had to and he wasn't the sort of patient the nurses wanted to tend for any longer than was necessary.

The registrar told him he was lucky to have escaped broken bones and advised him to stay under medical supervision for another day whilst they checked out his concussion, but Darren had heard enough and endured enough. He discharged himself from hospital and went back to his bedsit and his packet food and his television, like a wounded animal retreating to its lair and gathering its strength to meet the challenges of the hostile world outside it.

He would go back to selling drugs in due course. Dealing was lucrative and it was a world he felt he knew. Like most petty crooks, Chivers was far more confident than he should have been, incapable of taking the long view of his position in a dangerous trade. In the end, such people almost always fail. They are used for as long as they are useful, and then dispensed with ruthlessly.

The fact that he could not see his position on this wider canvas did not mean that Darren Chivers was stupid. His intelligence was above the average; moreover, experience had developed in him the low cunning which is an aid to survival. He would not give up his blackmailing activities, which could be highly rewarding, even if more dangerous than he had realized at first. He would need to be more careful, that was all. He would avoid the sort of lonely late-night backstreet situation where those thugs had waited for him.

He would also need to equip himself with some form of protection.

Each day his injuries hurt a little less. Over the weekend, he dug out the newspaper cuttings he had squirreled away for occasions such as this, and quickly found the one he sought. He read it several times, until he could recite it almost verbatim.

You didn't want to have to produce bits of newspaper to explain yourself – that would make you look like a novice.

The weather broke over the weekend, so that there was a thin drizzle dampening the air and shining the streets as he collected his unemployment benefit. The sour-faced young woman behind the counter scarcely glanced at him. He was a little disappointed. If she had challenged his failure to find work, he would have enjoyed showing her the plaster he had kept on his head and then perhaps revealing the vivid green and yellow bruising on his body.

The clouds were very low now, seeming to peer into the narrow streets of the old city and follow his movements as he left the centre and padded his way to the gun shop. He was pleased to find a man behind the counter who did not look much older than he was.

He knew exactly what he wanted. 'Could I see a Brocock ME 38 air pistol, please?' Darren Chivers found it difficult to deliver this precision with the casual attitude he was aiming for.

The assistant looked at him warily, as if committing his image to memory. 'May I ask what you will use this weapon for, sir?'

'Just a little hobby of mine. Shooting practice on paper targets in my cellar. Nothing more. I use harmless pellets. Perhaps a little plastic ammunition occasionally.' Darren delivered the prepared phrases between stiff lips. He needed to seem relaxed. He tried a smile, then gave up the effort when it wouldn't work for him. He would assert his citizen's rights if it came to it, tell the man he had no right to question him like this.

But the young man behind the counter nodded. He had been through the motions of checking. The purchase of air pistols was perfectly legal and there was a good profit on them. 'I think you've made a good choice, sir. Precision instrument, the Brocock is. Made in Germany and imported through our Birmingham supplier. Excellent value at one hundred and eighty pounds.'

Darren made a token inspection of the pistol, holding it in his palm for a moment, testing the weight and squinting along the barrel with what he hoped looked like expertise.

'I am required to warn you that these things can be dangerous

if not handled carefully. They should be stored well away
from any place where children might get hold of them.' The
assistant dropped his formal tone as if it were an embarrassment to him and moved comfortably into the sales flattery he
thought worthwhile even for this unpromising customer. 'But
I can see that you are an experienced man who is well aware
of such things.'

Darren concluded the deal quickly, accepting the offer of
some plastic ammunition as a goodwill gesture with a forced
smile of gratitude. He wanted to be out of the shop with his
purchase as swiftly as possible.

Michelle de Vries lay back exhausted on the blue silk sheet.

'You're good for me, Guy Dawson!'

'And you for me, Michelle. I've been looking forward to
Tuesday evening ever since you were last here.'

Even in her present state of relaxed, uncritical, post-coital
bliss, Michelle wondered if that was really true. She stretched
her arms luxuriously above her head against the headboard
and said, 'I must take a shower, Guy.' But she made no move
to vacate the bed in which she was so happy.

Although the bedroom faced the west, the sun had set some
time ago and only the very last of the summer daylight was
left in the room. Guy reached his hand out towards the bedside
light, but she put her hand upon his arm to stop him, running
her fingers down the inside of it in a last, lingering caress.
'We don't need the light. Light isn't kind to a woman of
forty-four.'

It was a daring demonstration of her confidence, speaking
her age like that. He knew how old she was, of course, but
voicing it was another assertion of the intimacy which she
had savoured so boisterously with him over the last two hours.
He said, 'You're pretty fit for an old 'un! Very fit indeed, I'd
say!' He took her in his arms again, running his fingers down
her spine, holding her hips and pressing her firmly against
him.

She felt the familiar surge of desire, stirring deep within
her. 'You can't, Guy, you surely can't! Not again. And I've
got to leave!'

He held her for a couple of seconds, then rolled away with
a secret relief that his manhood was not to be re-tested. 'I

could, but I won't. It might not be as good, because you've exhausted me, you young hussy!'

She loved the way he breathed the words into her ear, turning even the most facile of statements, even the small jokes of the sexual ritual, into declarations of intimacy. She stretched again, making herself as long as she could, thrusting her toes as far as she could towards the bottom of his bed, wanting to retain the feel of it for the rest of her week. Then she stared up at the almost invisible ceiling and said very quietly, 'Someone knows about us, Guy.'

He reached across and switched on the light beside her, and this time she did not attempt to prevent it. 'Who? Is it Gerald?'

'No. That's the threat, though.'

'The threat?'

'He's threatening to tell Gerald.'

'That mustn't happen.'

She was a little put out. She would have liked him to say, 'Let him tell him! Let's have it out in the open, let's have this sham of a marriage of yours out of the way! I want to marry you more than anything in the world, Michelle!' But she knew those words belonged in romantic novels, not in real life. That wasn't Guy Dawson, and she didn't want him any different from what he was, she told herself firmly. And she didn't want a divorce herself. She was fond of Gerald, in a very different way from Guy, and she certainly needed his money to fund her life. Boutique Chantelle might eventually prosper and be self-supporting, even highly profitable, but she needed her husband's money to get it off the ground and sustain it through the early, crucial years.

But she did want Guy to share this crisis with her. She said firmly, 'Of course we can't allow it to happen.'

He was staring hard at her now. The mood of luxurious relaxation, with their limbs comfortably entwined, felt days behind them, not minutes. 'You'd better tell me all about it.'

She told him about the shifty man who had come into her shop, the man who had seemed such an unlikely customer and proved to be so. 'He wants two thousand pounds. He's coming back for it tomorrow.'

'And have you got it for him?'

'Yes. I've got an account just for the shop and I've taken it out of that.'

'Is there any chance that Gerald will spot this?'

'No. I think I can cover it up, for the present. The auditors won't be in until the end of the financial year. I've got months to bury it under orders and receipts.'

'That's good.'

He nodded and relaxed a little, and again she had that little tremor of disappointment. She said, 'But I can't go on doing it, if he comes back for more.'

'They always do, people like that.'

'So what are we going to do?' She was determined to make him see that they were in this together.

'I don't know.' He shook his head irritably. 'How did he find out about us?'

'I think he must have been watching us for some time.'

'You, you mean? It could only have been you coming here.'

That was true. Guy had been very reluctant to enter into her life, making sure instead that she came always to him. They hadn't even been away together, though he kept promising her that they would, when her marital arrangements allowed it. She said, 'He gave me the number of this house. Quoted the time I left here last week.' She shivered beneath the sheets, could not help noticing that Guy did not move to comfort her.

'Yet you came here tonight. Even though you knew he might be watching you.'

'I looked out for him on my way in. I didn't see him.'

'And when you go out? Will you spot him if he's hanging about in the dark?'

'Probably not.' Michelle didn't like Guy's reaction. He was behaving as if he wished she had not come here – almost as if he wanted to call the whole thing off after this setback. 'It doesn't matter whether he's there or not now, does it? He knows about us.'

'I suppose you're right. What are you going to do about it?'

'I don't know. I've racked my brains for almost a week without coming up with anything. I hoped you might have an idea.'

He thought for a minute, then shook his head glumly. 'There isn't a solution, is there? Once he knows, we can't alter that. Even if you stopped coming here, even if we stopped seeing each other, he'd still know what we've done, if he's got the times and the places the way you say he has. He'd still be able to tell Gerald if you didn't pay up, wouldn't he?'

'Yes . . . Is that what you'd like to do then? End the whole affair because of some dirty little snooper?'

'No, of course it isn't. I'm just trying to get the facts clear in my mind.'

Michelle wished he sounded more convincing. 'I'll give him his two thousand tomorrow and tell him that's it. We'll just have to hope he doesn't come back for more.'

'He will.'

'We could go to the police, I suppose. I'm told they haven't much time for blackmailers. Perhaps they'd protect us from exposure.'

Guy shook his head vigorously. 'You mustn't do that, Michelle. Even if they kept your identity secret you'd have to go to court as a witness. Gerald would be sure to find out.'

She wanted to ask him if that would be such a disaster, to make him avow his unconditional love for her. But she sensed he wouldn't do that, and she knew that she had too much to lose herself from any such romantic declarations. She had a bleak sense of her own worthlessness as well as of the shallowness of her lover.

She was getting dressed after her shower when Guy Dawson said quietly, 'The only way out of this is to get rid of this sneaky sod altogether.'

The sneaky sod in question did not hear this dialogue of course, but it would scarcely have ruffled him if he had.

Darren Chivers enjoyed examining the weapon he had purchased, enjoyed the feel of it even more. He even enjoyed looking at the picture and reading the written details on the box. He took out the pistol and put it away again with great care, so that even the container of his splendid purchase would remain in pristine condition. Darren had had very few brand new things in his life. When he was a boy, his toys as well as his clothes had been hand-me-downs, things his feckless mother had acquired from other parents. He had been grateful for his few presents at Christmas and birthday, but they had come from charity shops or other, more mysterious, sources. They had rarely been boxed or wrapped.

On Wednesday morning, he pressed the trigger a couple of
times without ammunition, enjoying the crisp click of the
mechanism, the feeling of smooth oiled metal beneath his
fingers. Then he put the Brocock in the pocket of his anorak
and set out for the centre of Gloucester.

His exchange with Michelle de Vries was swift and efficient. She had the money ready for him and she paid up with
scarcely a murmur. He made a token show of counting the
notes, but he knew she wouldn't short-change him on the two
thousand – she had too much at stake for that. She looked
rather pale, he thought, but she gave no trouble. That was
almost a pity, for he would have enjoyed emphasizing how
he held all the trump cards to a haughty, expensively dressed
woman like this, the kind of woman who would have treated
him like dirt in other circumstances. Life was changing for
him, and he liked the changes.

She said, 'You promised me this would be a one-off
payment. I must emphasize that it is exactly that.'

'Of course.' He gave her a knowing smile, tried to convey
by his manner that both of them knew that she couldn't possibly
control this. But he had enough sense to leave it at that, to
get out of Boutique Chantelle as quickly and quietly as he
could. It was fine now, with a promise of sun to come above
the clouds. He mounted his bike cheerfully, secure in the
knowledge that one pocket of his anorak held two thousand
pounds and the other one the instrument which would secure
his continuing safety in his new ventures.

His ribs still ached, but the pain was a little less severe with
each passing day. He took his time, but the three-mile ride
did not have any severe ascents to add to his discomfort. The
sun was breaking through the cloud and there was a patch of
blue sky by the time he reached his goal. There was a man
talking to the garage owner, detailing the sort of service he
wanted on his car and the make of the two replacement tyres
it needed to pass its MOT.

Darren rode his bike round the side of the garage and waited
beside the high brick wall, silent and invisible, until the car
owner departed. Darren Chivers was good at waiting in the
shadows. He had done a lot of it in his short life.

The man in the garage workshop recognized him immediately and motioned him through to the smaller room at the

back, where a different sort of engineering was conducted. The fifty-year-old man with the straggling moustache was expecting this visitor and did not waste time on preambles. 'What is it you want?'

Darren took the Brocock ME 38 from his pocket and laid it carefully on the workbench in front of the man's oil-blackened leather apron. When the big man did not immediately react, he said, 'It's not stolen. I bought it over the counter on Monday.'

The man smiled for the first time. He said grimly, 'Anyone over seventeen can do that, Mr Chivers.'

Darren liked that form of address. He didn't like it from the police, when the title seemed to carry an ironic ring and meant they were trying to rig up a charge against you. But from this man it made him a customer, with a service to buy and money to spend. Money brought you the sort of respect he had rarely experienced. 'I want it converting. I want it made into a shooter. I've got the money.'

The man gave him a different sort of smile, with narrowed eyes and a sly connivance. 'Now that's not legal. That will cost you.'

'I can pay.'

'I have to narrow the barrel. Insert a metal rod.'

'Whatever. I know you can do it. That's why I came to the best.'

This bit of shameless flattery amused the man in the leather apron, who picked up the new weapon and examined it, though he did not need to do so. 'Two hundred pounds.'

'It's half an hour's work. One hundred.'

The man laughed. 'It's skilled work and it's illegal. I'm taking a harmless pistol from you and putting a lethal weapon back in your hands. I'll do it for one fifty for you, for old time's sake. It'll be a good job. I'm off the sauce now.'

'Done.' Darren stretched out his hand impulsively and grasped the much stronger paw of the man who was to give him protection against future beatings. The gesture felt odd but uplifting. He had never shaken hands on a deal before.

'I'll do it whilst you wait, if you want that. All part of the service, like our MOTs in the garage. You'd better go to our waiting room, though. I don't let people watch me working – might make me nervous, and we wouldn't want that, would we, on a precision job like this?'

Darren went obediently back through the garage and thence through a small door into a carpeted office area. There was a coffee machine in the corner. A woman secretary came out and asked him what sort of coffee he wanted. He ordered a cappuccino with as much aplomb as he could muster and she put in a coin and brought it over to him with a practised, professional smile. 'It's free to customers.'

He sat with his hands round the coffee, thrusting his back against the armchair, managing not to wince as the posture gave him a sharp twinge of pain in his bruised side. It was good to be treated as a valued customer. He patted the money in his anorak pocket and listened contentedly to the sharp sounds of metal work from the room behind the garage area.

TWELVE

Saturday evening. The end of a windless, humid day, with the temperature in the eighties and everyone telling one another what wonderful weather this is, whilst they sweat uncomfortably and find breathing difficult. Don't grumble, be British. We don't get many periods of sustained high temperatures and plentiful sun, so don't complain. It's your duty to enjoy this weather.

But by ten o'clock, with darkness dropping in on the ancient city and, the atmosphere still oppressive, the weather is taking its toll. In taverns, ancient and modern, the sales of alcohol and beer to the males and white wine to the females are reaching record levels. The streets are full of noisy revellers, and in the hours to come women will become more provocative as well as more attractive, men more argumentative as well as more hilarious, and trouble will follow. There will be the tiresome squalor of vomit, the repetitive obscenities of challenge, the rising tide of aggression.

The Gloucestershire police have seen it all before, but that does not make their task on this sweltering night less tedious, less challenging, or less dangerous. They will try to keep rival gangs apart, to relax tensions rather than encourage them. Contrary to the popular view amongst the young people here, the police, most of whom are scarcely older than those they are attempting to control, are not looking for arrests. They would rather send the inebriated home to peaceful beds and morning hangovers than carry them away to a night in the cells and the ensuing paperwork of minor charges.

The police in the centre of Gloucester are fully occupied with preventing the escalation of violence and with trying to preserve the law against the binge drinkers. But outside the city centre, there is plenty of scope for the quieter sort of criminal activity.

In the area where Darren Chivers rents his flat, there are lights behind curtained windows, but otherwise no signs of human presence. People here keep themselves to themselves; most of them do not move outside their residences after dark unless they have to. Many people live in the block which contains Chivers's flat. Yet there is no observer of the presence which steals softly into the building and up to the door of that flat.

The person who gains entry here has done this sort of thing before. The worn Yale lock is little protection against the credit card in expert hands. With scarcely a sound in the quiet corridor, the intruder is inside the flat and the door is shut again. There is no need for a torch. A little fumbling finds the switch by the door. After the darkness outside, the light shed by the single, shadeless bulb seems dazzling for a moment or two.

The interloper is in no hurry. It will not take long to search these two small rooms and there is little fear of interruption. Darren Chivers has taken no real precautions against snoopers; the danger of anyone coming into his lair had seemed minimal. There are no large metal filing cabinets here; indeed, there is not even a locked drawer.

On the table, there is a box with a life-sized illustration of the Brocock ME 38 air pistol on its lid, which the interloper notes but does not touch. A swift, efficient examination of the battered kitchen cabinet and the sideboard with the damaged mirror reveals nothing. In the tiny bedroom with its shut curtains, the infiltrator pauses for an instant in surprise before the lurid framed picture of the Sacred Heart, surrounded by flames on the breast of Christ, wondering whether this is a relic of a Catholic upbringing in the occupant or just a picture which came with the furnishings of this mean little pad.

The material this uninvited visitor wants is discovered in the chest of drawers beside the narrow bed. The top two drawers reveal nothing, but in the bottom one, beneath two threadbare shirts and an unworn sweater, is a small one-drawer filing cabinet with the key in the lock. It contains a collection of documents, accompanied by pages of notes compiled by Darren Chivers in a small, surprisingly neat, hand. The interloper sits for a moment on the edge of the bed, examining what has been unearthed, checking swiftly but efficiently through the sheets of paper. The material which prompted this intrusion has been found.

One section in particular gets more attention than the rest. It is stowed away carefully into the large plastic bag which is the burglar's only baggage. The raider returns the other material to the cabinet, then, on second thoughts, retrieves it and puts in the plastic bag with the rest. The shirts and sweater are folded neatly, then returned to the drawer by the gloved hands, which slide it softly shut.

Two minutes later, after a final check to ensure that there are no other papers of interest here, the light by the door of Chivers's apartment is switched off as quietly as it was activated. The whole process of search and removal has taken no more than a quarter of an hour. The door is opened an inch; the raider checks that all is silent and unsuspecting in this rabbit-warren of a building.

Then the intruder slips quietly away into the warm, oppressive darkness.

THIRTEEN

Monday morning again, and Chief Superintendent Lambert was on the prowl around the CID section of his police station.

His paperwork was up to date, he had checked his overtime budget and found there was money to spare, and the meeting he should have had with the Chief Constable at ten o'clock had been cancelled because of a conference of the top brass in Oxford. Bert Hook found him flicking through the Missing Persons pages on the computer which was usually the preserve of DI Rushton.

'Every one of these represents a personal heartbreak for someone,' John Lambert said to his detective sergeant, without taking his eyes from the screen. 'And all we do is register the names and details and hope they choose to get in touch.'

'You know the argument . . . we're police officers, not social workers.'

'I know.' John Lambert logged off carefully. 'I'd be saying the same thing myself if anyone challenged me with neglect. I know MISPAs are far too numerous for us to do much about them. But when you see how young a lot of them are, you wonder what domestic tragedies lie behind the statistics on that screen.' He sighed. 'I have the old-fashioned view that we're a public service, needing the public's support and providing them with solid value in return. It makes you feel very helpless, when you look at those details.'

It was at that moment that the young officer on the switch-board put the call through to his office and Lambert arrived there a little breathless to receive it. 'A suspicious death, sir. Outskirts of Highnam.'

'Has the Scene of Crime team been sent in?'

'Yes, sir. It's the SOCO officer who said you should be alerted.'

'Tell him DS Hook and I will be there in a quarter of an hour.'

He and Hook were in his car and reversing out of his space within two minutes. They had the faces of men who already had the scent of the chase in their nostrils. The rest of the station relaxed a little with their departure. Keep the old bugger out of their hair, a decent murder would, they thought. Let's hope it's not a simple domestic, with an arrest made within hours.

There was little prospect of that. The man who lay behind the hawthorn hedge in that quiet spot had long since ceased to have any family around him.

The area was already cordoned off with the plastic ribbons which denoted a scene of crime site. This was an isolated place, so that there was no sign yet of the ghoulish curiosity which often assembled round the place of a suspicious death.

But the area had to be isolated and defined, so that whatever clues lay within it would not be contaminated by any unofficial presence. A bicycle lay with its wheels in the air in the brambles on the far side of the clearing, as if a rough attempt had been made at concealment.

Lambert and Hook donned the paper overalls and plastic foot covers and followed the path designated by markers to the centre of this quiet scene of tragedy. The civilian Scene of Crime officer knew Lambert well enough. He nodded toward the corpse which lay face down in the undergrowth. 'Suspicious, all right. Possible suicide, but almost certainly murder, in my view.'

Lambert walked around the corpse, stooped a little stiffly towards it and smiled grimly at his informant. 'A bullet through the head is pretty conclusive.' He brushed impatiently at the flies he had disturbed as they rose round the damaged head. 'How long has he been here?'

The SOCO shrugged. 'A day or two at least, I'd say. But I'll leave that to the pathologist. Probably not long enough for the labs to play their delightful little games with maggots.'

When corpses had lain undiscovered for a week or two, the scientists could pinpoint the time of death fairly accurately by the state of development of the larvae upon the corpse. Lambert, despite many years of experience, had never developed the iron stomach which would have been useful at times like this. He said firmly, 'He doesn't smell to me like a man who's been here that long.' He glanced down at the lank hair above the bloodstained temple. 'It is a he, I suppose?' You could never be sure, these days. They had questioned the grubby inhabitants of a squat a few days earlier. Gender had not been apparent until they spoke.

'Yes. Not a prime specimen, but certainly male.'

Bert Hook stooped on one knee beside the corpse, as if genuflecting in the face of death. He put his face almost at ground level, so as to stare into the features of the cadaver without disturbing it. He stood up heavily. 'This is Darren Chivers. Small-time drug dealer. DI Rushton and I had him in for questioning a couple of weeks ago. I thought we'd warned him off. It appears not.'

The SOCO said, 'This might not be drugs-related. We haven't found anything illegal in his pockets.'

Lambert nodded. 'Forensics will test that anorak for drug traces. Whoever did this might have taken the drugs and fled, if it was a meet for an illegal transaction.'

'But why kill him?'

'Because the user didn't have the money for drugs? Because a minor disagreement transformed itself suddenly into a life and death struggle? Heroin addicts are notoriously unpredictable. All that matters is the next fix, especially when it's overdue. They'll sacrifice anything for it then, including a man's life, if he's holding back what they want. But all that is speculation. Hopefully the autopsy will give us more information. What have you found around here?'

He looked round at the crime scene. It had been a lonely place for a man to meet his death. The spot was no more than two miles from the centre of Gloucester, but it looked much more remote. They were on a country lane five hundred yards outside the village of Highnam, in a small clearing behind a six feet high hawthorn hedge. A picnic spot, perhaps, in happier times. The wood beside them cut off all views to the west and the Welsh hills, but when you looked the other way you could see the top of Gloucester Cathedral, looking deceptively close with nothing visible in between.

The SOCO officer looked at the woman and two men who were systematically searching the site they had cordoned off, working outwards from the body in the centre of it, then shook his head. 'Nothing which seems significant so far, Mr Lambert. We're bagging anything and everything found here, as per usual, but most of it will prove to have no connection with this crime. That includes a used contraceptive and a hair slide.' He shook his head with distaste. 'Couples, or at least one couple, obviously use this site for other purposes than murder. We've got a couple of fag ends, both of which look to me weeks old and equally useless as clues to your killer.'

Lambert stooped over the corpse. He was tempted to investigate the pockets of the navy anorak and the jeans beneath it, but until the pathologist had done his preliminary investigation at the scene, it was better to disturb nothing. Contamination of evidence at a scene of death had destroyed prosecution cases in court too often for him to take risks. He looked again at what had once been Darren Chivers. 'Did he die here?'

'I would say yes. We can't be certain yet, but my feeling is that the PM will establish that he did. We haven't found any evidence of a vehicle bringing a body here, but it's been so dry over the last three days that you wouldn't expect tyre marks. I suppose it's possible that he could have been killed on the other side of the hedge and dragged through to prevent more immediate discovery, but there's no damage to the hedge evident; you'd expect at least a few leaves to have been dislodged. He might have been dragged through the gap where all of us came in, but in that case you'd expect there to be blood or fibres from his clothes there. We haven't found either.'

It was at this moment that they heard a cry of excitement from a woman who was working her meticulous way along the base of the hedge which formed the boundary of the crime site. They went over and looked down at what she had found in the brambles which grew alongside the hedge, on the side away from the road. The sight of the thing she was preparing to extract with pliers and deposit delicately in a plastic bag stilled all of them for a moment.

Then Lambert said softly, 'It looks as if we have our murder weapon.'

The young woman who was so pleased with her find said reluctantly, 'It's only an air pistol, isn't it?'

Bert Hook smiled grimly. 'That's a Brocock ME 38. It not only looks and feels like a real gun in the hand, but a gunsmith can convert it to fire genuine rounds in twenty minutes by narrowing the barrel. I'd give long odds that it killed the man lying over there. If I'm right, that's a real bonus for us. When firearms are involved, it's not often we find the murder weapon at the site of the killing.'

The pathologist arrived as they spoke and began the process of recording information at the site. He took rectal temperatures, checked the degree of rigor mortis, and offered the opinion that death had occurred at least two days earlier. He promised that the post-mortem on this murder victim would be given priority at the Home Office forensic laboratory at Chepstow.

As they journeyed back to the station in Lambert's old Vauxhall Senator, both Chief Superintendent and DS felt elation at the discovery, at the very outset of the investigation, of what appeared to be the murder weapon. But years of experience temper optimism with a professional caution. The unspoken question both of them were wrestling with was why a killer should choose to leave this key evidence behind so conveniently for them.

The Reverend Peter Lynch arrived at the breakfast table on Tuesday morning to find his wife in a state of suppressed excitement.

'There's been a suspicious death,' said Karen.

'Anyone we know?' said Peter.

He was being flippant, but she took him seriously. 'The radio didn't give a name at eight o'clock. It was in Highnam. Put Radio Gloucester on. We might get more details there.'

Peter switched the local radio programme on and they carried on a muted conversation about the day ahead, whilst the resolutely cheerful announcer gave the forecast for the day's weather and details of local traffic hold-ups between the inane lyrics of the latest pop music. Peter noticed that the normally voracious Karen seemed to be toying with her cereal.

When the time came for the news bulletin, Karen reached across and turned up the volume. The announcer adopted the solemn tone appropriate for tragedy, though he could not prevent the excitement which accompanied a local scoop from creeping in as the item proceeded. 'Police have revealed that the body of a local man was discovered by a dog-walker early yesterday morning on the outskirts of Highnam. Radio Gloucester can reveal that in the last few minutes the identity of the deceased man has been released. He was Darren Christopher Chivers, a resident of Gloucester. Police are treating the death as suspicious. Anyone who has any information is asked to contact Oldford CID section as a matter of urgency.'

Peter Lynch tried to sound casual in the face of his wife's obvious intensity. 'He wasn't a parishioner. I didn't expect him to be – it's a relief in a way. Though I suppose I should be hoping that the poor man made what my mother used to call "a good death".'

'I knew him.'

'Eh?'

'I knew him. A long time ago, before I knew you.'

She stopped, staring at the packet of cereals between them.

He said, 'You don't have to talk about it, you know, love. It's all right. It's all gone.'

'It isn't really that long ago.' She spoke as if she had not heard him. 'It's just that it seems like another life altogether.'

'It is another life altogether,' said Peter quietly. 'And you really don't have to talk about it. Not even to me.'

'I can see myself as if I were another woman entirely. A woman living out a horror film. Wondering where the next fix was coming from. Prepared to do anything to get it. Prepared to steal to get the money for the next needle, the next lot of horse. Prepared to fornicate.' Karen tried the biblical word and apparently found it inappropriate. 'Prepared to fuck for it, to offer my miserable body to whoever could afford to pay for it.'

He reached across and took her hands, held them hard for long seconds without speaking, made her turn her agonized eyes upon his face. 'That's all gone. You were living a nightmare. Once you'd become an addict, you weren't responsible for your actions, you'd lost the power of free will.'

She was back with him now, looking into the face which was two years older than hers and yet so much younger, at the deep-set blue eyes and the nose which was a little too long and the wide, firm lips below it. 'You're very charitable. That's part of the job, though, isn't it? Comes with the territory, I suppose.'

He hadn't heard this note of self-disgust in her voice for years now. He couldn't cope with this distancing in the wife he loved. 'It's not charity. It's the truth. It's what I feel.' He wanted to speak on, to salve this lacerated spirit with words of comfort as he might have salved a wounded body with ointment. But the words which came to him so readily in other circumstances would not come to him now when he most needed them. He said desperately, 'Who was this Chivers man?'

'Darren Chivers. I never knew about the Christopher until I heard it just now on the radio. The bearer of Christ, Christopher, isn't it?' She smiled at the irony of that name for the sly, shuffling bearer of evil she had known as Darren Chivers. 'He was a drug dealer. Small-time, like me. A user turned dealer to get his fix, like me. Cleverer than me, though.'

Cleverer because he was finding other sources of income,

using blackmail to supplement his revenue from drugs. But in that moment she knew that she could not tell Peter about her meeting with Chivers a week ago. This man who had emerged from her past to torment her with his threats to unmask her unless she acceded to his demands could not be allowed into the vicarage. Even to report this intrusion of her past into a present life which was so idyllic would be to tarnish it, to risk its destruction. 'It might even have been me who recruited Darren. He was just beginning to deal when – when you rescued me from all that.'

'When you rescued yourself. I saw the hell you had to go through to get out of it, don't forget.'

'No. I won't forget.' She made herself look at him and forced a smile. She had the illusion that her blood was only now beginning to pulse again through her veins. She felt quite light-headed with the sensation. 'Sometimes this world and you seem like a wonderful dream which can't last, just as that world seems like a nightmare which comes back to haunt me at times like this.'

'This is the reality, Karen. This is no dream.' He grinned at her, knowing now that he was winning his strange, bitter battle against her past. 'We'd have a bit more money to throw about, if it was a dream!'

She stared at him wanly for a moment, then gladdened his heart by answering his smile. 'You're right as usual, of course! One glance at your stipend will bring us out of any dream. I'll go down to the hostel again this afternoon and see what I can do to help other poor devils out of their own nightmares.'

Peter Lynch frowned. 'Do you think you should, love? You've not been sleeping well, these last few nights, have you? There's nothing wrong with keeping the past at bay by ignoring it, you know, when it gets a little too close.'

His hands still held hers across the table. Impulsively, she picked up the right one and kissed his fingers. 'I'm all right, as long as I've got you. I really need your support – the kind of support you've just given me. But I'm all right, so long as I've got that. I'll get myself together this morning. By the time I get to the hostel I'll be ready for anything.'

She would, too, she thought when she was alone in the bathroom, looking in the mirror at the dark rings beneath her eyes. They had come during the last few disturbed nights, as she agonized about where she could possibly raise the money to buy off Chivers.

All that was over now. Karen Lynch tried hard to regret the death of Darren Chivers, but all she saw in that face in the mirror was relief.

FOURTEEN

The woman had a face which was prematurely lined and eyes which seemed permanently narrowed in suspicion. Her untidy grey hair needed a wash. Her thin lips turned downwards at the corners; they were set in a line of discontent which seemed to be her natural expression. In the car, she told the female police constable who was driving her to the mortuary that she was forty-eight. That was the first shock for the younger woman, who would have thought her nearer sixty.

Perhaps it was the stress of what she was going to do which was making the woman look older, PC Emily Johnson thought charitably. Being called upon to identify the shattered body of your son would surely affect the most undemonstrative of mothers. She chatted a little, trying to divert the woman's mind from the task ahead, but was answered only in curt monosyllables.

At the mortuary, the woman accepted the offer of tea and biscuits. She munched a digestive and thumbed unseeingly through a magazine, glancing twice at the clock and giving every impression of impatience. Perhaps she just wanted this to be over and to be alone, thought PC Johnson. It must be a terrible thing to have to contemplate. She had given up trying to talk to the woman. Her emollient little clichés seemed to have helped the two women she had accompanied previously on this wretched mission, but they were clearly useless here.

The corpses were presented behind glass nowadays, like stuffed specimens in a wildlife museum. PC Johnson made sure that she had an upright chair available, in case this previously unemotional woman felt faint when faced with the reality of death, as people often did. The morticians had told her tales of strong men collapsing under the stress of identification.

When the body slid into view, she was relieved to see that the worst of the damage was concealed. The sheet was drawn neatly under the chin, covering the worst of the multiple cuts of the post-mortem examination. The lank hair had been brushed forward to conceal the incisions in the skull; the side of the face which had been shot away was mercifully hidden on the far side of the damaged head. The thin profile which was presented was waxy and white. It might almost have been a model rather than what remained of a living human presence.

The woman gave a tiny gasp, but otherwise showed as little emotion as she had done since she was first apprised of this death. After no more than a second, she said in a perfectly even tone, 'That's him. That's my son.'

'You're sure of that?'

'Of course I'm sure. What's next?'

'Would you like a little time with him alone. I can—'

'No. What would I want with that?'

She signed the form of identification in the office, then went back to the police car with the young police officer.

They drove without speaking through Herefordshire lanes. Mrs Chivers was almost back at the supermarket and the resumption of her job there when she said, 'I hadn't seen Darren for three years, you know. It was a bit of a shock when I heard. But we were never close.'

It seemed a fitting maternal epitaph on the narrow, flawed, violently truncated life of the son she had left behind her.

When you were an ex-copper, you knew a wide cross-section of humanity. There wasn't much which could still shock you, after what you had seen in the job. You got used to keeping your emotions in check. Moral stances and moral judgements were usually better avoided. For a lot of the time, you didn't pass judgements, but just got on with what you had to do.

Daniel Steele found that this was for the most part a good preparation for the work he had to do at Gloucester Building Supplies. There were people who had worked here for many years, who had made him feel like an interloper when he had first come to the place. They had their own ways of working the system to their advantage, small ruses they had developed over the years, which most of them had ceased to regard as cheating.

So long as these were not major abuses, Daniel chose to ignore them. He had discussed things with the managing director, who was impressed that he had discovered these small depredations so quickly. They had agreed that he would monitor the situation and take no action, so long as the fiddles which people had come to regard as the perks of the job were not too blatant. Human nature being what it is, the men involved – it always seemed to be men who enjoyed playing the system – would devise equally ingenious and perhaps more damaging ways of peculation. A few bricks or a few lengths of wood in the boot of the car for do-it-yourself improvements at home did no great damage to company profits and made for a contented workforce.

Within three weeks of taking up his duties as security officer, Steele had exposed a more major offence and taken the appropriate action. A delivery driver had been loading more than the items ordered on to his HGV and selling the residue to small local builders. Like most people who find what they see as an easy way of supplementing their income, the man had grown both greedy and careless. For a man with Dan Steele's police experience, he had presented an easy catch. He had been duly exposed and sacked, sent on his way without the prosecution which neither the firm nor the offender wanted.

The incident had established the new security manager's position with both the owners and the workforce. This was a man who would ensure that the company was not being ripped off, the owners said, congratulating themselves quietly on this latest appointment. This was a man who was not to be trifled with, the workforce said, a man to be treated with respect. His exposure of the HGV driver even ensured him a certain degree of popularity as well as respect, for workers do not like to see people milking their firm to a criminal extent. There was a general feeling that the man had been allowed to get away with too much.

So Dan the Detection, as a couple of Welshmen in the workforce had dubbed him, had established himself quickly as an

efficient and likeable operator, a man who knew his job but
who exercised his knowledge with discretion. This reputation
was an important factor for a man who worked for much of
his time at night. He would otherwise have been a vague identity for most of the men it was his job to study; he was now
a real presence for them to take into their considerations.

This afternoon, he had his monthly meeting with the
managing director. It was as brief and efficient as usual. They
exchanged views on how the new procedures which Steele
had suggested were working and how best to implement a
couple of new refinements to the checking of vehicles leaving
the premises. Then Dan strolled among the workers in the
stores and the busy loading bays; when you were in charge
of security, it was always a good idea to present yourself at
unexpected times, to convey the view that you knew everything that was going on and were likely to turn up without
warning at any moment.

Then he left the works and drove swiftly for six miles to
a small parking bay beside the A40, as it wound its way
through the hills towards Ross-on-Wye. The grey Ford Focus
was there as he had known it would be. It was the only other
car in the parking facility. He eased himself from the driving
seat of his Vectra, then stretched theatrically for the benefit
of any curious eyes, as if he was pausing after driving a couple
of hundred miles. He walked swiftly to the near side of the
parked Focus, where he was shielded from passing traffic.

The window of the car had been wound down as he drew
in behind it. The transaction took no more than five seconds,
with scarcely a word exchanged on either side. The Focus
pulled away swiftly and immediately. Daniel Steele gave it
three minutes before he pulled out unhurriedly and turned for
home.

An hour later, Chief Superintendent Lambert was closeted in
his office with DI Rushton and DS Hook. They were studying
the PM report which had been emailed to them from the
pathology laboratory.

The pathologist was able to tell them little which they did
not already know or suspect. Death had been instantaneous,
the result of a head wound inflicted from a firearm at close
quarters, almost certainly the one found nineteen feet from

the body. The body was that of a male in his twenties, without serious malfunctions in any of the major organs. He had been a user of drugs but not an addict. The forearms showed evidence of sizeable but not daily injections of heroin, which had probably been more frequent at some time in the past than in more recent months.

The most useful information concerned the time of this crime. The stomach contents indicated that a meal of fish and chips and apple pie had been consumed about two hours before death. The crime had almost certainly been committed where the body was found; the hypostasis after death showed that the blood had settled on the front of the thighs, stomach, chest and face, indicating that the body had almost certainly fallen forward after the shooting and not been touched subsequently.

The state of the digestive organs and the development of rigor mortis indicated that death had probably taken place two to three days before the discovery of the body by a man walking his dog at 7.30 a.m. on the morning of Monday the 7th of July. Two to three days would have to be the parameters for any expert evidence delivered in court. However, if it was assumed that it had been an evening meal which had been consumed, the likeliest time of death would have been in the late evening of Friday the 4th of July.

'That makes sense,' said Chris Rushton. 'Someone shot him under cover of darkness, probably at a deliberately chosen isolated rendezvous on the edge of Highnam village.'

'It needn't have been premeditated,' said Bert Hook. 'We all know that druggies are unpredictable. This man was a dealer. His death might have been the result of something as simple and trivial as an argument over the price of drugs. Anyone desperate for a fix could easily lose control when he saw it being taken away from him.'

Lambert shook his head. 'We can't even be sure that there is a direct drugs connection yet. Chivers was a dealer, so that seems the obvious connection, but we can't rule out other motives. It looks at the moment as if the killer went there armed, which suggests that there is at least the possibility that this was a premeditated killing.'

Chris Rushton, who had been doing his usual job of coordinating house-to-house inquiries and logging information on his computer, said, 'Bert and I had warned Chivers off dealing and he seems to have been lying low over the last week or two. We released his picture to the local press last night and I've just had the first reported sighting, in the Cathedral, of all places – hardly the usual pitch for a drug dealer.'

'When was this?'

Chris consulted the note he had brought with him. 'A Miss Edwina Clarkson, civilian administrator of the Cathedral's commercial activities, thinks she saw Chivers there two or three weeks ago, talking to one of her vergers. He'll be contacted this afternoon.'

Lambert nodded. 'I'll interview him myself, with Bert.'

Rushton, who had not visited the scene of crime, was puzzled about what had been found there. 'Why would the killer leave the murder weapon at the site? If he didn't want to retain it, why didn't he sling it into the Severn or some such place, where we'd never have found it?'

It was at that moment that Lambert's internal telephone buzzed insistently. 'Sorry to interrupt you, sir, but there is a man at the desk who insists he has information relevant to the killing at Highnam.'

Lambert glanced at the other two. 'Send him in here,' he said grimly.

The man was in his early twenties, a little in awe of Chief Superintendent Lambert and his formidable local reputation. He felt suddenly less certain of his ground than he had when he had been speaking to the desk sergeant in the reception area of the station. He sat very upright on the chair which had been offered to him and said, 'The radio said anyone with information should come forward. It may be nothing. I just thought you should know.'

'I'm sure we should,' said Lambert briskly. 'We appreciate you taking the trouble to come in here, Mr . . .?'

'Jackson. Leo Jackson. I work in the gun shop off Westgate.'

'And what is it you have to tell us?'

'This man who was killed. His picture was in the *Citizen* last night. I recognized him. He came into the shop last week – I'm almost sure it was him.' He produced the newspaper from his pocket, folded to reveal the photograph of a slightly younger Darren Chivers, as if it was some sort of evidence of his good faith.

'And did he make a purchase, Mr Jackson?' Lambert's heart

was sinking. Any information, even of a negative sort, had to be useful, but he feared that he wouldn't much like what he was going to hear next.

'Yes. He bought an air pistol. A Brocock ME 38.'

'Did he say what he wanted it for?'

'He said he shot pellets at paper targets in his cellar. He said it was a little hobby of his.'

'But you didn't believe him.'

'No, I don't suppose I did, really. But there's nothing we can do, if someone assures us he's going to use the pistol for an innocent purpose.' He squirmed a little on the chair in the silence which followed this, then added irrelevantly, 'The Brocock ME 38 is a precision instrument. It cannot cause serious injury, if it is handled responsibly.'

'Unless it is converted to something altogether more lethal, as many of these pistols are.'

Leo Jackson gave a self-conscious shrug. 'We can't control that. We have to sell to legitimate purchasers.'

Lambert allowed himself a sigh. 'No, of course you can't. Thank you for acting as a good citizen and bringing us this information, Mr Jackson.'

The three officers stared glumly at each other for a moment after their informant had left the room. 'You have the answer to your question, Chris,' said Lambert. 'The murder weapon was left at the scene because it belonged to the deceased, not his killer. And none of us believes there'll be any prints on it.'

Their one useful clue had just been declared useless. 'Let's hope the forensic boys come up with something for us from the clothes and the pockets,' said Bert Hook. He did not sound optimistic.

Choral evensong in Gloucester Cathedral was one of Robert Beckford's favourite services. He loved the ethereal sound of the carefully modulated trained voices; it sounded to him like an echo from that heaven which the modern world was deserting. He glanced at his watch, finished setting out the chairs for the meeting of the cathedral chapter on the following day, and hurried back into the ancient church.

The choir were in their traditional surplices. The congregation was depressingly small, though supplemented by those few late-afternoon tourists who chose to sit down and listen rather than hurry out of the place with the advent of a religious service. Robert looked upwards at the slender stone vaulting shafts, soaring impossibly high above him in an unbroken sweep. He knew a lot about his workplace now, knew that this choir had been built in the 1330s, that even then it had been a remodelling and masking of the massive pillars of the old Benedictine abbey church.

For the professional soldier Beckford had been for so long, that seemed an impossibly long time ago. Soldiers were taught to exist in the here and now, to obey the urgent demands of a dangerous and perpetually changing modern world. He knew that the world in which these stones had been raised was as violent and even more brutal than his own – indeed, the tomb of Edward II, the king who had died the most hideous of all royal deaths, was but a few yards away from him. He turned his gaze upon the great east window, the size of a tennis court and the largest stone-traceried window in England, as he told any visitors who showed interest in it. Almost seven centuries ago, that had been constructed. He envied once again the certainty of the people who had built this place, the 'singing masons building roofs of gold', in that ringing phrase of Shakespeare's from a play he had never seen.

The archdeacon who was conducting the service today spoke a few words, reminding his listeners of an unchanging God and this unchanging House of God in a changing world. Then the choir took over again, and Rob looked up at the vaulted ceiling above him, where the notes and the voices seemed to hang, then seep away into the ancient stone. The men who had hewn those stones then had known their trade, secure in their faith as they moved around Europe, enjoying the patronage of a wealthy church which was certain of its ground and certain of the faith of the men and women who walked upon it.

Robert Beckford had a pleasant confusion in his mind which he felt no urgency to resolve. In the harsh setting of the Falklands and Iraq and the orderly, intensely disciplined army world which had framed his former life, he had thought himself an atheist. Gloucester Cathedral and his daily presence within it had changed him. He had become first an agnostic and lately the possessor of some sort of faith. He could not define it, and he would not have the confidence to defend it against the vigorous arguments of those who found Christian services so much mumbo-jumbo. But he was certain that what he had just savoured was a spiritual experience, something more than mere physical satisfaction. This job was important to him. It carried a significance far greater than the modest salary which was paid into his account each month by the cathedral authorities.

'Mr Robert Beckford?'

He still hadn't got used to that form of address. Only officers had been 'Mr' in the army which had been his working environment for so many years. Rob blinked a little as he moved out through the massive doors and into the bright sunlight. 'That's me. What can I do for you?'

The young man in uniform tried not to sound too pompous. 'We'd like a few words with you, sir. Well, not me, Chief Superintendent Lambert, actually. It's a CID matter, you see.'

For Robert Beckford, the bright day had suddenly darkened.

FIFTEEN

Mark Rogers never listened to local radio. He couldn't even find Radio Gloucester on the dial of the old set in his bedroom. His son George heard the discordant sounds of his struggle and bounded in to tune to the station with expert, eight-year-old's fingers. A set of those should be sold with every new piece of electronics, his father thought fondly.

He felt less doting when George announced a little while later over the evening meal, 'Dad was listening to Radio Gloucester in your bedroom, Mum.'

'Don't speak with your mouth full, please, George.' Samantha turned to her husband. 'You never listen to Radio Gloucester. You always say local radio is nothing but pop records and mindless chat.'

'I wanted the news and the local weather, that's all. I'd missed it on the way home.' He'd heard all of the Radio

4 *PM* programme on the car radio as he drove back from his meeting with the BT engineers who worked for him, but she wasn't to know that.

'And was there anything earth-shattering?'

'Nothing at all.'

'There's been a murder. Dad was listening to that. They're asking anyone who can help to get in touch with the police.' George turned his wide-eyed beaming face upon his mother, and awaited a reaction.

Samantha turned to Mark. 'You're not interested in murders.'

She sounded almost accusing, he thought. 'Not normally, I'm not. But this is local. It's the same man who was beaten up a couple of weeks ago. It rather intrigued me.'

'How do you know it's the same one?'

'I remembered the name.'

'Someone you know, is it?'

'No, of course not. I just happened to remember the name. Darren Chivers, he was called.'

Samantha Rogers let it go at that. She didn't like talking about things like this in front of the children, who as usual were watching them wide-eyed when she'd rather they lost interest.

But Mark was usually very bad on names.

'It's a nice place to live, this. Very cosy and very handy for the centre of the town.' Bert Hook tried to break the ice as they entered Robert Beckford's house.

'It comes with the job. We couldn't afford it otherwise. Goodness knows what a house in the cathedral close would bring on the open market.' Rob tried not to sound as nervous as he felt.

Lambert scarcely removed his eyes from Rob as he said to the man's wife, 'We need to see Mr Beckford on his own, I'm afraid.'

'You'd better use the front room, then. You won't be disturbed in there.' Gwen Beckford was not as good at concealing her feelings as her husband. She felt a little miffed to be excluded.

It was a comfortable room, with a tall Victorian fireplace and a picture rail running round the high walls. It was furnished as a dining room, with a highly polished mahogany table as its centrepiece. The CID men sat on the upright chairs beside it and looked at their man across the table without speaking for a second or two. He said, 'I'm willing to give you all the help I can – that goes without saying. But I can't think what this can be about.'

'Can't you, Mr Beckford? Haven't you been following the news over the last twenty-four hours? The local news, in particular.' Lambert was polite but brusque, even a trifle hostile.

'This murder, you mean?'

'I do indeed.'

'But that's nothing to do with me. I don't see how I can be of any help to you.'

'We are interested in talking to anyone who knew the dead man, Mr Beckford.'

Robert set his features to reveal nothing. One of the things you learned early in the military life was to keep an impassive face in all kinds of circumstances, such as when you were standing to attention on parade with some manic drill pig yelling in your ear. That training stood him in good stead now. He stared straight ahead of him, focused on the Worcester vase on the mantelpiece, and said, 'I can understand that. But as I didn't know the man, I can't see why you are here.'

'The dead man was Darren Chivers. Do you still maintain that you did not know him?'

'The name means nothing to me.'

'Yet you have been reported to us as speaking to him in the cathedral within the last two or three weeks.'

Edwina bloody Clarkson! It must be. Sticking her nose in and causing trouble for him as usual. He didn't think anyone had seen that little interchange with Chivers in the Lady Chapel, but she must have been keeping an eye on him after their little spat. Damn the woman!

Robert felt an overwhelming desire to tell them the truth, to tell them that the man had been blackmailing him and threatening to reveal events from his past to the cathedral authorities. The identity of blackmail victims was kept secret, wasn't it, even when such criminals were taken to court? But it would be bound to come out, even if the police didn't reveal it. Miss Edwina bloody Clarkson would make it her business to ferret out what was going on, once she knew that the police were involved. And if she knew, she would delight in conveying her knowledge to the bishop and the senior clergy as quickly as possible. And then she would make the maximum use of it. She would claim he had obtained his verger's post under false pretences, and both the job he loved and this house he and Gwen loved would be taken from them in a trice.

He said doggedly, 'I didn't know anyone called Darren Chivers.'

'You're saying our informant was mistaken?'

'Who was your informant, Mr Lambert?'

'We do not reveal our sources, Mr Beckford. With your military background, you would no doubt expect that.'

'Well, I do not know anyone of that name. Lots of people speak to me in the cathedral. Most of them just want information about the history or the layout of the buildings. If this man did speak to me, he was probably asking a question of that sort. I certainly do not know anyone called Chivers.'

His rather stiff military manner was serving him well. He didn't think his face was revealing much and his voice was quite even, sounding in his own ears much calmer than he felt.

The man who had been introduced as Detective Sergeant Hook now produced a photograph of Chivers and passed it across the table to him. 'Is this the man who spoke to you in the Lady Chapel?'

Robert made himself study the picture for a few seconds. 'It may well have been. I couldn't be certain. This would have been a casual exchange of the kind I conduct several times a day, as I've explained to you. I'm afraid I don't give close attention to the people I meet in those circumstances.'

Lambert studied him silently for a moment, in that way which often embarrassed members of the public, who were used to polite social exchanges where such scrutiny would have been positively rude. 'Our information was that this was quite a prolonged exchange, lasting for two or three minutes. I would have expected a meeting of that sort to stick in your mind a little more clearly.'

'I'm sorry that I don't recall it more clearly. I don't wish to be vague – I'd like to be more helpful to you, if I could.

May I suggest that your informant might be mistaken in her description of this chance encounter?'

Lambert smiled, acknowledging that with his use of gender the man had divined who had placed this information with them. 'That is always possible, of course. I take it that your recollection is that the exchange between you and our murder victim was much more brief.'

'As I do not recall the meeting at all, I cannot be precise.' He had not been caught out and contradicted himself, as this shrewd, persistent man had hoped; Rob allowed himself the suggestion of a smile. 'However, if the conversation had been as prolonged as your informant claims, I am pretty sure that I would remember it now.'

'And you had no previous acquaintance with Darren Chivers?'

'No. And I am still not convinced that I spoke with him on that morning.'

Lambert's grey, unblinking eyes were intent upon the face of the man on the other side of the mahogany table. 'I didn't mention that this exchange took place in the morning, Mr Beckford.'

'Didn't you? I must have assumed it, then.'

'And your assumption is correct. Interesting, that.'

Beckford didn't allow his irritation to show. 'Interesting, but scarcely significant, I'd have thought.'

Lambert stood up. 'Mr Chivers is a murder victim. Keep that photograph, please. You never know, it may eventually stir some memories.' His voice was tinged with irony for a moment. Then he said briskly, 'You will realize that it is your duty to get in touch with us at Oldford CID if anything occurs to you which might have a bearing on this case. Good night to you, Mr Beckford.'

Robert stood holding the wide blue front door of the house until his visitors disappeared from view at the end of the close. He was brusque and dismissive when his wife asked him what it had all been about – a case of mistaken identity, he told her.

Rob had taught himself to sleep in all kinds of uncomfortable and occasionally dangerous places around the world. But Gwen Beckford noticed how restless he was in their bed that night.

* * *

Michelle de Vries found that the conversation with Guy Dawson was very scrappy when she visited his house as usual on Tuesday night. Perhaps he was as anxious to get into bed as she was, she thought, with the self-deception which is always a lover's weakness.

In fact, Guy was as preoccupied as Michelle with the death of Darren Chivers, the man who had threatened to bring their world crashing about their ears. Both of them had listened to every news bulletin they could about the sensational murder of their tormentor. Yet for some reason neither of them cared to mention it to the other as they drank the gins and tonics which were a prelude to their retirement to the bedroom.

'Does Gerald suspect anything?' Guy ran his fingers round the edge of his glass, deliberately casual.

'No. I'm sure he doesn't.'

'There's no reason why he should, now.'

That small three-letter word was the only reference either of them made to the events of the last few days during the first hours in which they were together.

Much later in the evening, Guy Dawson sighed a sigh of gratified exhaustion and murmured into Michelle's ear, 'You're insatiable!'

There was no doubt from the awed tone in his voice that he intended it as a compliment. Michelle stretched her toes luxuriously towards the bottom of the bed and murmured, 'Only with you, my darling! I've never felt like this with anyone else!'

'I think you're a wanton harlot! And what's more, you're my wanton harlot!' They were both lying on their backs and satiated, but he now rolled on to his side and took her again into his arms, stroking the small of her back in that tentative, experimental way he had. Each caress felt as if it was the first time he had ever touched her; she enjoyed the sensation that he was each time feeling his way anew into her body and her affections.

She felt the familiar stirring of desire, even at this moment when she was so fulfilled, but she said as firmly as she could, 'We can't, Guy! It's time I was getting home.'

'That's a relief! I'm only human, you know, as King Kong said to Fay Wray. There are limits even to my stamina.'

But he went on gently stroking her back, so that Michelle still felt a little shaft of disappointment that she could not stay the night. She detached his hands and rolled on to her back. She was gazing at the ceiling of Guy Dawson's bedroom when she voiced the thought that had been in both their minds earlier in the evening. 'I won't be seeing that man with his demands for money again, thank God!'

'And so say all of us! Well, both of us, in this case. And God knows how many other poor sods whom we don't even know and don't want to know.'

'You think he was extorting money from others? That we weren't the only ones?'

'Good word that, "extorting". I like it when you display your technical expertise. You're a woman of many parts.'

He let his hand move on to her hip. She took it firmly in hers and squeezed it. 'I suppose he could have been black-mailing others as well as me. When he came into the shop, I somehow thought it was a one-off.'

'He sounds like the sort of sly sod who would have a lot of dubious irons in the fire. Not that I've ever met him, of course.'

That seemed to Michelle an odd qualification to make. She said without any great emotion, 'You missed nothing. He was scum.' She had a sudden, disturbing thought. 'You don't think he left anything behind, do you? Anything which might get back to Gerald, even now?'

'No, I'm sure he didn't. I don't suppose he ever meant to tell Gerald, so long as you went on paying him. Because he'd have been back for more, you know. He wouldn't have stopped at that first two thousand.'

'I expect he would have come back again, yes. And I wouldn't have been able to give him any more, without Gerald discovering that money was mysteriously disappearing.'

'It's just as well he's gone then, isn't it? We shouldn't spend much time mourning a bastard like that.'

It was a conventional enough reaction to the death of a black-mailer. But as she showered in Guy Dawson's bathroom, Michelle de Vries could not rid herself of the feeling that she was cleansing herself of something secret and evil.

SIXTEEN

The post-mortem report on Darren Chivers had revealed very little, beyond the fact that he had almost certainly been killed with his own weapon, by person or persons unknown. Less than twenty-four hours later, the three men at the heart of the investigation met again, hoping that house-to-house inquiries and the forensic laboratories might have come up with something more helpful.

Rushton always tried to give the least helpful information first. Occasionally he enjoyed presenting something startling with a conjuror's flourish at the end of their exchanges. 'No one saw Chivers on Friday evening in Highnam,' he began gloomily. 'It rather looks as if he arranged to meet someone at the isolated spot where he was killed. That was his bike which was found at the scene.'

Lambert nodded. 'If he went there on a bike, he was much less likely to be spotted than if he'd gone there by car. Two cars meeting usually get attention; one car at the side of the road in darkness is assumed to enclose a couple out for a snog.'

'Friday night seems the likeliest time for this death, when we put the PM report next to other findings. Chivers was seen going into his flat on Friday afternoon – that's the last sighting of him we have so far. The old lady in the flat next door usually saw him on Saturday mornings. Last Saturday he didn't turn up.'

Bert Hook looked surprised. 'He was a drug dealer, Chris. Small-time, but dangerous. You and I know that. When we interviewed him, he didn't seem the type to visit old ladies.'

'He used to do a bit of shopping for her on Saturdays, when he was getting things for himself, she says. Apparently he was always very kind to her – sometimes he'd have little chats with her when he brought her shopping back.'

The three of them were silent for a moment, contemplating this tiny window of human kindness in Darren Chivers, the man they had known only as a criminal and a murder victim.

Then Lambert said, 'Did the team turn up anything useful in his flat?'

'No. But we think we know why. The place was illegally entered, probably on Saturday night. It was left very tidy – perhaps too tidy to be convincing. The handle on the outside of the door and every significant surface and handle within the flat had been wiped clean of prints. We don't know what was removed, but it wasn't an ordinary burglary. Money was left undisturbed in the kitchen drawer, though we're sure it had been searched. The likeliest time for this break-in was Saturday night. The murder wasn't discovered until Monday morning, or the team would obviously have been to the flat earlier.'

Lambert sighed. 'No sightings of an intruder?'

'No. There are plenty of people in that house, which is a bit of a rabbit warren, but they keep themselves to themselves, especially after dark on a Saturday night.'

'Did the team come up with any suggestions about what might have been removed from Chivers's flat?'

'There was a small one-drawer filing cabinet in the bedroom with the key in the lock. It had been investigated and was empty when our team got to it. Whatever papers were within it were almost certainly removed on Saturday night. The forensic boys have examined it, but found nothing useful.'

Hook said slowly, 'So it looks as if whoever killed Chivers on Friday night went to the flat on Saturday to remove something which might incriminate him.'

'Or her,' said Lambert automatically. 'But why would someone buying drugs raid the flat of his dealer? What would he be trying to remove?'

'Evidence of his identity?' asked Rushton unconvincingly.

Bert Hook said suddenly, 'We've been presuming so far that this crime was drugs-related. But Chris and I had tried to scare Chivers off dealing, by pointing out what it might mean if he was caught again. What scanty evidence there is suggests that he'd heeded us. The drug squad have no sightings of him dealing in his usual haunts over the last three weeks. I checked yesterday.'

Rushton nodded slowly. 'Chivers had no previous history of violence. That implies that he bought that weapon to protect himself, not to attack someone else. Presumably the person or persons who put him in hospital a fortnight ago. Who we can also presume is the person who murdered him.'

'Probably, but not necessarily,' said Lambert. 'We have to ask ourselves why someone who thought a beating was sufficient two weeks ago should think he had to murder the same man only nine days later. How had the situation escalated in that period? You and Bert don't think he was dealing much in that time. What else could he have been doing?'

'Blackmail?' suggested Bert Hook. 'That's the sort of crime that drives victims to take desperate action. Chivers was the kind of bloke who might blackmail, from what we've seen of him.'

'Anne, my fiancée, saw him apparently spying on someone near her school.' Rushton was still a little self-conscious about describing Anne Jackson like that, and he hastened on before the older men could make any comment. 'She watched him because she thought he might be a paedophile, but he wasn't at all interested in the children, she said.'

'So what was he doing there?'

'He seemed to be checking an address. He made a note of the number and name of a house almost opposite the school, as far as Anne could see.'

'Did she challenge him at all? Ask him what he was about?'

'No. Anne's not a police officer, is she? As soon as she realized that the children coming into school were in no danger, she went back to her classroom.'

Lambert grinned at Rushton's resentment. 'Of course she did. She went and got on with her job, and quite right too. Just as a policeman, getting on with his job, would have asked Chivers what he was about. So what have forensics come up with?'

'They've emailed me their findings about the material gathered at the scene of crime,' said Rushton. 'Nothing very useful from that pistol, as you might expect, just confirmation that it's the murder weapon. And nothing from the bike. It's been identified as belonging to Chivers, but, as with the pistol, there are no prints other than his upon it.'

'Contents of pockets?'

'Traces of coke and heroin in the anorak, but probably not recent, the laboratory staff think. It's difficult for them to be absolutely certain, because the body had probably lain for three nights and two days before it was found.' He hesitated, then decided to keep until the end the one piece of material which might possibly be significant. 'His keys, a ten-pound note and a few coins were still in the pocket of his jeans.'

Bert Hook spoke as if ticking off possibilities on his fingers. 'So there was no robbery motive for the crime, and his assailant didn't think to take the keys and give himself easy entry to his flat. Perhaps the searching and removal of material from there was an afterthought.'

'There was a single sheet of paper in the left-hand pocket of his jeans. It looks like a list of names.'

Lambert frowned. 'And do we know any of these names?'

'If they're local, we'll trace them pretty quickly. One of them at least we already know. The man you interviewed last night is the third name there, the one who claimed never to have met Chivers. Robert Beckford.'

The church was hardly changed from the days when it had been crammed with Victorian worshippers, secure in their faith and contemptuous, as their clergy encouraged them to be, of that Godless man Charles Darwin and his ridiculous theories.

But the high, ivy-clad vicarage which had once housed their pastor in comfortable affluence had been sold ten years ago and converted into luxury flats. The vicar was now housed in a raw brick cube of a detached house, which looked even smaller because it was crammed on to a small plot between the lofty elevations of the church on the one side and the former vicarage on the other. The rows of regimented lobelia and antirrhinums which filled the small flower beds around the square of front lawn seemed to emphasize the regularity which was a feature of the house, as if even colour had to be disciplined here.

The Reverend Peter Lynch was in his study at the front of the house. He saw the police car park outside and opened the front door as the two big men in plain clothes came up the path. 'I'm Chief Superintendent Lambert and this is Detective Sergeant Hook,' said the taller and older of the two.

Lynch gave him a firm handshake. Policemen didn't phase him. He was used to being contacted about fringe members of his congregation and their offspring; you didn't just minister to the middle classes, and sometimes he found sinners easier to deal with than the consciously righteous. But his police visitors were usually in uniform, and never before as high in rank as this. He said briskly, 'What can I do for you, Mr Lambert?'

'You could tell your wife we're here, please. It's her we need to see.'

Now Peter Lynch was shaken. 'You're sure about that? I've often helped your colleagues before, and if it's a parish matter I'm sure—'

'It's not a parish matter, Mr Lynch. Is your wife at home?'

He had an absurd wish to tell them Karen was out, to deny them access to the wife he suddenly felt was vulnerable. Then reason took over. 'I think she's in the back garden. I'll get her for you.'

He left them in the study and went through to the rear of the house. They observed the room as CID men do automatically, recording anything which would suggest things about the occupants. They noted the cheap, functional modern furniture, the prints of Rome and Venice and St Petersburg on the walls, the wedding photograph of the man who had just left them and a woman smiling in a white dress, holding his arm with shy pride.

It was a full two minutes before Peter Lynch returned with his wife. She limped into the room, smiled at them with what they saw was an effort, and said, 'I'm Karen Lynch. I believe you wanted to see me.'

Her husband drew up a chair for her and prepared to sit down beside her. Lambert said firmly, 'I'm afraid we need to see Mrs Lynch on her own.'

'We have no secrets from each other. I know everything about her past,' protested Lynch stiffly.

Lambert thought that a curious way to phrase his protest, but he said only, 'This is standard procedure.'

'You mean people are more vulnerable on their own. That's why you don't want me here, isn't it?'

Lambert gave the man a small, reassuring smile. 'Mrs Lynch has surely nothing to fear, if she cooperates with us.'

'Forgive me, but my experience of the police is—'

'Leave it, Peter. I'll be all right. As they say, if I've done nothing wrong, I've nothing to fear, have I?' She gave him a wide, reassuring smile, which lasted until he had left the room.

But as the door closed behind him and she transferred her attention to the visitors, she appeared suddenly very tense. 'Would you tell me what this is about, please?'

'It is about the death of a local man. A man called Darren Chivers.'

'The man whose body was discovered on Monday in Highnam.'

'Correct. What was your connection with him, Mrs Lynch?' Lambert dropped the quiet words like a hand grenade into the sunlit room.

'I didn't know the man. I know his name because it's hardly been off the news bulletins since Monday.' She looked very pale and very determined.

'Then can you explain how your name came to be on a list found in his pocket at the scene of his death?'

'No I can't. There must be some mistake.'

'I don't think so. I advise you to think very carefully, Mrs Lynch. This is a murder inquiry. The courts would regard any refusal to cooperate with us very seriously.'

She had short dark hair and was dressed neatly but economically in a shirt and jeans. Her clothes, like the furnishings, said that there was little money for luxuries in the modern vicarage. Hook wondered if she was always as pale as she was this morning. There was quite a pause before she said hesitantly, 'Could – could you tell me anything about this man Chivers?'

Lambert looked for a moment at Bert Hook, then gave him a quick nod.

Bert said, 'I interviewed him with one of our detective inspectors not long before his death. He was a drug user and a drug dealer. He already had a conviction for dealing and we warned him about the probability of a custodial sentence if he was arrested again on dealing charges. We think that worked as he seemed to have suspended his dealing. He didn't have regular employment, so he would have had to do something else to support himself.'

'Or live on benefits.'

Hook smiled grimly. 'He claimed those, all right; we've checked with the employment offices. But he was only drawing unemployment pay for a single man. Yet he had a considerable sum of money in the bank and quite a lot of cash in his flat at the time of his death. And before you suggest it, he had no history of burglary offences.'

She gave this more sympathetic face of the two a thin smile. 'I wasn't going to suggest that. I can think of one place where I might have met him.'

'And where would that be?'

Her leg was aching, the way it often did when she was tired or under stress. She stretched it for a moment, then picked her words carefully as she said, 'St Mary's Hostel treats addicts. They are people who have lost out on society, who are at the stage of their lives where they either recover or destroy themselves within a year or two. Unfortunately, only about one in five are brought back, once they get to that stage, but Father Ryan and his voluntary helpers do wonderful work. I give a few hours whenever I can spare them, which is usually on weekday afternoons.'

'I know St Mary's. We have to go there on occasion.'

'To make arrests?'

'Sometimes to make arrests. Sometimes to question people about what they might have heard or seen.'

'I don't blame you for that. I know some of the people there commit criminal offences and your job is to protect the public. Once they're hooked, they can think of nothing but the next fix and how they're going to get it. They lose all the concepts of right and wrong which they once had. I know you have to enforce the law, but the real criminals are the drug barons who have reduced them to this state and made millions in the process.'

'Believe me, we're well aware of that, Mrs Lynch. These men usually operate at a distance; even when they're caught, they have the best defence lawyers, so that it needs a cast-iron case to put them away. In the meantime, we have to try to stop dealing on the streets and the back streets and protect the public as best we can.'

Lambert said with a hint of impatience, 'You say you think that you may have met Darren Chivers at St Mary's.'

'I said it's the only context in which I can think I might have come across him.'

'But he wasn't an addict. I would be pretty sure that he was never a resident of St Mary's.'

'And I'm not conscious of ever having met him there. But

that's the only place where I have any contact with drug-users, so it seemed possible that he might have picked up my name from there.'

Hook said thoughtfully, 'Do you think Chivers might have picked up your name from one of the addicts there?'

She gave the possibility a few seconds' thought. 'It's possible, I suppose. I spend a lot of time talking one-to-one with addicts there, trying to get them to undertake rehabilitation. They're quite unpredictable and, as I said, most of them carry on using. I suppose it's possible that one of them might have mentioned my name to this man Chivers, if she was getting her supplies from him.'

'You mean he had you down as an enemy, someone who was trying to destroy his trade?'

She gave a little shiver. 'I hadn't thought of that, but I suppose it's possible.'

Lambert stood up. 'Possible but unlikely, I'd have said. Darren Chivers was a shifty character, but he had no previous history of violence. I don't think you'd have anything to fear from him, even if he were still alive. Thank you for your thoughts. If you have any further ones about how your name got on to that list, please ring this number immediately.'

The police were gone, almost as abruptly and unexpectedly as they had arrived. Karen Lynch told her husband that it was nothing but a routine inquiry and that she hadn't been able to help them. She insisted that Peter went back into his study and resumed the work the police had interrupted.

Then she sat alone in the small, aseptic kitchen at the back of the house, considering her options.

SEVENTEEN

Chris Rushton enjoyed demonstrating his mastery of the computer and the efficiency of his administration to his Chief Superintendent. Early on Wednesday afternoon, the DI told John Lambert, 'We've pinned down most of the people on the list found in Chivers's pocket. One of them is proving a little difficult. There are five Mark Rogers who live locally. But one is an infant and another is a pensioner confined to a home. We should have the right man by the end of the day.'

'Good. Bert and I saw Mrs Lynch this morning but didn't get very far. She's slightly disabled and a vicar's wife; she is also one of those young women who seem instantly likeable. All in all, it's difficult to think of her being involved in a crime like this, but both of us felt she was holding stuff back from us. Unless one of the other names provides us with an obvious killer, we'll need to go back to Karen Lynch.'

'There's one interesting name on that list. Daniel Steele.'

Lambert frowned, then shook his head. 'The name rings a vague bell, but I can't place it.'

'He used to be in the job. He was CID, in fact. But I can't see from the records that he could ever have operated with you. He spent most of his career working the Cheltenham area.'

'Steele.' Lambert shook his head irritably, then looked suddenly concerned, as some mysterious connection took place in that most complicated of machines which is the human brain. 'Wasn't there some talk of corruption?'

'There was. But there isn't much on the records, because there was no official inquiry and no court case. Officially, Steele merely retired from the police force. But he left suddenly, and several years earlier than he would normally have done.'

'And went where?'

'Like many an ex-copper, he got security work. It was initially quite a humble position, which again suggests he got out in a hurry and was glad to take whatever work he could get. There seems to have been an internal investigation, but because he eventually resigned and the matter wasn't pursued, not much is recorded of the findings.'

Lambert looked at the scanty details Rushton had so far recorded under the name on his computer. 'I'd like rather more information before we confront this Daniel Steele – if he's anything to hide, he'll know the system and be fully prepared. Who was his superior officer at the time he was investigated?'

Rushton consulted his notes. 'Superintendent North.'

'Jack North?'

'That's the man. Doesn't mean anything to me – this was well before my time here.'

'I know Jack North. He gave me my first breaks, when I was a sergeant. Old school, but a good man. Solid as a rock and reliable as the day is long. I saw him only last month.'

Rushton was wondering why Lambert looked so grim. 'That's a good thing, then, that you're still in touch. You'll be able to discover the facts of the case – as I say, there's very little in his file, because no legal case was ever brought. Human rights legislation, I suppose.' He smiled ruefully at the unrealism of the legislators, always a solid source of agreement amongst policemen.

Lambert's smile was even more doleful. 'I visited Jack North in a home, Chris. His wife asked me to go, for old times' sake. He's got Alzheimer's. He scarcely knew me, the day I saw him. Whether he'll remember anything about Daniel Steele, I very much doubt, but I'd better go to see him again.'

They paused for a moment outside Boutique Chantelle. Their collective CID career experience now spanned over forty years, so that there were very few situations into which neither Lambert nor Hook had ventured to conduct inquiries. This appeared to be one of them.

They took deep breaths and entered the shop. A stout woman was paying for a highly expensive and beautifully packaged dress. She looked at the two big men very suspiciously, as if venturing into this exotic female world automatically declared them to be peeping Toms at best, and more probably some much more devious sort of pervert.

The two large men stood at one side of the floor and stared at the dove-grey hat which was the nearest item to them as if it was of surpassing male interest, waiting patiently for the proprietor to be free. This apparently confirmed the customer's worst suspicions. She dearly wanted to know what they purposed, but she had to collect her credit card and depart with a final baleful glance.

They showed their warrant cards and announced themselves. Then Lambert said with a glance at the door and the vanished patron, 'I feel we may not be doing your business and reputation much good, Mrs de Vries. Is there somewhere more private where we could talk?'

She took them through to what had once been living accommodation but which in these more affluent days was now merely storage space behind the shop. It was surprisingly spartan, even squalid, after the sumptuous gentility of the window display and the shop interior. A kettle and three mugs stood on the side of an old porcelain sink. The wallpaper was at least twenty years old and the two armchairs in the room were designed for comfort rather than style.

The elegant figure who invited them to sit on two of the upright chairs beside a battered table seemed wholly out of place in this environment. She offered them tea, apologized for the fact that she did not have fresh milk because it went sour too quickly in here in the summer heat, then glanced round the room, as if seeing it for the first time. They divined in that moment that she did not spend much time in here, and was probably preoccupied with other concerns when she did.

With her obviously expensive beige dress and her carefully coiffured ash-blonde hair, her sparingly but expertly made-up face and her shoes in soft tan leather, Michelle de Vries was clearly designed to inhabit the front section of the premises rather than these unlovely private quarters. Lambert was reminded of the occasion years ago when he had interviewed a famous and debonair actor and found him in full Shakespearean costume, but smoking one of the now long departed Woodbines before a cracked mirror in the green room.

Both men noticed that Michelle de Vries seemed so far neither surprised nor disconcerted by their arrival here. She sat down opposite them, looked round again, and said, 'I must spruce this place up a bit, I suppose. I haven't been here that long.'

'How long, Mrs de Vries?'

'Eighteen months, since I opened. A little longer since I took the lease.'

'It's nice to see a new enterprise amidst all the big chains. Is it a success?'

She wanted to tell him to mind his own business, that she realized that he was only doing this preliminary fencing to find out more about her. But something told her to treat this watchful, experienced man with extreme caution. 'It takes time to establish a business like this, which doesn't depend on the popular taste. Advertising isn't much use, beyond letting people know that we are here. Most of our recommendations come by word of mouth.'

'You speak as if there are others involved. But this looks very much a one-woman business.'

She forced a smile. 'I have an assistant, at present part-time, until we see more clearly how business is developing. The initial capital to set up and stock the shop came from my husband. That is why I tend to think of it as a joint enterprise.'

'And what do you know of a man called Darren Chivers?'

His tone had not altered; his delivery was as low key, almost conversational, as it had been in his previous questions. That made the sudden switch all the more devastating. Michelle felt the skin on her face suddenly hot as she strove to retain the same control of her own voice. 'He's the man who was killed at the weekend, isn't he? The man whose body was found at Highnam.'

'Indeed. But I was wondering whether you didn't know rather more than that about Mr Chivers.'

'No. He wasn't the sort of man who would come in here, was he?'

'And how would you know that, if you hadn't met Chivers, Mrs de Vries? Our press officer hasn't released any details of his personal circumstances or his lifestyle to the media yet.'

Michelle had never played these deadly games before and she was no good at them, she realized. Certainly no good against a skilled man like this. She said dully, 'He came into the shop a fortnight ago. I'd never met him before that, and I didn't meet him again.'

'And why did he come here?'

'He was demanding money with menaces. I sent him away with a flea in his ear and he didn't come back.'

'And you didn't report the incident to the police?'

'No. I told you, I'd sent him away with his tail between his legs. I didn't see any need for further action.'

Lambert nodded slowly, weighing the information, and for a moment Michelle thought that he was accepting what she had told him. Then he said, 'Does that sound very believable to you, Mrs de Vries? It doesn't to me, and I'm sure it doesn't to Detective Sergeant Hook. I think a woman alone in a shop like yours would feel very vulnerable. I think that if a man demanded money with threats of violence she would accede to his demands. In the unlikely event of her successfully repelling such an attack, I think the first thing she would do is inform the police of the incident. I find it incredible that she would not do so. So I suggest that you abandon this fiction and tell us the truth.'

Michelle felt a variety of emotions, but the overwhelming one was of humiliation. She hadn't felt so small and worthless since a nun had exposed her in a lie when she was fourteen and left her standing in front of her desk, twisting her toes in an agony of embarrassment, willing the floor to open beneath her and remove her from those relentless eyes beneath the starched white wimple. She could see the lines on the forehead of this interlocutor, whereas she had not been able to see the nun's brow at all. That only made the unblinking grey eyes seem even more threatening.

She was looking at the scratches on the table as she said, 'He did demand money, but not with threats. Not physical threats.'

'Chivers tried to blackmail you, didn't he?'

She nodded, unwilling to trust herself with further words.

The quiet, relentless voice said, 'We need the details of this threat, Mrs de Vries.'

From somewhere deep within her, she found the will to resist, to defend that flame in the darkness that was her and Guy. 'I'm not prepared to tell you that. I've told you all you need to know. All you're going to get from me.'

Lambert and Hook had operated for so long together that they were like football strikers with an instinctive, unspoken understanding of when to move. Bert Hook, whom Michelle had almost forgotten in her contest with Lambert, now said quietly, 'Chivers was seen checking the number and address of a house near Park Road primary school on Monday the twenty-third of June. What can you tell us about that, Mrs de Vries?'

It was a bow at a venture. He had no evidence that this sighting was related to the woman in front of them, but something had suggested to him that this was a likely connection. It worked. She shrugged hopelessly, assuming as members of the public usually did that they knew far more than they actually did. 'I have a lover.' She glanced up at them on that bold word, for the first time since her initial lie about Chivers had been exposed. 'My husband does not know about this. Darren

Chivers was threatening to reveal it to him. He wanted money to keep his mouth shut. I said I needed time. Fortunately for me, he died before he could collect.'

For some reason she could not at first analyze, it was important to her that she concealed the payment she had made. Then she realized that secrecy was surely important, if nothing of this was to get back to Gerald. She looked up into the comfortable, weather-beaten face of DS Hook and could almost believe that he was on her side. He said sympathetically, almost apologetically, 'We are here because we are conducting a murder inquiry. You realize that this gives you a motive for removing Darren Chivers?'

'I suppose it does. I didn't kill him.' It sounded flat, even fatuous.

'We need the name of this lover, Mrs de Vries.'

'Why? So that you can go and accuse him of murder?'

'So that we can eliminate him from the inquiry.'

She sighed. It was hopeless. They seemed to hold all the cards. 'You have his address. You might as well have his name from me as from anywhere else. His name is Guy Dawson. And he knows nothing about this death.'

Just when she had got used to answering Hook, it was Lambert who now asked, 'Where were you last Friday night, Mrs de Vries?'

'That's when he was killed, isn't it?'

'We think so. Answer the question, please.'

'I was at home with my husband, I think.'

'He will confirm that?'

'No. You can't ask him that. He'll want to know how I'm involved in this.'

'Unless we arrest someone else for this crime quickly, we shall need confirmation of your whereabouts at the time it took place.'

'Gerald couldn't do that anyway. I've just remembered, he had a business meeting in Birmingham on Friday. He didn't come home until late on Friday evening.'

'I see. If you can think of anyone who can confirm to us that you were not in the Highnam area between the hours of eight and midnight, it would obviously be in your interests to give us the details. As it would to furnish us with any other information relating to this crime. Good day to you, Mrs de Vries.'

A woman came into the shop as they left, looking at them as curiously as the earlier customer had done. Michelle was glad to move straight into the process of selling a wedding outfit to the prospective bride's mother. She felt thoroughly at home with this conversation, just as she had felt out of her depth with the CID officers. If all went well, she was assured, there was the possibility of two bridesmaids' dresses to follow today's sale. She was giving a performance, of course, just as her stuttering display to the police had been a performance, but this one was altogether more assured. It was a smooth and practised performance, which came very easily to her. She felt that her tongue had been loosened and her brain unlocked with this return to her normal world.

It was welcome because it postponed her return to that uneasy position she had never had before, suspect in a murder inquiry. Once she was alone with her thoughts again, uncertainty, doubt and eventually dread took over her mind. She forced herself to sit absolutely still and breathe evenly in the empty shop for a full two minutes before she picked up the phone.

'Guy? I'm sorry to ring you at work, but it's urgent. The police have been here. They left about half an hour ago.'

'We knew that was possible. At least you've got it over with. What did you tell them? As little as possible, I trust. That's what we agreed.'

'I know it is. And I tried to keep to it. But they knew things. Knew a lot more than I thought they would.'

'What sort of things?'

'Well, they knew that Chivers had been here. Apparently my name was on a list in his pocket.'

'But they didn't know why.'

'I had to tell them, Guy. I told them at first that he'd come in here demanding money with menaces, that I'd seen him off, but they wouldn't buy that. I had to tell them that he'd been trying to blackmail me.'

There was a theatrical sigh at the other end of the line. She could almost feel his disapproval coming down it, but he made no comment.

'I didn't have a choice, Guy. I couldn't afford to be seen to be holding back information from them, could I? I didn't tell them that I'd actually paid him two thousand quid.'

'That's something, I suppose.'

'Yes. They pointed out that being blackmailed gave me a murder motive.'

'They can't make anything stick, though, so long as you keep schtum. You didn't tell them about us?'

'I had to, Guy. I tried not to, but Chivers had to have something to blackmail me with, didn't he?'

That sigh again, as if he was dealing with a troublesome child who couldn't obey simple instructions. 'But you didn't tell them about me, did you? You kept me out of it?'

'I had to tell them, Guy. They already knew a lot more than I thought they would. Someone had seen Chivers outside your house, checking on the number and the name.' She wondered why she was so desperate to account for herself to him, why they could not just be fighting this battle together. 'If I hadn't given them your name, they'd have had it from the electoral register, wouldn't they?'

'You've dragged me into it now, haven't you?'

She wanted to tell him that he should want to be with her in whatever trouble was around, to scream at him that she was only in this because of him. Instead, she said meekly, 'I had no choice, Guy.'

'They'll want to see me, now. They'll be treating me as a murder suspect.'

Michelle rang off then. She stared at the phone for a long time after she had put it down. For the first time, she wondered where Guy Dawson had been last Friday night.

EIGHTEEN

'You arrested anyone for this murder yet, Dad?' Jack Hook was full of the sensational case which was dominating the local press.

'Eat your cereal,' said his mother sternly. It was a totally unnecessary demand, as the cornflakes were disappearing with their customary lightning speed, but she didn't like her boys to concern themselves with unsavoury crime.

'They used to hang people for murder,' said twelve-year-old Luke in wide-eyed wonder. '"You will be taken from this place and hanged by the neck until dead",' he intoned, then clasped his hands around his throat and popped his eyeballs alarmingly. 'Do you remember those days, Dad?'

'No, they were long before my time. And you're going to be late for your piano lesson,' said Bert Hook sternly. 'You wouldn't have risked that in my day.'

'Birch you for it, did they?' said Jack. 'Does he still have the marks on his bottom to show for it, Mum?'

'Albert Pierrepoint, the hangman was called,' said Luke dreamily. 'Must have been a good job, that.' He made his throttling gesture with his hands again, holding his breath and threatening to project his eyeballs on to the breakfast table.

'Hanging wasn't his only job,' said his elder brother magisterially. 'He ran a pub as well.' Jack shook his head sadly at the thought of these vanished opportunities. 'Ideal sort of life, it sounds to me.'

'Mr Armitage says he taught this chap Darren Chivers at one time,' said Luke. 'He thinks he came from a broken home. Do you think we could pull that one, Jack?'

His parents refused to rise to the bait, and Jack was driven to his favourite remark. 'I expect Dad will be playing a hunch, Luke. Producing some brilliant insight when John Lambert is baffled.'

Bert Hook did not snub this as he would usually have done. It felt uncomfortably close to what he had been doing on the previous day. He was reduced to snapping, 'It's Mister Lambert to you, Jack, and don't you forget it.'

Mark Rogers decided to emphasize his status to the police. They didn't need to know that he had only acquired this office a month ago, or that he shared the PA who greeted them in the outer office with another, female, executive. He would play the busy and important man, who was squeezing them into his day only because he was an exemplary citizen and wanted to give the authorities all the help he could in their pursuit of a serious criminal.

'See that we're not disturbed for as long as this takes, please, Julie,' he said loftily. 'Explain to my appointments that an emergency has cropped up and I shall be available to them as soon as possible – I don't anticipate that this will take very long. And rustle up some coffee for my visitors a.s.a.p., will you?'

They sat down carefully in the easy chairs he had set out for them and studied the office unhurriedly, noting the neutral company prints on the walls, the absence of any of the individual touches which would have made this room a personal province. Mark felt compelled to break the uncomfortable silence. 'You said when you rang that this was in connection with that mysterious death in Highnam at the weekend. I'm anxious to give all the help I can, of course, but I can't think that will be anything worthwhile.'

'You're obviously a busy man, so I shall come straight to the point, Mr Rogers,' said Lambert dryly. 'Can you account for your name on a list found in the pocket of a murder victim?'

Mark made himself smile. 'The short answer is no. Are you sure that you have the right Mark Rogers?'

'Yes, we are. This has been thoroughly checked.'

'It's odd, this, because I don't recall any meetings with a . . . Derek Chivers, was it?'

'Darren Chivers, sir. We have a possible sighting of you with Mr Chivers a little while ago.'

He was shaken out of the urbanity he had planned. 'Are you positive about that? I'm sure I don't recall any such—'

'On the evening of Monday June the twenty-third, it was,' said Bert Hook, his notebook open in front of him in anticipation of this denial. 'The informant was one of our plain clothes drug squad officers. If you are now telling us that it was another man entirely, we can soon sort the matter out.'

Detection is a serious business, so that you have to accept simple pleasures where you can find them. The sight of a thoroughly discomforted BT executive gave an unworthy satisfaction to his visitors. Rogers said eventually, 'I expect you're right. The name didn't ring any immediate bells, but—'

'Even when you realized it belonged to a murder victim, Mr Rogers? I find that difficult to believe,' said Lambert sternly. 'I think you had much better be honest with us from now on, don't you? This is a murder inquiry, and any attempt to mislead us constitutes a serious offence.'

'I've a lot at stake here. I've a wife and two children who mean the world to me.'

'All the more reason to be honest with us and safeguard them, I'd say.'

'All right.' As he spoke the words, coffee arrived. Rogers gave his PA a weak, abstracted grin and said that he would see to the pouring of it himself. His hands were quite steady as he filled the cups and added milk as directed, but he did not trust himself to speak until they each held a cup and saucer. 'I was a little wild in my youth, before I settled down. But which of us is not?'

He waited for an assenting phrase or nod from the two men opposite him, but none came. The two looked to Mark Rogers as grave and serious as if they had never been through youth at all. 'Darren Chivers was a dealer. He supplied me with drugs. Pot, of course. A little cocaine, but nothing—'

'How long ago was this, Mr Rogers?'

'I told you, in my wild youth.'

'Which must have lasted until you were around thirty. Darren Chivers was twenty-seven when he died. He had been dealing for no more than eight years at the outside.'

Mark cursed himself for improvising such an unlikely story. He had thought Chivers much older. He shrugged, trying hard to loosen his shoulders and make it convincing. 'I suppose I wanted it to be longer ago. I used drugs a lot in my youth and I still turned to them when I felt the need of a high, even in the early years of my marriage. I'm not proud of it and I didn't want either my employers or my wife and children to know about it. Chivers knew that. He was threatening to tell both Samantha and BT about the trades I had done with him.'

'And trying to extract money from you by doing so.'

'Yes. That is why I had to meet him on that Monday you mentioned. He'd been ringing the house, saying he wanted to speak to me. Samantha was getting curious about who this man was.'

'What happened at that meeting, Mr Rogers?'

'I gave Chivers a small sum of money.'

Bert Hook flicked to a new page in his notebook. 'How much was that, Mr Rogers?'

'Two hundred pounds. I made him promise that that would be the end of it.'

'And did you believe that it would be?'

'Yes, I think I did. He was a small-time operator with drugs, and I didn't think he'd have the nerve to come back to me again. I may have been naive, but—'

'Blackmailers almost always come back for more. Are you not aware of that?'

'I don't think I even thought of it as blackmail. He seemed too pathetic a creature to be really threatening.'

'Pathetic, and yet you handed money to him. You must have felt threatened.'

'I have a stable job and a happy family. It seemed at the time a small price to pay to keep the situation stable.'

'When did you last see Darren Chivers?'

'On the night you mentioned. Monday the twenty-third of June, I think you said it was.'

'Two days after that, Mr Chivers was beaten up so badly that he ended up in hospital. What do you know about that?'

'Nothing at all. This is the first I've heard of it.' He looked at the sceptical faces, aware that all three of them in the room were thinking of his earlier denials. 'I'm sure I can account for my whereabouts at the time of that attack, if you give me the time and the place.'

'I'm sure that you could do that, Mr Rogers. What happened to Mr Chivers on that night had the hallmarks of a beating by professionals – thugs who hire out their services to whoever is prepared to pay for them.'

'Then they weren't hired by me. I don't have contacts like that.'

'Do you know where Mr Chivers lived?'

Mark wanted to deny all knowledge of the man, but he had been caught out once and he did not know what else they knew about him. 'I do, as a matter of fact. That's if he still lived where he used to do years ago. He had a flat in Collingwood Street. Why do you ask?'

'Because someone entered that flat illegally last Saturday night and removed certain materials which could well have become significant items in a murder trial.'

'It wasn't me.' It felt very banal. He wanted words which were much stronger, but they would not come to him.

'Where were you last Friday night, Mr Rogers?'

'We had a company policy meeting in Birmingham on Friday afternoon. It finished much later than I'd hoped it would.

I stayed and chatted with a colleague until about seven, I think. We both wanted to let the traffic get away.'

'So what time did you get home on that night?'

He licked his lips, well aware of what they were about, anxious to present this as well as he could. 'I knew the children would be in bed well before I got there, so I'd missed them. I went for a drink in Gloucester before I went home, because I wanted to unwind a little. My section of the company is going through a difficult time, and I don't like taking my worries home with me. The pub was pretty crowded, at that time on a Friday night – I don't suppose anyone would remember me being there.' He knew even as he formed the phrases that he should not have uttered that last sentence. It sounded far too defensive.

Hook, pen poised over his notebook, let that thought hang in the air for a moment before he asked Rogers for the name of the pub and the time he had arrived home, which was some time after eleven. Then they left him, with an injunction to get in touch immediately when – not if, he noticed – any further thoughts on this death occurred to him.

Mark Rogers put his coffee cup back on the tray and rejoined the bustling world of BT, which was oddly reassuring to him after the last twenty minutes. He was noisily cheerful to his PA, making the routine jokes about not being behind bars after all, hoping he was not overplaying his nonchalance in the face of interrogation by senior CID officers. Back in the privacy of his office, he decided it had gone as well as could be expected, after his initial gaffe in denying all knowledge of Darren Chivers.

He would have been less sanguine if he could have heard the conversation of his visitors in Lambert's car. They had driven a couple of miles in thoughtful silence before Hook said, 'I didn't buy his story about the drugs. He might well have bought from Chivers in the past, more or less as he told it, but I don't see him allowing himself to be blackmailed over that. Half the younger executives in the country would be at risk, if things like that were going to ruin their careers.'

Lambert eased his foot down on the throttle as the old Vauxhall cruised west down the A40. 'I agree. I found myself trusting hardly anything the man said to us. It's interesting that he knew where Chivers lived and can't really account for where he was at the key time on Friday night. I think we shall need to have further dealings in due course with the shifty Mr Rogers.'

There was only the lightest of breezes to temper the heat of the sun, and people were sitting out in the gardens of the retirement home. The lobelia and alyssum and the vivid geraniums were at their best now; the first of the spectacular dahlias were beginning to show colour.

John Lambert found the tiny figure of Mrs North sitting alone at the far end of the rose garden, a very small, motionless figure on a sturdy garden bench which seemed much too big for her. 'I'm sorry this isn't just a routine friendly visit,' he said awkwardly, as he sat down beside her.

'You told me that on the phone. There's no need to apologize. Jack won't mind; he won't know the difference. I'd like to say he'll be glad to see you, but he might not even recognize you. We have to take it day by day, now. They're trying a new drug. I think it's making him a bit better, but I'm trying to teach myself to expect nothing. That way, any little improvement is a nice surprise.'

Lambert marvelled again at the courage and resilience within this tiny, bird-like creature. 'He was a good boss to me, you know. The best I ever had. He taught me a lot of things.'

'Including one or two you've had to forget, I expect. He was as honest as the day's long, Jack, but I reckon he took a short cut or two, didn't he, when he was anxious to see justice done?' Her voice was full of tenderness, not condemnation; even her man's frailties were loveable, after the years of uncomplaining support which had bound her to him.

John Lambert smiled, wanting to put his hand consolingly over the tiny one on the bench beside him, afraid that it would be too intimate a gesture, which might bring on the tears which were not too far beneath her sturdy surface. 'The police service has changed like the rest of the world, Amy, and not always for the better.'

'He's having a nap. He usually does after his lunch. Do you want me to come in with you to see him?'

Strictly speaking, anything the man could tell him was confidential and for his ears only, but he'd be floundering, out of his depth, if Jack North couldn't communicate. 'I'd like that, Amy, if you wouldn't mind.'

'I was a police wife for long enough, John. I know what doesn't go beyond the walls.' She rose and led the way towards the big Victorian mansion, her shortness even more marked in front of the tall man who followed her lead.

She had to wake her husband, stroking his hair as gently as if he were a sleeping child, holding his large gnarled hand in hers until she felt his grip tighten upon her. Jack North knew her immediately, but when he eventually realized he had another visitor, standing awkwardly behind her, he peered at him uncertainly and said, 'You should be at work, Ben.'

Amy made him look up at her as she said, 'It's not your son, Jack, not today. This is John Lambert, who used to work with you. He needs you to help him.'

'John Lambert.' North repeated the name carefully, as if trying to commit it to his shattered memory. Then a gleam of recognition lit up the rheumy eyes. 'Did you get him, John? Do we have a collar?'

The old police word North had always used for an arrest, for the successful conclusion to a case. Lambert was encouraged. 'I need your help, Jack. I need you to tell me things, if we're going to get a collar. It's a big one, this, the biggest of the lot.' He glanced at Amy North, wondering if he should be bringing talk of murder into this quiet world, but felt her willing him on. Perhaps it was important to her that Jack North was able to help, to provide her with the crumb of comfort that his usefulness might bring.

North was looking at him with an open-mouthed trust which he found searing. Lambert said softly, 'Dan Steele, Jack. Remember him?' No understanding lit up the tired face. He wracked his brains, remembering that the police always dealt in nicknames, usually not very original ones. 'Danny Boy, Jack?'

A shaft of recognition in the blue pupils, a smile of delight twisting the mouth. Lambert wished all the faces he interviewed were as revealing as this one. 'Danny Boy, that's him. Danny Boy Steele.' Then the face darkened and the brow furrowed. 'Don't trust him, Jack. He's a bad lad, Danny Boy.'

'That's right, Jack! A bad lad. What did he do, Jack?'

'Bungs, John.' The old familiar word which he had not used

for years came quickly to North on the heels of the name. 'Don't have him, John. He takes bungs. Get rid of him. Don't have him back.'

'Who gave him the bungs, Jack?'

'Druggies. Thieves. Seccy . . . Seccy . . .' He shook his head hopelessly.

John Lambert, concentrating fiercely, had his own moment of inspiration. 'Securicor, Jack? Was it a raid on Securicor?'

'That's it! Bungs. Securicor.' He repeated the four syllables carefully, than cackled suddenly at his cleverness. 'I got rid of the bugger, John. Don't you have him back now!'

'I won't, Jack. And you've been a big help to me. You're a good copper, Jack. You were the best boss I ever had, you know. And you're still a good copper.'

Jack North repeated the phrase happily as he sank back into that half-world of confusion in which he lived his life now. Lambert held the old hand in his for a moment, trying to continue some sort of conversation, feeling guilty because now that he had what he had come for he wanted to be away.

The tiny tower of strength which was Amy North edged him aside and told him to be off catching villains. He looked back from the door of the room to see her smoothing her husband's hair and plumping up his cushions, talking the while as if to a child who had done an unexpectedly clever thing. Not for the first time in his long career, he saw heroism in an unlikely physical casing.

NINETEEN

L ambert had an excellent memory for faces, though the names did not always stick as easily as they had done when he was a young copper on the beat. He was fairly sure that he had never met Daniel Steele before, even though the man had once been a police officer working within thirty miles of him.

The man who was now in charge of security at Gloucester Building Supplies was a powerful, stocky man, just under six feet tall. Thirteen stones plus, Bert Hook's experienced eye told him, with the build of a rugby prop forward and deep-set, watchful eyes, the pupils of which were almost black.

He led them into a small dining room at the front of his house and said, 'We won't be disturbed in here. My wife's gone to work. She works four mornings a week in an office, now that the kids have left home.'

'And you work nights.'

'Not always, but quite often. It's the nature of the job. Petty pilfering during the day, sometimes by our own staff. The danger of major thefts by professional criminals comes at night. I'm confident daytime security is now under control. Night work makes for a happy marriage, I always say – we don't see enough of each other to get on each other's nerves!'

'You were in the job.'

'I was a copper for twenty years, yes. I don't miss the paperwork, nor the odd hours, nor being buggered about by twats who never leave their desks. Present company excepted, of course.'

Lambert allowed himself the faintest of smiles whilst keeping his eyes steadily on the swarthy face. 'I feel no great attachment to my own desk.'

'Aye. I've heard that of you, Chief Superintendent Lambert. Bit of a dinosaur, they say, but one who gets results. I like the sound of that.'

'How well did you know Darren Chivers, Mr Steele?'

'The man who was killed at the weekend? I didn't know him at all.' Steele stared steadily at Lambert, challenging him to disprove it. He would give them as little as possible, make them demonstrate to him what they knew. He had bluffed criminals often enough in his police days to know that CID men often made a little knowledge go a very long way.

'So how do you account for your name being on a list found in his pocket?'

Damn! Daniel had been pretty confident they'd find nothing to connect him with Chivers. He couldn't possibly have fore-seen this. He looked suitably puzzled, then said dourly, 'Perhaps he was planning to contact me. I can't think why. It wouldn't be for a job, and I've never done drugs.'

'And how do you know that Darren Chivers, this man you'd never met, supplied drugs?'

He kept cool. Revealing nothing on his square face was a

skill he had learned a long time ago, in his days as a young DC. 'It was in the reports of his death, surely?'

'It was not. Our press officer has not released that information.'

Steele shrugged, deliberately keeping the temperature of the exchange down, when he should have been disconcerted. 'I was a police officer for years. I'm still involved in security work. One picks up all sorts of random information and it sticks. You two should know that better than most. I expect someone at the works mentioned it when we were talking about the man's death.'

Hook made a note of this reply, his face as serious and unrevealing as the one opposite him. Then he said, 'We now know that Chivers was also a blackmailer. We think the sheet of paper found in his pocket listed some of his victims.'

Daniel Steele raised his eyebrows; the movement to indicate surprise was a little too elaborate on his hitherto impassive face. 'A blackmailer, eh? I don't suppose you've any more time for those bastards than I had when I was a copper.'

'He's a murder victim, now. And we have to wonder whether he was trying to blackmail you.'

'Pure conjecture that, isn't it? All you have is my name on a list. And what would he have to blackmail a security man who didn't even know him?' He jutted his jaw and gave them a defiant smile.

'Perhaps something from your time in the police, Mr Steele,' said Lambert quietly. He made it a statement rather than a question.

Daniel wasn't going to show them embarrassment, still less temper. Rage made you lose control, and he needed control more than he had ever needed it in his life. 'I had a good police career. I enjoyed most of it. As I said, I got out a year or two earlier than I might have done, because I was being buggered about by silly cunts who were still wet behind the ears and I wasn't prepared to put up with that.'

Lambert too was not going to lose his temper, though he felt himself on the verge of doing just that. He hated bent coppers, who brought contempt not just upon themselves but upon the police service itself. 'Was it not the police who got rid of you, Danny Boy?'

Steele started at the name he had not heard for years, then

lapsed without thinking into an automatic denial. 'I had a completely unblemished record during my police career.'

'Not what the grapevine says, Danny Boy.' Lambert let his dislike of the man come out in his taunting use of the name.

Steele told himself again that he must not descend into anger. He forced a smile. 'Prove it, Lambert. There's bugger-all on the records.'

'There's a damned good copper says you took bribes, Danny Boy. That's good enough for me. If it had been left to him, there'd have been charges at the time.'

'I don't believe that. Jack North was my DI at the time. Vindictive sod he was, too. He's in the funny farm with his brain gone now, and I can't say I'm sorry.'

'Correction, Steele. Jack North is in a retirement home with mild Alzheimers. The drugs are working well. I spoke to him yesterday. His recall of you and your character was gratifyingly accurate.'

'You can prove nothing.'

'Darren Chivers must have thought he could. Or had he some other facts with which to blackmail you?'

'I told you, I never knew the sod. If he was a blackmailer, the world is better without him.'

'As it would be without bent coppers. But if someone murdered you, I'd still hunt him down.'

'Thanks for nothing. And I hope whoever killed a blackmailing drug dealer gets away with it.'

'Where were you last Friday night?'

'Is that when the sod was killed? Well, I'm in the clear then. I was at the works last Friday night – I work one weekend in four. Sorry to disappoint you. Better make a note of that, DS Hook. I don't want you fitting me up with anything, do I?'

'And where were you on the night of June twenty-fifth?'

He paused for a moment, appearing to give the matter thought before his face brightened. 'I was on nights that week, so I was at work again, Lambert. Ten p.m. to six a.m. I do. Sorry to disappoint you!' He smirked at Hook as the DS noted this reply. 'What happened then, anyway?'

'Mr Chivers was badly beaten up and put in hospital.'

'What a shame! From what you tell me, he had it coming to him.'

'And no doubt you know nothing about an illicit entry to Mr Chivers's home on Saturday last.'

'Certainly don't, squire. If it was at night, I'd be working again, wouldn't I?'

Lambert rose abruptly. 'Don't leave the area without informing us of any new address, Mr Steele.'

'I've no intention of going anywhere, Chief Superintendent Lambert. I've nothing to be ashamed of, you see.'

The middle of the day was the quietest time at St Mary's hostel. Father Ryan was grateful for Karen Lynch's assistance in making up three beds with newly washed sheets.

'You shouldn't be doing this,' she said to him.

'Needs must. Two of my voluntary ladies who come in on a Friday have sick children.'

'Couldn't you have left the sheets another day?'

He gave her a wry smile. 'Not really. When addicts piss their beds, there isn't much room for manoeuvre. I'd have got them to help me with this, but they were too far gone. Thank heavens for washing machines.' He folded his side of the sheet into a hospital corner with an expertise which came from much practice.

'How's Lisa getting on?'

'She's doing well. She found the first week in rehab very hard, but she's still there. I think she'll make it. Which will be in no small measure thanks to you, Karen. I don't think she'd even have gone there without you.'

She shook her head. 'I told it like it was. Told her as one who'd been through it. I told Lisa she'd scream her way through the first days, but that she must stick with it. I'll try to visit her again tomorrow.'

'Do, if you can. She appreciated your visit last week.'

They continued working in companionable silence for a full two minutes, the rhythms of mindless physical movement an escape from the anxieties of their lives. Then Karen said suddenly, 'Do you still hear confessions, Father?'

He glanced at her sharply, then went back to studious contemplation of the fraying sheets in the big linen cupboard. 'I don't nowadays, no. My work here has taken over from any parish work.'

'But you still believe in it?'

Father Ryan smiled fondly at her. 'What kind of question is that to ask a Catholic priest? Do you want me to get into trouble with my bishop?'

She grinned at him. 'You'd never do that. They'd never get anyone to take on what you do here. But I've never been a Catholic, never even known one closely. Telling all your thoughts to a person you may not even know, even with a screen between you, always struck me as quite horrific. I don't think I could ever do it.'

'Ah, sure you weren't brought up in the Faith, my child!' He mimicked the kind of Irish priest he had grown up with. 'You're right, in most ways. People do find it difficult. Perhaps that's part of the idea. You're supposed to remember that the priest is just an intermediary in the confessional, enabling you to say you're sorry to God. It's God who really forgives you, so long as you are genuinely penitent.'

'Then why not let people speak directly to God? Why is there the need for anyone in between?'

He laughed, finding he was enjoying this need to justify his position as a priest, to conduct the kind of theological debate he had not done for years. 'This is like being back in the seminary! You make a good point. The sacrament of penance has probably come under the spotlight most of all, in the ecumenical debates. Curiously enough, the psychologists, most of whom are probably atheists, have come up with some incidental benefits. They think confession is often good for the soul, whatever their doubts about Catholic dogma. People feel better when they've got something off their chests, and tend to behave better as well.'

She nodded thoughtfully, earnest as the young girls he remembered making their first confessions and first communions when he had been a curate. How long ago that seemed to him now, how much part of a different and more innocent world! He wondered how many of those earnest young eight-year-old girls and boys eventually ended up as addicts, stealing to support the habit, with all clear ideas of right and wrong forsaken as they scratched for the money for their next fix.

And Father Ryan wondered also about something more specific, as he saw this sturdy young woman who gave her time so selflessly limp away from him. He wondered quite what it was that she would like to confess to him.

*   *   *

Robert Beckford had known that they would be back. As three days stretched themselves out after his Tuesday night meeting with the CID without any further contact, he had tried to persuade himself that his replies had satisfied them. But in his heart he had always expected that that tall, gaunt man whose face he could not erase from his mind would be back.

Late on Friday afternoon, his fears were justified. The bad news was brought by the worst herald he could imagine. Robert was sweeping the cloisters, marvelling as he always did that the delicate tracery of the fan-vaulting above him had been carved with such pride and expertise by masons almost seven centuries earlier, when Edwina Clarkson materialized unseen behind him. Her voice sounded louder and clearer than usual as she announced with satisfaction, 'Those senior police officers are here to question you again, Mr Beckford.'

She allowed herself an impressive sniff of disapproval towards the ancient stones above her. 'I expect this will be in connection with their murder investigation. In view of the seriousness of this matter, I have offered them the use of my office for their interrogation. It's inconvenient, but perhaps you will be able to convince them of your innocence and send them on their way quickly.'

As Robert turned to face her, it was apparent that this was the last outcome she wished for. Her sour face was full of righteous disapproval, her small eyes studied him eagerly for any admission of discomfort, her prim mouth turned down even more steeply than usual at its corners.

He said coolly, 'That is most considerate of you, Miss Clarkson. Perhaps I should make it clear that I have not been accused of any crime. As you say, I can't imagine that this will take very long.' It was like some dusty verbal minuet, with the formal steps of surface politeness used to conceal the real dislike of each other beneath their movements.

She followed him to the entrance to the cathedral, watched his every action as he made formal acknowledgement of his visitors and took them into her office. He shut the door quietly but firmly upon Miss Clarkson, looking her boldly in the face as he did so.

Robert discovered that the civilian administrator, as the notice on the door designated her, appeared to have set out the room for this interview. She had placed chairs for the

detectives behind her big desk, with a slightly lower one for
him in front of it, so that they had their backs to the morning
light from the window and he was facing it. It seemed that
she had been given more notice of this meeting than she had
volunteered to him.

Lambert studied his man without speaking for a moment.
Then he said, 'We now know a lot more about Mr Chivers's
activities than when we spoke to you on Tuesday evening, Mr
Beckford. We wondered if on reflection you might wish to
modify your statement to us then, or even to change it
completely and begin again from scratch.'

Robert had not expected anything so direct. He kept his
face as impassive as he could as he said, 'And what is it that
you have now discovered about Darren Chivers which makes
you think that?'

Without any apparent consultation between the two men,
DS Hook took over the dialogue. 'We're here to ask questions rather than to answer them, Mr Beckford. But it might
help you towards more honest replies to be aware that we
now know that Mr Chivers was building up quite a network
of blackmail victims. It seems to us that his visit here to see
you was almost certainly in connection with these activities
rather than with the sale of drugs.'

'His connection with me was very tenuous. I feel that the
relationship has been exaggerated by the person who has
volunteered this office to us today. Frankly, Miss Clarkson
and I just do not get on. I'm afraid that when she mentioned
your murder victim's visit to the cathedral, she was more interested in embarrassing me than in anything else.'

'It may interest you to know that Mr Chivers was also seen
in the cathedral on that day by a teacher accompanying a
school party on a visit. Mr Beckford, I think we should now
warn you formally that concealing information in the course
of a murder inquiry is a very serious offence.' Hook's weather-
beaten, countryman's features were unusually grave.

Robert's natural inclination was to defer to authority. He
had spent over twenty years in army life, where rank had been
supreme, when the key theme in your training was to defer
unthinkingly to orders from above. Now a very senior
policeman and his aide were pressing him to divulge what he
wanted to hide and he felt them wearing down his resistance.

He put on what he now thought of as his parade face, staring straight ahead of him and freezing his features into an emotionless mask. Yet in this more intimate context, he sensed that his attitude was neither appropriate nor convincing. He said through lips which barely moved, 'I'd like to help you. It's just that I'm not able to do it.'

Lambert's calm, unemotional tone now took him back through the years to that of the presiding officer at the court martial. 'Then how do you explain the presence of your name on a list found in the pocket of the dead man's anorak?'

'I can't.' Rob felt his head swimming, his brain drowning beneath the tide of evidence rising against him.

'I think you can and you will, Mr Beckford. Before you issue any further denials, I will tell you that we are now confident that the names on this scrap of paper are those of people being blackmailed by Darren Chivers.'

Robert realized now that he wasn't going to get away with this. He couldn't continue to deny any connection with Chivers, not when they had his name on a list of blackmail victims. He said dully, in a voice which seemed to belong to some other pathetic, defeated person, 'All right. He was blackmailing me. I'm sorry I denied it. I – I have a lot at stake.'

Lambert let the admission hang in the air for a moment, allowing the knowledge that he was beaten to seep into the man's consciousness. 'How much did Chivers have from you?'

'A thousand pounds. Two separate five hundreds. I told him that was the end of it, but he'd have been back for more, wouldn't he?'

'He almost certainly would, yes, if someone hadn't removed him from the scene. Was that someone you, Mr Beckford?'

'No.' He wanted to offer them a more convincing rebuttal, but the words would not come. He moved his hands vaguely, hopelessly in front of him and then dropped them back into his lap. He had the feeling that he should be standing stiffly to attention, staring straight ahead of him, taking the inevitable condemnation of his dishonesty like a soldier, instead of sitting limply in a chair.

'When did you last see Darren Chivers?'

'When I handed over the second five hundred pounds. A fortnight last Tuesday morning. In Kenyon's coffee bar in the city centre.' He piled detail upon detail, trying to offer some compensation for his earlier dishonesty. Hook made a note of them. Beckford watched his round, unhurried hand moving over the page and wondered what was coming next.

It was what he most feared. The DS looked up at him, sympathetically now, and said, 'What information was Chivers using to extract these payments from you, Mr Beckford?'

Robert felt uneasy with Hook's use of the title. They should be reviling him, flinging his earlier lies back in his face, bespattering him with contempt for wasting their time. 'Mister' was for officers, not for the likes of him. He would have been happier with the ritual obscenities of military life, which he had once used so freely and unthinkingly himself. 'I killed a man once, a man I should not have killed, a prisoner. Well, the men under my command did – it's the same thing, in military law.'

'In the Falklands?'

'No, in the Gulf War. The first one. 1991.' The familiar details he had struggled and failed to forget came out as if from an automaton.

'There was a military inquiry into this, no doubt.'

'There was a full army court martial. I was found guilty, but with mitigating circumstances. The prisoner was causing trouble in a theatre of war. We were being fired upon by the enemy, and we couldn't afford to turn our backs on this man. It all happened in a flash. He got hold of one of my men by the hair and he turned and shot him.' It seemed easy, almost a relief, to spit out the awful, familiar details to this concerned, sympathetic, village-bobby face.

Hook nodded. 'And what did "Guilty but with mitigating circumstances" mean, in a military context?'

'My previous unblemished record of service was taken into account. I was given a severe reprimand and reduced from Staff Sergeant to Sergeant.'

Surely the lightest sentence which could have been given once a man had been found guilty. Hook felt a surge of sympathy for this man who had had the bad luck to be placed in an impossible military situation and paid the penalty for it. Who, in a bizarre and unforeseen extension of that relatively light penalty, might now have committed murder. 'No doubt you concealed this incident when you were applying for the post of verger at the Cathedral.'

'Yes. I'd been promoted to staff sergeant again by then.

The people who advised us when we were leaving the service to go back into civilian life said that what had happened nine years earlier was over and done with, that I'd paid the penalty at the time in terms of military rank.'

'But Chivers found out about it.'

'Yes. He got the story from a soldier who was buying drugs from him. A lot of ex-military men get the drugs habit, in the years after they've left the service.'

'And Chivers threatened you with exposure to the bishop?'

'Yes.' Robert allowed himself a wan smile and looked round the office. 'He wouldn't have needed to go as high as the bishop. The woman who works from this office would have made sure that I lost my job and my house in the Close, once the secret was out. I know blackmail victims are supposed to have protection, but Miss Edwina bloody Clarkson would have made it her business to find the skeleton in my cupboard. Still will, I expect.'

'She won't find out from us, Mr Beckford. If it becomes evidence in a prosecution for murder, we will then have no control over court reporting.'

'I didn't kill Chivers. I'm glad he's dead. I suppose that gives me a motive.'

Lambert had studied the man's reactions intently throughout this exchange with Hook. He now said calmly, 'Where were you last Friday night, Mr Beckford?'

Beckford appeared to give the question some thought. 'I was at home. In the house in the cathedral close, where you talked to me on Tuesday. I'm sorry I lied to you then.'

Lambert ignored the belated apology. 'Can anyone confirm this for us?'

'No. My wife was babysitting for our daughter in Newent. She wasn't back here until just before midnight.'

'Did anyone speak to you on the phone in the later part of the evening?'

'No. Not that I can recall. That's when he was killed, isn't it?'

'It is. Where were you on Saturday night?'

Again the appearance of innocent thought. 'At home. My wife's sister came over and had tea with us – her marriage broke up and she lives alone.' His face clouded. 'I ran her home in the car – she doesn't drive. She lives in Ross-on-Wye.

We left here at about quarter to ten, I suppose. I was probably out for an hour or a little more. She likes me to go into the empty house before I leave her, to make sure there is no one in there.'

'And where were you on the evening of Wednesday, June the twenty-fifth?'

'At home, I expect. What happened then?'

'Darren Chivers was beaten up and put in hospital for a couple of days. Two men were involved – maybe hired thugs. If so, they were probably employed by one of the man's blackmail victims.'

'By the man who killed him last Friday night.'

'Quite probably, but not necessarily. Had you anything to do with that beating, Mr Beckford?'

'No. This is the first I've heard of it. Someone was presumably trying to warn him off.'

'Then either they weren't successful, or some other victim decided to be rid of the man altogether. No policeman likes blackmailers, Mr Beckford. They cause their victims much anguish and give us a lot of work. Unfortunately, the law dictates that we like murderers even less.' Lambert gave him a thin smile. 'You made a bad start with us, Mr Beckford. I hope you are now being completely honest. Is there anything else you feel we should hear?'

'No. I've a lot at stake here. I stand to lose not only a job I've grown to love, not just my work, but a house where my wife and I are very happy.'

'DS Hook has already explained that we treat all the information we acquire as confidential. Unless we arrest you, there is no reason why your employers should learn anything of what you have told us. If you think of anything which may have a bearing on this investigation, it is your duty to contact us immediately.'

Bert Hook lingered for a moment after his chief had left the room, knowing that he would find him gazing at the huge tower of the cathedral from where they had parked the car. 'Your wife knows all about the army stuff.'

'Yes. You can't hide an army court martial, with officers in blues and the married quarters alive with gossip. Not that I'd have wanted to. Gwen stood by me and was a massive help to me at that time.'

'But I expect she doesn't know about the blackmail.'

Robert wondered how this harmless-looking man could have such insights. 'No. That was one of the problems. I was taking the money out of our joint account. I couldn't have concealed any more payments.' He realized in horror that he was building up his profile as a suspect.

But all Hook said was, 'You should tell her, you know. Tell her about the strain you've been under. Secrets don't help a marriage. I don't believe you'll have kept many things from her, until now.'

'You're right. I'll tell Gwen all about it. She knows there's something up, of course, but I haven't told her about the blackmail, until now. Thank you.' He reached out impulsively and grasped his adviser's strong right hand. For a moment, they were comrades in the sergeants' mess, rather than on opposite sides in a murder inquiry.

Lambert was studying the stone tracery on the massive stone cliff of the cathedral's front elevation, as Bert had known he would be. He glanced at his colleague and friend curiously but not unkindly. 'Been doing your counsellor act, Bert?'

'Something like that, yes,' said Bert Hook gruffly as he slid into the driving seat of the police Mondeo.

'The human face of the police. I like it. I just hope you haven't been counselling a murderer.'

'So do I,' said Bert. Then, as he started the engine, he added, 'I've known one or two murderers whom I quite liked, over the years. I hope I don't have to add Robert Beckford to the list.'

TWENTY

Christine Lambert was too experienced a police wife to ask her husband about his work. If he wished to speak, the initiative must come from him. Twenty years and more ago, he had hugged his work to him like protective armour, working long hours and shutting her out completely from that part of his life. It had almost fractured the marriage which nowadays seemed so secure, such a model for more junior men, who so often found the exigencies of police work a passage to divorce.

In his fifties, John Lambert had become much more relaxed, confident that not a word of what he uttered would pass beyond the walls of the home where he had once found it so difficult to relax. He was a different animal now, Christine sometimes insisted. She said to him on Saturday morning, 'You'll be working this weekend, I expect.'

He glanced up from *The Times* and his perusal of the account of the Ashes test match. 'I'm afraid I will, yes. We're making progress, but it's already a week since the man died.'

That old police watchword: if you didn't have an arrest within the first week of a murder inquiry, the chances were that you wouldn't get one at all. Christine couldn't remember the statistics, but she understood the implications. 'Try to make it for tea tomorrow, if you can. I was planning a family gathering. Jacky says she hasn't seen Caroline and the children for months. It will only be salad. That's not an invitation to be late, by the way.'

He grinned. 'I'll do my best to be there. Even for salad. Jacky's well rid of that Jason.'

It was some months now since Lambert's elder daughter had been deserted by her husband for a younger woman. Christine smiled a rueful smile. Despite her own more private doubts, she had always stood up for Jason against her husband's misgivings, as long as he had been around. 'She probably is well rid of him, but that doesn't make it any less painful for her. Try to be there tomorrow, John – you know how close she's always been to you.'

'And I to her.' He thought irrelevantly, uselessly, of the years when he had held Jacky's small frame tight against his chest as she sobbed her eyes out over some crisis at school. How far away those years must seem to her, and how close they still were to him! The familiar lament of the ageing parent. He would be an old man before he knew it. 'I must be about the work of the state and the detection of murder,' he said with mock self-importance.

'The cricket test highlights are on at seven fifteen,' Christine reminded him. You had to encourage a proper sense of perspective in husbands.

*   *   *

Karen Lynch polished the brasswork of the altar rails vigorously, trying to dissipate her nervousness through the force of her physical energy. She limped over to Florence Jenkins, who was deftly arranging large pink carnations in two vases to be set in pride of place on the main altar.

'I don't know how you produce an effect like that so quickly,' she said, as the older woman slipped an extra piece of asparagus fern behind the blooms to show them off to optimum effect.

'You get used to it, after the first few hundred efforts!' said Florence, who was a consistent winner in the floral arrangement classes at the local horticultural shows. 'Ted doesn't know yet, but I raided his greenhouse for these. He'll grumble a bit, but he won't really mind, if it's for the church. I might even be able to drag him along to the service tomorrow, if I promise him his blooms will be on the high altar. Of course, he appreciates your husband's sermons as well,' she added hastily.

'There's no need to be polite, when you put in the time and the effort that you do, Florence – especially when you bring along your husband's prize blooms as well!' Karen assured her. She liked seventy-year-old Florence, who was ultra-conservative in temperament but tried to remain resolutely open to Peter's modern and liberal ideas. 'I think Peter's preparing his sermon in the vestry at this very moment, as a matter of fact. I've sent him over here to get a little peace – you'd be surprised how many visitors we get at the vicarage on a Saturday morning.'

Including two she knew were coming at ten o' clock. She didn't want Peter or anyone else in the house when the CID men arrived.

She took them into the square, characterless room with the cheap modern furniture and the conventional prints of Rome and Venice on the walls. She rather liked this bright modern room. Its clean, aseptic character and the sunlight which flowed in through its window were an assertion of the blamelessness of her new life, a physical contrast to that darker world of drugs and crime she had left behind her. But today the room seemed to her bare and clinical, a context where these men could concentrate on her weakness and mercilessly expose her past. She felt now as vulnerable as she had felt in those police interview rooms which had, years ago, been so familiar.

Perhaps Lambert sensed this, for he attacked immediately. 'Mrs Lynch, I should tell you that we now know much more about Darren Chivers than when we saw you on Wednesday. Enough, in fact, to question the reliability of many of your statements to us at our last meeting. We know that Mr Chivers was not just a drug-dealer but a blackmailer. We think the list we found in his pocket contained the names of some of his blackmail victims. I have to remind you again that your name was on that list.'

This was as bad or worse than anything Karen had expected. She resisted automatically, trying to gain time to think. 'Do I look like a woman who could be blackmailed?' She looked down hopelessly at her jeans, at the smear of silver polish on her blouse from her cleaning in the church. 'Do the furnishings in this place, the clothes I wear, speak of a woman with the resources to attract a blackmailer?'

She thought she caught the slightest inclination of Lambert's long intense face towards the softer one beside it. Detective Sergeant Hook said, 'Karen, you told us that the only possible place where you could have met Chivers was at St Mary's Hostel, through the addicts that live there. That the only way you could have got on to that list in his pocket was because one of those people might have mentioned your name to him. We now believe that you had a much earlier acquaintance with Darren Chivers. I think you should take this opportunity of telling us about that and putting the record straight.'

He was quiet, insistent, seemingly sympathetic, so that even in her turmoil she heard his every word. She wondered if this was a speech he had prepared before they came here, whether this avuncular figure was playing a predetermined role even when he seemed so genuine in his concern. Whatever the reality was, Hook's concerned tone seemed only to emphasize the hopelessness of further attempts to conceal the realities of that life she had sought to leave behind her. She said with dull resignation, 'You know about how I once lived.'

'We know a certain amount from police records, yes. We are not interested in mining them. What we need to know about is your previous and present dealings with Darren Chivers.'

'I was an addict, Chivers was a dealer. The life I led then is part of another world, but it's come back to haunt me, hasn't it? I suppose I always knew it would. I'd like you to know that my husband knows all about the life I led then. Peter knows that in those days I'd have done anything for the next fix – that's what being an addict means. I stole for heroin. I fucked for heroin.' She spat out the obscenity she had not used for years, as if in a desperate attempt to purge herself. 'That's the way you are, when you're an addict. All decent behaviour disappears.'

Hook wanted to hasten her on, but he sensed that this was a necessary first stage of her revelations. He said softly, 'We're not drug squad, but we've seen enough of horse and coke and the rest to know what they do to people. We know also that the cure is sometimes worse than the addiction. You came through that and fought your way back to a normal life.'

She looked up at him again, as if registering his presence anew through her private agony. 'I'm older than Chivers was, you know. I was a dealer myself once. I'm not sure, but I might even have introduced him to dealing. When you were recruiting, you were told to look for users who would become dealers to get their next fix. It was the way the system worked. I expect it still is.'

'So Chivers knew all about your previous life.'

'I suspect Darren Chivers knew as much about my life at that time as anyone else on earth.'

'And he decided to make use of that knowledge. He decided to add you to his list of blackmail victims.'

Hook made it a statement, not a question, as if it were the most natural thing in the world that she should admit it. It worked, because it suddenly seemed to Karen Lynch hopeless to deny it, though she had intended to do so when she entered the room. 'I go down to St Mary's Hostel to help Father Ryan on most Tuesday afternoons. Chivers tackled me in the street as I was walking back into the city centre. He told me he wanted money to keep his mouth shut about the life I had led, the person I had once been.'

'And you paid him.'

She gave him a withering smile. 'He wanted five hundred pounds. I told him he might as well ask for the moon. I can't raise money like that. Peter and I live from hand to mouth as it is. I'm proud of what he does, proud that he regards money as secondary. But Darren Chivers told me I'd manage to raise the money from somewhere.'

'And did you?'

'No. I scratched together two hundred.' Suddenly and unexpectedly, she found herself in tears. It took her a full half minute to regain control, during which neither of the men spoke. They had seen much human misery, but they knew full well that misery, like other extremes of human emotion, is often a prelude to revelations. Eventually Karen managed to explain her breakdown. 'I'm sorry. It's just that this was the beginning of what Peter called our "baby fund". We want to start a family as soon as we can afford it. This was the only money we had, and I was going to give it to a man like that to keep his mouth shut about the woman I'd been.'

'You'd a lot at stake.'

'I'd everything at stake, DS Hook. Peter knows all about my past life, but no one else does. If Chivers had exposed me, it wouldn't just have been my life ruined, it would have been Peter's. He's making a success of things here, bringing people back into the church. All kinds of people. But his reputation as well as mine would have been ruined. The important people who run things here would think he'd deceived them. That he'd brought a junkie and a harlot into their vicarage without warning them.'

'I think people might be a little more forgiving than you think. There's great admiration for someone who's made the kind of recovery you've made.'

'The Mary Magdalen effect, you mean? People find that idea romantic, until they have to take on such a woman themselves. Peter says they'd welcome the reformed sinner. I wouldn't like him to have to test that theory.'

'But in the end you didn't have to take your two hundred along to Chivers.'

'No. Someone kindly removed him. I can't rejoice in the death of anyone, but I can't deny my relief.'

She had almost forgotten the intense attention of John Lambert in her preoccupation with reliving her own agony through Hook's promptings. It was the chief superintendent who now said, 'Let's be clear about this. Are you telling us now that the single occasion when you saw Darren Chivers was when he approached you in the street after you left St Mary's Hostel?'

'Yes. He said I had a week to get five hundred pounds together. As I said, I'd scratched together two hundred in the ten days before he was killed, but he hadn't contacted me again.' She was staring straight ahead of her, as if she could still not believe that her agony was over. 'Will it come out now? My past, I mean. Will it all come tumbling out when you arrest someone for this?'

'Not from us it won't. If you're involved in a murder inquiry, all kinds of things become public. In the meantime, if the press come sniffing around, you should resolutely refuse them any kind of comment.'

Michelle de Vries should have been exultant. It had been a busy Saturday at Boutique Chantelle and she had made several lucrative sales. The shop was becoming known. Two of the customers had journeyed over forty miles to examine the latest stock and make their purchases.

She was grateful for such success, of course. Perhaps within a year the shop would be making a reasonable net profit and no longer relying on her husband's financial support. But Michelle could not get Darren Chivers and the murder investigation out of her mind. Those polite, watchful detectives who had come to her shop on Wednesday loomed like spectres in her mind, so that she constantly expected them to reappear and confront her with the evidence of her dishonesty.

Instead of the CID men, she had another, more unexpected, visitor as the crowds began to thin in the streets of the ancient city. It was a visitor who in happier times would have filled her day with joy. Today she would quickly sense that it was something very different from joy he brought.

Guy Dawson, normally so confident, slipped like a fugitive into her shop, glancing theatrically behind him to make sure he was unobserved before he shut the door on the world outside. He said, 'I'm glad you're on your own!' and gave her a passionless peck on the cheek before leading her through to the storeroom behind the shop, where they would be unobserved.

'It's good to see you, Guy! This is a bit of a bonus for me.'

She reached out both arms towards him. 'I've already had a good day in the shop, and now that you've come—'

'Have the police been back?'

'No. I think they must be satisfied with what I told them. Perhaps we—'

'Not "we". You're on your own in this. I don't want you implicating me with them in any way.'

She recoiled as if he had struck her. 'I didn't implicate you. They knew Chivers had been watching your house. They knew that it was because of you that he was able to blackmail me.'

Like many weak men, he wouldn't accept logic when he was confronted with it. 'All I know is that you told them about us. Dragged me into this.'

For the first time that she could remember, she lost her temper with him. 'That's ridiculous! I might as well say that you dragged me into it. We're conducting an extramarital affair, and you take risks when you get into such things. Of course, you could come out into the open and let Gerald know about it. Then no one would be able to blackmail us.'

In that moment, she willed him to do just that, to scream at her that he wanted her, wanted to live with her, that she should be rid of her rich husband and live more modestly with him for the rest of her life. It was an absurd notion, of course, and she would have probably have rejected it if he had voiced it, but it would have been wonderful to hear it.

There was not the remotest chance of that. Guy Dawson slicked back his hair in the nervous gesture she had once loved, then glanced automatically at the door to the shop, as if anxious to be done with this before they were interrupted. In that moment, the scales fell from her eyes and she saw him for what he was: a man on the make, a sexual predator with an easy, surface charm who picked up what he could and disappeared when the going got tough.

He said petulantly, 'You've dragged me into the middle of this. The police came round to see me yesterday.'

'You should have expected that.' She was suddenly weary of his weakness. 'Who came to see you?'

'A detective inspector – Rushton, I think he said his name was. He had a young detective constable with him who made notes. They wanted to know where I was last Friday night when Chivers was killed.'

'And what did you tell them?'

He looked at her sharply. 'The truth, of course. That I was having a drink at my local, the way I often do on a Friday—'

'You told me you were delivering a car to Birmingham, when I rang to say that Gerald was away and we could meet.'

'I – I got back earlier than I thought I would.'

It had been a lie, then. He had been available, if he had wanted to see her. She felt not the pain and sorrow she should have felt but only an immense weariness with this shifty, craven man who was her lover. 'Did they believe you?'

'I don't know.'

'I'm not even sure I believe you. Didn't you tell me you were going to find out about Chivers? Perhaps you did and took the opportunity to get rid of him. To preserve your precious skin from anything Gerald might do to it, if he found out about us.' She wanted to make wilder and wilder charges, to fling anything at him which might hurt him, to punish him for not being the man she had thought him in the excesses of her stupid infatuation.

'Don't be silly. I didn't kill the man. Though thanks to you, it now seems that the police think I might have done.' He reached out and took her clumsily into his arms, as she had been willing him to do only minutes earlier. He did not even notice that for the first time ever she did not respond to him. 'I need your help, Michelle. You mustn't tell the police any more about me than you have. And you certainly mustn't let Gerald know anything about us.'

She pushed him away, holding her arms against his chest for a moment before she dropped them to her sides. 'It's all about protecting you, isn't it? Guy Dawson mustn't be affected, whatever happens to anyone else. Don't you ever think of me, of what I must be going through? It's me the man tried to blackmail. Me the police came to first, me they had as a suspect.' She looked at the regular, handsome face, thinking for the first time how weak the mouth looked, how those lips she had kissed so often now trembled with apprehension. 'The people who came to see you were small fry. I had the man the papers call the "super sleuth", Chief Superintendent John Lambert. That's who I had to deal with!'

He gaped at her, totally taken aback to see her like this. She felt a preposterous delight that her interrogators should outrank his. He was pitiable in his fear, and she wondered suddenly if he had other things he wanted to keep away from the police. 'Look, we're both upset. Let's give this some thought and discuss it more rationally when we meet on Tuesday.'

He dropped his gaze to the table, so that she was beset with contempt for him. He could not even look into her face to do this. 'We won't be meeting on Tuesday, Michelle. I think we should end this, before things get any worse.'

'That's what you came here to say, isn't it?'

'I think it would be best for both of us.'

'For you, you mean.'

'I'm sorry you're taking it like this. Perhaps, when all this murder business is over, we can get together again.'

He was into the statements he had prepared, she thought. Trust him to think in clichés. She felt dangerously calm as she said through clenched teeth, 'Get out, Guy! Get out now! Don't say any more.'

'You meant a lot to me, Michelle, I want you to know that I—'

The sound of her palm against his face was like the crack of a whip. She hadn't known that she was going to do it, but she must have hit him hard, for she felt the angry sting of the hit in her hand, even as she saw the shock in his eyes and his fingers lifting to the weal on his cheek.

He muttered, 'You bitch!' as he turned away from her, stumbling in his haste to open the door and be gone.

She stood perfectly still for a few moments, then followed him through the shop, dropped the lock on the outer door, and put up the closed sign. She felt the blood pounding in her temples and sat down hastily as giddiness overtook her. She didn't know that she was crying until she felt the first drops on the back of her hand. They were tears not of sorrow but of rage, of anger at herself that it had taken her so long to see the reality of this weak, venal creature.

She didn't know how long she had been sitting there when the phone rang, but she felt perfectly composed when she had to speak. It was Detective Sergeant Hook, informing her that he and Lambert needed to speak to her again on the morrow. They could come to her home, or if she preferred it she could come in to the station.

Her mind worked quickly and well, she thought. She said, 'No, I'd prefer it if you came here, I think. I can make sure that we won't be disturbed.'

TWENTY-ONE

Mark Rogers wanted to answer the door himself, but his wife was too quick for him. By the time he got into the hall, Samantha had opened the door and was greeting Chief Superintendent Lambert, about whom she had recently read so much in the local press.

She was being dutifully polite, waving aside the police apologies for calling at this time on a Saturday evening, gushing a little in her consciousness that she was in the presence of a strange kind of celebrity. Mark took over as quickly as he could. 'These are the detectives I told you about the other day, dear. Mr Lambert and DS Hook. I'm trying to help them fill in some of the detail on this murder case.' He switched his attention to the two men who were watching him so expectantly. 'We'll go into the dining room, I think. We shan't be interrupted in there.' He led them through the first door in the modern hall and shut the door on the sound of childish excitements at the rear of the house.

Mark tried not to find Lambert's unwavering gaze disturbing as he installed the two men in the chairs he had set out before they came. 'Working late, I see.' He heard his nervous giggle and cursed himself for it.

'Murder overrides the normal priorities, Mr Rogers. It doesn't help when people try to deceive us. I hope you will see the importance – from your own point of view as much as ours – of being completely honest with us today.' Lambert allowed himself the ghost of a smile. 'Working at weekends may make us a little less patient than usual with any evasions.'

Mark decided to take as firm a line as he could. It wasn't easy, in view of their years and their obvious seniority in the police hierarchy, but he tried to imagine that these people were junior employees. He said as loftily as he could, 'I'm not aware that I was anything other than honest with you when we talked on Thursday. I told you that I had bought drugs from Darren Chivers in the past. I told you that he had extracted a blackmail payment from me because I did not want him to reveal that. I gave you an honest account of my whereabouts on the night when it appears he was killed.'

Just when he had focused all his attention on the gaunt, sceptical face opposite him, it was Bert Hook who looked up from his notebook and said, 'If your account of the blackmail relationship was full and accurate, Mr Rogers, we would find it easier to believe your account of your movements on that Friday night.'

'What I told you about that night is absolutely true. As is what I told you about Chivers and his blackmail, DS Hook.' He put a slight emphasis on the rank, hoping thus to remind the man both of his junior status and the respect he owed to the executive whose integrity he was questioning.

Hook was distressingly unperturbed. 'You told us on Thursday that you had made a blackmail payment to Chivers of two hundred pounds. Would you now care to revise the sum involved?'

Rogers glanced automatically at the door and the rest of the house behind it, and they knew in that second that he had told his wife nothing of this. 'All right, I gave him more than that. I don't see that the sum should greatly matter, but I gave the bastard a thousand pounds.'

Hook flicked to a new page of his notebook and made a note of that. It seemed to Mark that it took him a long time to do it; the silence stretched long and heavy, whilst Lambert's grey eyes observed him steadily. It was the Chief Superintendent who then said calmly, 'I'm glad we have established a more reasonable figure. It also seemed to us that your account of the background to this blackmail payment was frankly not credible. We don't believe that you would have made such a payment in the hope that Chivers would not reveal your purchases of cocaine. In the present climate of opinion, we don't think such revelations would be very damaging to you at BT. There would be many vulnerable executives in the country if past experiments with cocaine could damage them.' He looked at his man with no sign of a smile now. 'Perhaps I should point out to you that in a murder investigation all sorts of financial and other information which would not normally be accessible will be made available to whoever is directing the inquiry.'

'You don't have access to employment records?' Mark meant it as an assertion, but it emerged as a question, and he knew as he heard himself speak that the last shreds of his deceit were being stripped away from him.

Lambert knew it too. 'Frankly, Mr Rogers, you have made yourself a murder suspect by your earlier dishonesty. I'd say that in these circumstances, we could obtain access to whatever normally confidential records seem relevant. However, that would excite considerable interest among the people who would have to grant us such access. I should have thought it would be preferable for you to be completely honest with us this evening.'

Mark had given them two easy chairs, with himself in a third he had brought through from the sitting room. He had felt at the time that he would keep this meeting informal, hopefully with himself dictating the pace and content of it. Now he felt totally without defence, sitting in a chair with nothing but air between him and these two practised adversaries. He should have sat them on upright chairs at the table, with four feet of wood between them, and his twisting feet kept invisible beneath it. He stared at the carpet as he said dully, 'I was a bit imaginative when I filled in my original application form for my first job with BT.'

'You told lies, you mean.' Lambert let some of his dislike for the man seep into his contempt for his evasions.

Rogers shrugged hopelessly. 'Economical with the truth. Everyone does it. Or I thought they did, at the time.'

'Everyone puts the most favourable interpretation on what they have done.' Lambert thought grimly of promotion boards long ago, when your every statement, as well as every comment from your superiors on the form in front of the panel, had been relentlessly picked over by fellow professionals who had seen every dodge and heard every bland cliché before. 'But you must have done more than merely state the best case for yourself, to lay yourself open to blackmail. You must have altered certain facts.'

'Yes. Look, is this really necessary? Even my wife doesn't know about this, let alone anyone at the company. I'd obviously prefer to leave it that way. I've given you the reason why Chivers was able to blackmail me and confessed to the payment I made to him. Surely that's enough?'

'You made a mistake when you did not tell us all this on Thursday, Mr Rogers. I'm afraid we need to know the full details. Mr Chivers is a murder victim. We need to know the exact nature of the hold he had over you.'

Mark had known even as he made his protests that it would come to this. He said hopelessly, listlessly, 'I changed the class of degree I'd had. Gave myself a first where I'd actually had a third. And I said I'd had a managerial post abroad for eight months, when I'd actually been unemployed for most of that time. I'd lost a couple of jobs through drugs – I could hardly write that down, could I?'

'And what would you have done if the company had asked you to produce evidence of your degree?'

'I'd have given back word on the job. Resigned, if they'd asked for such things after I'd actually taken up the post. Look, it didn't seem that serious at the time. I've got on well since at the company, so I must have ability, mustn't I? That's what really matters, isn't it?'

'How did Darren Chivers come to know about this?'

'I didn't know he did, until he stopped me coming out of the pub six weeks ago and told me I was going to have to pay him to keep his mouth shut. What I told you about his supplying me with drugs years ago was correct. What I didn't tell you was that in those pre-BT, pre-family days, I used quite a lot of crack. I was never an addict, but I came pretty near to being dependent on it, when I look back at it now. I was off my head quite a lot of the time. Chivers was supplying me, and I must have told him what I was doing when I filled in that form. I didn't realize it at the time, but I was high and worse than high for a lot of the time. Darren Chivers is – sorry, was – a more intelligent man than you'd think. He even claimed he'd helped me to fill in that application form, but I'm not sure that he did that.'

'At any rate, he knew enough about it to demand a thousand pounds to keep his mouth shut, as a first payment.'

'He said it was a one-off.'

'But you didn't believe that. You're by no means stupid, whatever you did all those years ago to get a job. It wasn't as if you could pay him to return photographs or other evidence and be done with it. You must have known he'd be back.'

'You know that, deep down. You've heard all about blackmail. But when you're a victim, you just hope against hope that it will be different for you.'

'And when that doesn't work out and he comes back, you should go to the police and demand protection. Instead of which, you chose to meet the blackmailer and remove him with his own weapon.'

'No! No, I didn't do that!'

Panic eventually roused him from his submissiveness, so that he found himself shouting the denial at them. It was Bert Hook who said calmly, persuasively, 'Maybe you didn't go there intending to kill him. Maybe it was an argument which got out of hand when he made impossible demands.'

'No, it wasn't like that. I didn't meet him. I had nothing to do with his death!'

'Maybe it was even accidental. Perhaps you didn't even mean to kill him. You could almost certainly get away with manslaughter, if that is how it happened.'

There was the merest pause before he said, 'No! That isn't how it was! I didn't even see Darren Chivers on that Friday night.'

'Mr Rogers, our officers have checked out the pub where you claim to have been drinking at the time when Chivers died. I have to tell you that the landlord does not remember you. So far, our team has not turned up a single customer who remembers seeing you there on that Friday night.'

'I told you, it was very crowded. I expect it always is, at that time on a Friday. It isn't a place I visit regularly. I knew the kids were in bed and I just felt like a drink after a hard day in Birmingham.'

There was a shrill scream of childish pain from the back of the house, then a murmur of maternal consolation and laughter from the other child, as if to remind Mark of that family life which was physically so near and yet in other respects now so far from him. Lambert studied him for another moment before he said, 'Have you anything further to add or any amendments to make to what you have told us tonight, Mr Rogers? In view of the radical revisions to what you told us two days ago, you would be most unwise to withhold anything now.'

'No. How far will this need to go?'

'That will depend largely upon what happens in the next few days. If you are not the killer of Darren Chivers, we will not willingly release anything, but there can be no guarantees.'

'I can't afford to tell them at work. Not at the present time, when everyone's job is at risk.'

'I can't make decisions for you on that, Mr Rogers. Please do not leave the area without informing us of any address, other than this one.'

At ten to eleven on that Saturday night, a grey Ford Focus car pulled into a dimly lit street behind a pub in the dock area of the city of Gloucester. The pub had a car park and there were spaces vacated in there as the customers began to leave, but the driver preferred to park on the street. A swift getaway after your business was concluded was much easier from there.

Several other people left the pub in the twenty minutes which followed, calling noisy goodnights to their companions of the evening. Most of them had had enough drink to blunt their powers of observation, and none of them paid any attention to the two men sitting in the car. This wasn't the sort of area or the time of night where you stopped to ask questions.

It was warm enough for the men in the Ford to have the windows open, so that the myriad sounds of the central city carried faintly to them over the intervening roofs. But it was the human sounds from the immediate vicinity which interested the men in the Focus. They gave more acute attention to them as the minutes passed and there were fewer people left behind the brightly lit windows of the public house.

Eventually the man in the passenger seat breathed, 'That's him!' and they eased themselves silently from the car in readiness.

Their unsuspecting quarry's voice sounded extra loud through the darkness. No doubt it was made louder by his cheerful inebriation. 'I'll see you on Wednesday, Denis, all being well!' he called back to some invisible companion, as the exit door swung shut behind him. He settled himself comfortably into his voluminous sweater, feeling his head swim a little and his knees unsteady for a moment as the fresh air hit him after the warmth of the crowded room he had left. Then he smiled to himself, ducked his head a little, and moved through the car park and into the narrow street behind it.

The two men with baseball bats knew he had not got the money. Perhaps, indeed, keyed up as they were for violence, they would have been disappointed if he had. But they went through the motions of challenge, playing out the prelude to the sordid little drama in which they were acting. 'Last chance to pay, Barker. You owe five hundred. You've had your warning.'

James Barker's senses cleared miraculously as fear surged through his veins. 'I haven't got it. I told him, I'll pay next week. By the end of the month at the very latest!'

'You've had your warnings. Last night was the deadline. He told you that.'

'I need a little more time, that's all. Only a little. Business is picking up and—'

They hit him then, as they had always known they were going to do. Hit him systematically, unemotionally, with brutal efficiency. He fell quickly and went into the foetal crouch with which they were familiar. They beat him about his back, his thighs, his calves and his buttocks, resisting the impulse to kick the defenceless heap beneath them, knowing that blows from the sticks were more anonymous.

The men were practised and experienced and their work took no more than forty seconds in all. Then they were back in their car and away, leaving their victim moaning quietly behind them.

It was at the end of the street that things went wrong for them. The police car pulled across their path as they accelerated, forcing them to halt. The four coppers were out of the car before they had left theirs, pinning them against the doors with their arms across the roof, yelling the words of arrest as they slipped the handcuffs around the men's thick wrists.

The two men were in the police cells within fifteen minutes.

TWENTY-TWO

On Sunday mornings, the Reverend Peter Lynch often had the equivalent of stage fright. His sermon was prepared, he knew exactly how he wanted the service to proceed. He had even planned what to say to one or two members of the congregation individually when they were leaving the church at the end of the service. Once the main business of this sunlit summer morning was under way, he would be calm and confident. But in the time before that, he was trying to feel properly appreciative of his cereals and toast.

Then he looked at the white, strained face of his wife and felt guilty about his own preoccupations. Karen hadn't been her normal cheerful self in the last week; it seemed that the death of this man Chivers had brought her past back vividly before her and affected the zest she usually brought to her life. 'Things are looking up financially,' Peter said with sudden determination.

'Is your stipend going to be increased?'

'I live in hope. The bishop was most encouraging about the work we're doing here when I saw him last week.'

'The work you are doing here, you mean.'

'No, I don't. We're a partnership. You've got strengths that I will never have. Everyone appreciates the way you muck in and turn your hand to everything.' He was going to mention her sterling work at the hostel with Father Ryan, then thought better of it, sensing that anything which brought that unfortunate man Chivers back into her thinking would not be a good idea.

He looked at her anxious, abstracted face and said on impulse, 'It's time we got on with this family we're going to raise.'

'We can't afford it, not yet. I thought we'd agreed on that.'

'I think we should just take the plunge and put our faith in God to look after us. You're thirty-four and your biological clock is ticking. Partly thanks to your work, more people are coming into the church than have done for years. I'm sure we're going to have a little more money soon.'

'Perhaps we should wait and see.'

She was listless, when he would have expected her to be delighted. He knew how much she wanted children, how she normally enjoyed discussing even the possibility of them.

He said forcefully, 'I think we should initiate the project right away. I think we should go for lift-off tonight.' He came round the table and stood behind her, feeling the tenseness in her neck as his fingers massaged it gently. He let his hands run down gently over the familiar breasts. 'Stop playing hard to get, you little minx!'

She roused herself at last. 'Be off with you and get on with your work, you randy vicar, you!' She stood up and smiled at him, then began to gather the dishes together on the table. She tried not to let him see her limp. Her leg always hurt most when she was under stress.

She was relieved when he did as he was bid and left the room to get on with his public Sunday morning duties. She would not have liked him to see the tears beginning to flow.

The centre of Gloucester was a quiet place at this time. Michelle de Vries could not recall that she had ever been there at quarter to nine on a Sunday before. Apart from a dribble of worshippers making their way towards the cathedral, there were few people on the streets.

The CID men came promptly, even at this time, their silhouettes outlined for a moment against the eastern sun as if they were angels of death. Michelle let them into the shop and then locked the door firmly, making sure that the 'Closed' sign remained clearly displayed. 'I told my husband I was coming in for a couple of hours to do a little stocktaking,' she explained to them, picking a thread of cotton off a dark green dress that seemed altogether too elegant for the shabby storeroom behind the shop. 'I'd be grateful if we could preserve that fiction.'

Lambert did not comment directly. He merely said, 'This need not delay any of us very long, if you choose to tell us the truth.'

'I have already done that. Obviously I want to help you as much as I can, but—'

'You told us on Wednesday that Darren Chivers had been here a fortnight earlier and that you hadn't see him after that. You told us first that he had demanded money with menaces, then changed your story to admit that he had come here to blackmail you. You said that he had demanded money from you to remain silent about your affair with Mr Dawson, but that fortunately for you he had been killed before he came back to collect the money from you. We now have reason to believe that, apart from your admission that you were a blackmail victim, your statement is a string of lies.'

He was suddenly impatient with her Paris dress, her hundred-pound leather shoes, her unspoken assertion that the squalid world of murder was something beneath her comprehension. She felt in him an open hostility she had not experienced for years, and it shook her.

She said, 'I have a husband I love, who supports this shop and will continue to do so until it is properly established. I am not proud of my association with Guy Dawson, which I concluded last night. Surely you can understand that I felt the need to—'

'What I understand and what you should understand, Mrs de Vries, is that this is a murder inquiry. It is no place for embarrassment, especially if that embarrassment leads you into lying to those conducting the inquiry.'

'I'm sorry! I didn't kill the wretched man!' She found herself shouting, had to make a real effort to lower her voice. 'You don't see things as clearly as that, when you have your own concerns. I was anxious because I didn't want to lose a good husband and the lifestyle I have.'

It was Bert Hook, notebook open on the table in front of him, who at this point said quietly, 'Perhaps you should now tell us the real truth of the matter, Mrs de Vries.'

She looked at him for two or three seconds in silence, as if finding it difficult to refocus on this very different, less threatening face. Then she said, in a lower voice which became almost a monotone, 'Chivers did come back here again. A week after his first visit.'

'That would be on Wednesday, July the second.' Hook's voice was as calm and unemotional as if he were compiling a grocery list.

'Yes. He came to collect the money he had demanded. I paid him two thousand pounds. He said that would be the end of it.'

'But you didn't think that would indeed be the end of it.'

'I wanted to. I suppose the victims of blackmailers always want to believe it. But no, I don't suppose I really believed him. I feared he would be back.'

'And two days later he was dead.'

'So you tell me. I didn't kill him.'

'But there is no one who can vouch for your whereabouts at the time of his death.'

'No. I expect many innocent people have that problem.'

It was her first and last flash of defiance in the whole of the encounter.

Lambert stood up and said, 'If you can think of any means of establishing where you were on the night of Friday the fourth of July or any information which might help us with this investigation, it is your duty to contact us.'

'I should obviously be delighted to do that, Chief Superintendent Lambert. Unfortunately, I don't think it is likely.'

Michelle saw them out of the shop and shut the door behind them, moving like an automaton. Then she went back into the storeroom and sat for a long time with her head in her hands.

The two men both had previous convictions for violence. They knew the score when they were brought up from the cells. They were going to be charged with Actual Bodily Harm at the very least. They were taken to separate interview rooms and left in isolation for ten minutes to get more nervous.

The CID decision was to allow the more experienced officers to interview the younger of the two, purely because he had appeared the more nervous when breakfast had been delivered to the cells an hour earlier. Rushton set the cassette turning and announced that Matthew Green was about to be interviewed by DI Rushton and DS Hook, with the interview commencing at 9.48 a.m. He regarded the man with undisguised hostility for a few moments before he spoke.

'You're in trouble, Green. We shall throw the book at you, unless you choose to cooperate. GBH is on the cards. You're going inside. The only question is for how long.'

'Get lost, copper.'

The ritual defiance, as predictable as the sun rising and setting. Rushton nodded happily. 'That's the attitude we'd expect. I didn't think you'd have the sense to look out for yourself.'

'Whadyermean, look out for myself?' A glimmer of interest flickered in the narrowed eyes, despite himself.

'I should have thought even you could see that. Your only chance to get off lightly is to cooperate with us, give us a few things we might like to know. We might even be able to tell the judge you've been a good boy, if you have the sense to do that. But I don't expect you will.'

'I don't shop people to pigs. Never have, never will.'

Rushton nodded. 'I'd expect that sort of attitude from the likes of you. Can't say I'm sorry, really. It will be good to have you off the streets and behind bars for a good few years.'

Green said sullenly, 'I don't shop people, copper. I want to help myself, I'm not stupid. But I don't shop people.'

Bert Hook smiled at him. 'Bit of a contradiction there, Matt, isn't there? You want to help yourself, but you don't want to give us any help. Nothing is for nothing. You must have learned that by now.'

Green peered at him suspiciously whilst the irrefutable logic of this worked its way into his mind. He said slowly, 'I wasn't the man who set the jobs up, you know. It was Jim who was in charge.'

'And it's Jim who's being questioned next door at this very minute, Matt. Probably straining every nerve to put the blame on you.'

'He wouldn't do that.'

'Oh, I wouldn't rely on it, Matt. Our experience is that when people see the chance of cutting down the years in the big house, they blame anyone and everyone except themselves.' Hook shook his head sadly. 'It's understandable, I suppose. If I was facing the prospect of slopping out every morning for month after month, I'd be frantic to put the blame on someone else.'

'You don't slop out. It's been abolished.'

'Really? Well, I wouldn't rely on that either, if I were you, Matt. Which fortunately, I'm not, of course.' Bert shook his head in slow motion, in sad recognition of the plight of the wretched man on the other side of the small, square table. 'Our lads are round at Frank Lee's house this morning, talking to him. Nasty piece of work, Frank Lee. There'll be a lot of people in the town glad to see him get his comeuppance.'

The name had been dropped in casually, as if he was merely repeating something already established between them. In fact, it was an attempt to determine the name of the man who had employed these brutes to do his dirty work on the previous evening, and it worked.

Green nodded his head slowly. 'No one likes a loan shark. But he pays well.'

Chris Rushton registered no emotion as he made a careful note of this. The first witness in the court case against the slippery Frank Lee, who had caused so much misery in the town with his loans at exorbitant rates, had just been established. He said sternly, 'You realize we can charge you with much more than this one, Green. Frank Lee isn't the only man you've worked for.'

'He pays best!' A ludicrous smile flitted across the coarse features.

'And he's landed you in trouble, Matt,' Bert Hook reminded him. 'Big trouble, as DI Rushton told you at the beginning of this interview. But maybe not the worst. The worst charge against you may come from beating up a man who was subsequently murdered. Darren Chivers, Matt. We have to ask ourselves whether his subsequent death is also down to the two men who put him in hospital nine days earlier.'

'We didn't kill Chivers!' The eyes which had previously been hooded stretched wide in panic.

'Remains to be established, that, Matt. You know how anxious we coppers are to get convictions. Well, we've got you banged to rights for last night's job, and it seems to me you've just admitted to the assault on Chivers. You can see how tempting it would be to put the lot on you. I don't think a couple of thugs with baseball bats are going to command a lot of sympathy in court. Do you?'

'You can't fit me up for murder!' But his voice thrilled with the fear that they might do just that.

'Fit you up, Matt? Oh, DI Rushton and I wouldn't want to

do that. We're honourable men, the Inspector and I. But we need something to convince us, you see, or we might be carried along by events.'

Slyness suddenly took over the brutish face. 'It was one of yours that set up that beating for Chivers.'

'A copper, you mean?' Hook was studiously impassive.

'Ex-copper. Jim told me that.'

'We'd need his name, Matt, to be convinced, wouldn't we?'

'I don't shop people. I told you that.' Green made a belated return to his criminal philosophy.

'Well, perhaps you don't need to, Matt. We know all about Daniel Steele.'

'How'd you know that? I didn't tell you, did I?'

'Oh, we're very interested in Dan Steele, Matt. Very interested to have confirmation that he set you up to give Darren Chivers a beating.'

'But we didn't kill him!'

'Do you know, Matt, I'm rather inclined to believe that? But I think we shall need to have further discussions with Mr Steele.'

Chris Rushton was inordinately pleased with his findings when Lambert and Hook joined him in the CID section to review the latest state of the Darren Chivers case.

'I thought Sunday morning was a good time to put our heads together, whilst the place is pretty quiet,' said Lambert.

'We made a great leap forward this morning,' said Chris, scarcely able to contain his excitement. 'Well, Bert did. He was the one who wormed the information out of the man.' At one time, he had been so keen on promotion, so insecure with John Lambert, that he would have claimed the credit for himself. He was more relaxed at work as well as outside the station nowadays.

'Joint effort,' said Bert stolidly. 'You set him up, I knocked him down.'

Lambert looked at the pair quizzically for a moment. 'Are you offering me a murderer trussed up ready for the Crown Prosecution Service?'

Rushton was deflated. 'Well, not quite that, no. There's a little more work needed before we have the case ready for that lot.'

'In that case, let's review things as planned. Preferably with an open mind.'

Rushton sighed inwardly, flicked up a file on his computer, and tried not to sound frustrated. 'All the major suspects are blackmail victims. Robert Beckford is the first.'

'Yes. Skeleton in the cupboard from his army days. Prisoner killed when he shouldn't have been. As far as I can tell, Beckford was just in the wrong place at the wrong time. Most people would have been caught out as he was. Understandably, he concealed it when he applied for the post of verger at Gloucester Cathedral.'

'Is it a strong enough motive for murder? I haven't seen the man, but wouldn't the Cathedral authorities have been sympathetic if he'd simply made a clean breast of it?'

'Possibly. But the key thing is how Beckford sees this. He's far more wrapped up in the job than he expected to be when he took it, and he really loves his little house in the cathedral close – as most people would. As far as he was concerned, Chivers was threatening his whole life. He'd already paid him one thousand pounds and he hadn't the resources to go on paying him the bigger sums which we know would have been the pattern.'

'He's also the only one of the suspects who we know has killed before. He'd seen lots of violence in the Falklands and Iraq, so he might have been more prepared than the others to see the elimination of Chivers as a way out,' pointed out Hook sturdily. He'd liked Rob Beckford, found himself hoping at the end of their exchanges that he wasn't their man, but he had long since learned the danger of letting personal feelings influence professional judgements.

Rushton glanced at his monitor screen. 'Motive and opportunity, then. He was out in his car at around the time when Chivers died. We've checked his story, and he took his wife's sister back to Ross-on-Wye as he claimed, but he certainly had time to meet Chivers and dispatch him in Highnam on his way back to Gloucester.'

Chris flicked up another file, anxious to run through these people and get to the man he was increasingly certain was the one they would arrest. 'The vicar's wife, Karen Lynch. Can we really entertain her seriously as a suspect?'

Lambert smiled. 'Until she is eliminated, we must do

just that. If we disregard Mark Rogers, who claims to have been off his head when he dealt with Chivers, Mrs Lynch is the only one who seems to have known Chivers intimately in a previous life. She says she might even have recruited him as a dealer, when she was an addict and dealing herself.'

Hook said determinedly, 'We've all seen what drug addiction can reduce you to. Karen Lynch is one of the few people who've come through it and made something of her life. More than something, really. The people in the parish think she's a gem and Father Ryan at St Mary's Hostel can't speak too highly of the work she's doing there with addicts and drug-users.'

'The more complete the recovery she's made from what she was, the more she now feels she has to lose,' Lambert pointed out gently. 'She's terrified of being exposed, not just for herself, but for her husband. She feels it would destroy him and the work he's doing in his parish.'

For a seasoned police inspector, Chris Rushton still had an appealing naivety about him at times. He said, 'Surely it would be the Christian duty of everyone in the parish to support her, if all this came out. The sinner that repenteth, and all that.'

Lambert gave him a grim smile. 'The kinds of things addicts do to support their addictions would be a revelation to a lot of people who have led more sheltered lives. I'm not sure they could ever bring themselves to accept a vicar's wife who had been a thief and a prostitute to pay for heroin. But that's irrelevant. It's Karen Lynch's horror at the very thought of such revelations that sets her up as a blackmail victim.'

'But not a very promising one,' Hook said. 'I don't think money is very important to the Lynches, but there plainly isn't very much of it around. I don't see how she would have been able to scrape up the sort of sums Chivers would have been demanding.'

'Which could make her a more likely candidate for his death,' Lambert insisted. 'Her very despair in knowing she couldn't raise the sums he wanted might prompt desperate action.'

Hook shook his head disbelievingly, whilst Rushton said,

'We shall present you in a few minutes with a much more convincing murderer.'

'Mark Rogers,' said Lambert abruptly. 'What do you make of him? Another reformed character, according to his own account.'

'Now a dutiful family man with two charming children. That's according to himself,' said Hook. 'We only have his own word for quite a lot of things. Including his whereabouts at the time of the murder.'

Rushton was looking at his screen and the new file he had flashed up for Rogers. 'Yes. So far, we haven't come up with anyone who sighted him in the pub where he claims to have been drinking on that Friday night. To be fair, everyone agrees that it was very crowded at the time.'

'Even if we come up with a sighting, it won't be conclusive,' said Hook. 'If I were planning murder, I'd have made sure I was briefly in the pub as I claimed to be before or after the event, to establish some sort of alibi.'

Lambert nodded. 'For what it's worth, Chris, I don't think Bert and I trusted a word Mark Rogers said. When we saw him on Thursday, he gave us a cock and bull story about having bought coke from Chivers in the past; probably true, but not strong enough to leave him open to blackmail. When we saw him again last night, he wriggled a bit, then admitted that he'd falsified facts on his application form to BT. Apparently Chivers knew all about that. Rogers also admitted that he'd given him a thousand pounds, not the two hundred he'd claimed at our first meeting. Chivers would almost certainly have been back for more, and Rogers knew it.'

Rushton frowned at his monitor. 'So he had motive and opportunity.'

Hook nodded. 'And a hell of a lot at stake. He's done well since he joined BT and he's got an excellent executive post there. He also has a wife and two children of whom he's genuinely fond. He'd almost certainly be sacked if BT found out that he had lied on his application form – and he wouldn't find it easy to get another post in those circumstances.'

Lambert smiled. 'I didn't take to Rogers any more than Bert did. However, it's a big step from being a cheat and a liar to becoming a murderer. He hasn't any previous history of violence or criminal record. But again we have to remember that desperation can lead to quite uncharacteristic violence.'

Rushton was anxious to get to the suspect who he was increasingly convinced was their man. He put up a new file and looked at it without conviction. 'Michelle de Vries. I haven't seen her and you two have, but on paper she doesn't look like a killer.'

Lambert frowned. 'One of the difficulties of this case is the man was killed with his own weapon. It's possible, perhaps even probable, that his killer didn't meet him with the intention of killing him. There may have been a quarrel which went wrong.'

'But whoever killed him chose an isolated place for the meeting, where violence would go undetected – as it did, for two days and more.'

'We mustn't presume that it was our killer who set up this meeting. It may well have been Chivers. He's been a drug-dealer for years, used to looking for quiet spots for his transactions. He was now a blackmailer, but that too is an activity which has to be conducted in secrecy.'

'But he'd been beaten up and put in hospital only ten days earlier. Surely he would have been cautious about setting up meetings in isolated places?'

'He may have been meeting someone he was confident wouldn't be a threat. More importantly, he'd acquired a Brocock ME 38 and had it converted into a deadly weapon. He probably felt well able to protect himself.'

'So he wouldn't have felt in any danger from Michelle de Vries,' admitted Rushton reluctantly.

'He'd have felt he was calling the shots. According to what some of his victims tell us, the feeling of power was important to him.'

Hook said, 'Michelle de Vries is one of the victims with access to large sums. Chivers must have felt she could be tapped indefinitely, in view of her husband's riches.'

Lambert nodded. 'I'm sure he did. But of course the whole basis of the blackmail threat was that Mrs de Vries was terrified that her husband would discover the secret of her liaison with Guy Dawson. She'd given Chivers two thousand pounds. She's now admitted to us that she felt she couldn't make more payments without her husband wanting to know where this money was going.'

Rushton looked at his screen. 'This man Guy Dawson has been interviewed. He claims to have an alibi for the time of the death, which is being checked out. Frankly, he looks like a sexual con artist who persuades women he's in things for the long term when he's really out for a quick bit on the side. He admitted that he knew his lover was being blackmailed, but denied any connection with Chivers himself and said he was planning to call time on his affair with Mrs de Vries. He's divorced and he certainly wouldn't go to the wall to keep things secret. I think he just wants out of any trouble – I can't see him committing murder to hush up his affair.'

'But Michelle de Vries might,' said Bert Hook. 'She's a cool customer and very determined to make a go of her shop. She's completely dependent on her husband's financial support to get the venture off the ground and intensely anxious that he shouldn't get to know about the Dawson liaison. She also has no alibi for the night of the murder. She claims she was alone at home.'

'All of this may be overtaken by something Bert and I heard this morning,' said Rushton impatiently. He put up his file for Daniel Steele. 'Two men were arrested for assault last night. They were giving a man a beating on the orders of a loan shark, who uses their services quite regularly. But they admitted under interrogation that they were also the pair who put Darren Chivers in hospital ten days before he was murdered. And Bert tricked one of them into revealing who employed them to do that: Daniel Steele.'

There was a pause whilst the pair looked at Lambert to assess his reaction.

Hook said quietly, 'A bent copper who was allowed to leave the service without prosecution. He's got form, even if it's unofficial form.'

Lambert sighed, feeling the excitement which the others felt at the prospect of putting this one to bed, sharing their feeling that if a bent copper was belatedly brought to justice, this would be a satisfactory outcome. 'The two crimes aren't necessarily connected, of course. But there is a strong possi- bility that someone who employed his thugs to do his dirty work might escalate the violence, if his warning didn't have the desired effect.'

'In other words, if Chivers didn't learn his lesson and insisted on coming back for more, Steele might have shut him up for good.' Hook seemed to be reassuring himself that this one was nearly over.

'I think you and I should go and see what Daniel Steele has to say for himself,' said Lambert grimly.

TWENTY-THREE

They didn't give Daniel Steele any warning that they were coming to his house. Surprise was a small weapon, and they were prepared to use every weapon they had against this man.

He lived in a neat modern detached house with a weedless front garden, which was bright with geraniums and petunias and lobelia. It was three o'clock on a warm Sunday afternoon, that hour when two thirds of the nation indulges in postprandial drowsiness, but Mrs Steele told them that her husband was working in the back garden. 'We have some questions to ask him,' said Lambert.

She looked at them curiously as she led them into the little room which she said was her husband's study. 'Not that he does much studying nowadays,' she said nervously. 'It's more of a den, really, where he can lock himself away from the grandchildren and me when the house gets too noisy.'

There was a piano with music on the stand which looked as if it was regularly played, a reminder that hard men could have unexpected hobbies in their domestic lives. On top of it were photographs of a formidable-looking young Steele in rugby kit, of him standing with a slightly embarrassed smile beside his bride in front of a gothic church door, of his grandchildren at various stages of their development, of Steele himself smiling broadly and holding the silver rose bowl from the local gardening show.

The most recent picture showed him with all of his immediate family, in what was presumably the back garden where he was working now, his long arms encircling the shoulders of his two daughters, with the grandchildren holding small tools and smiling obediently in the forefront.

'Apparently most of the most ruthless Mafia bosses are enthusiastic family men,' said Lambert acidly.

There was not a single photograph or any other remembrance of that twenty-year police career which had ended in hasty retirement under clouds of suspicion. Lambert walked across to the small metal filing cabinet in the furthest corner of the room. It was locked, as he had expected. It would be easy enough to get a search warrant, if the man was arrested for murder.

They were sitting patiently by the time Steele came into the room. He looked at them suspiciously, then went and sat down opposite them. 'This must be something important, to bring a chief superintendent into my home on a Sunday,' he said. He nodded briefly at Hook, but otherwise did not acknowledge his presence. He had washed his hands and face when he came in from the garden, but he was still in a short-sleeved shirt, his powerful torso straining against the cotton.

'We wouldn't need to disturb your Sunday, and ruin ours, if you hadn't lied to us on Friday,' said Lambert.

Steele glared back at him steadily, pausing to let them see that he was not to be thrown by this uncompromising opening. 'I didn't lie. I'm ex-job, aren't I? I'd have more sense than to lie to the great John Lambert.' He allowed the slightest of grins to flicker across his swarthy features, to reinforce his sarcasm.

'You will very shortly be facing serious charges. The least of these may be of causing Grievous Bodily Harm to Darren Chivers, a man who was murdered nine days later.'

A gleam of fear in the dark eyes, but no hint of it in the calm, contemptuous voice as he said, 'You should be careful of what you say, Lambert. False accusations can lead to hefty compensation nowadays. And considerable harm to your spotless reputation. I should hate to have to sue.'

'You won't be doing that, Mr Steele. But you will be facing very serious charges in court. Perhaps the most serious one of all.'

'You told me about that sod Chivers being beaten up when we spoke on Friday. I can provide you with chapter and verse about where I was at the time.'

'And I can provide the Crown Prosecution Service with a cast iron case against you.'

'Oh, I very much doubt that, John Lambert. And I shall enjoy—'

'The two thugs whom you employed to beat up Darren Chivers are in the cells at this moment. They were caught red-handed delivering another beating last night and arrested.'

'You forget that I was a copper myself for twenty years. These thugs sound like professionals to me. One of the things about people like that is that they don't bleat about the people who employ them – they know better than to do that. Not that I'm admitting anything, of course.'

'Oh, they're bleating, all right, Mr Steele. Singing for all they're worth, to try to save their miserable skins, or at least cut down their sentences. And it looks as if we shall be able to tell the judge that they have been highly co-operative. They've given us the name of the man who used them last night. And they've told us how you employed them to beat up the late Mr Chivers on the night of June the twenty-fifth.'

'Watch my lips. I'm saying nothing, Lambert.'

The man was good at this, Lambert admitted to himself reluctantly. Steele must by now be really alarmed, and his brain must be working furiously to know what would come next. But his exterior remained calm. His face was frozen into impassivity, his dark eyes stared steadily at his questioner, and his powerful folded arms moved not an inch.

Hook, who had been recording his replies, now looked up and said, 'Where were you on the night of Saturday, July the fifth, Mr Steele?'

For a moment, he was disconcerted. He had been concentrating all his attention and all his venom on the attack from Lambert. This question from an unexpected quarter threw him momentarily off balance. But he recovered, even allowed himself a small smile as he prepared to deliver the answer they would not want to hear.

'I was at work, wasn't I? I was doing nights and the weekend, so I was at the works on that Saturday night. Make a note of that, would you, DS Hook? Ten p.m. to six a.m., I was there. You can check with the man I relieved and the man who relieved me in the morning, if you wish.'

'We've already done that, sir.'

'Then why are you pissing me about like this?'

'Because we have reason to believe you left the premises for a period during that time. For perhaps half an hour or even a little more. It would have been easy enough for you to do so, as you were in sole charge of the premises during that night.'

This man Steele had thought he could dominate was a sturdier foe than he had anticipated. He found himself working hard to convey the derision he wanted as he said, 'And what heinous crime am I supposed to have perpetrated during this highly theoretical absence from my duties?'

'The residence of Darren Chivers was illicitly entered on that night, we believe at around eleven o'clock.'

'So rather than look for a candidate among the local petty villains, you choose to harass a man who was legitimately at work at the time. I don't give a lot for your chances. I should think your clear-up rates are pretty grim, if this is an example of the way you go about things.'

Lambert came back at him now, his voice like ice in the warm room. 'A man answering your description was seen entering the building by a neighbour, Mr Steele. You know as well as I do that we will have no difficulty in getting a search warrant. I should be surprised if we do not find items removed from the flat of the deceased in this room – probably in that filing cabinet over there.'

He did not take his eyes off Steele's face to indicate the cabinet by a glance, and he was rewarded by a flash of fear on the squat features. The man's gaze flashed rapidly, revealingly, to the cabinet and back again, and Lambert knew he had scored a bull's eye. He said quietly, 'It's time to come clean, Danny Boy.'

The old police nickname rang like a knell in Daniel Steele's ears, reminding him that he could expect no quarter from these men, that the things he had done as a bent copper were stacked against him now.

He licked his lips, forced himself to speak evenly. 'All right,

I'll admit it. The bastard had been blackmailing me. He knew some of the villains I'd dealt with during my police days, some of the drug dealers who'd given me backhanders to turn a blind eye. Chivers had the evidence in his flat and he was threatening to reveal it to my boss at Gloucester Building Supplies. I removed it, that's all.'

'Having removed him on the previous night.' Lambert nodded, as if completing a complicated tale to his satisfaction.

'No! I didn't kill him! You're not pinning a murder rap on me, Lambert! I told you on Friday, I was at work when he was killed.' Steele could not disguise his fear now. He was leaning forward with his hands on his desk, his dark eyes wide with alarm, almost imploring them to believe him.

Lambert regarded him with undisguised distaste. 'We know you had Chivers beaten up and put into hospital nine days before he died. You have just admitted that you illegally entered his flat and removed incriminating documents on the night after he died. You could have left your post at Gloucester Building Supplies for half an hour or more on Friday night, exactly as you have just admitted to doing twenty-four hours later.'

'But I didn't! I didn't kill the bastard.'

'You have lied to us consistently throughout this investigation. There is no reason why we should believe this latest lie, any more than the others.'

'Look, I didn't kill the sod. I want a brief.'

'You're going to need one, Mr Steele. You're going to need a very good one.' Lambert stood up, looked at the photographs on the piano, then glanced briefly out of the window at the innocent Sunday afternoon scene in the suburban street outside. 'I suggest you put your house in order, whilst you have the chance. Don't leave the area. You will be informed of the exact nature of the charges against you very soon.'

Sometimes Lambert thought he was a better grandfather than he had been a father. When his own children were small, he had been preoccupied with his job, not so much anxious for promotion as simply to prove to himself that he could do it, could win what sometimes seemed to him a very personal battle against serious criminals and what they did to pleasant, ordinary people.

His own children had suffered as a result. It had been left to Christine to give them the love and the concern and the sheer hard work that went with parenthood. He had meant well, had usually been able to come in and do the right things in a crisis, but it was Christine who had expended the time and the relentless effort which had been the basis of the family. His two daughters both thought the world of him and he knew that – sometimes, indeed, he felt guilty that they should turn so instinctively to him when things went seriously wrong, when it was Christine who had put in the work and deserved the attention.

There was no crisis today. Caroline was chatting happily with her mother in the kitchen, whilst Lambert played with her two sons in the garden. They had a tennis ball and Lambert was patiently trying to teach them to catch it. He threw the ball a gentle five feet to the four-year-old, congratulating him extravagantly each time he managed to hang on to it, whilst the infant clutched the ball to his chest and smiled delightedly. Then he threw slightly more difficult lobs to the six-year-old, making sure that he caught his due share, well aware that no male child could afford to be upstaged by a younger sibling.

He found it no problem now to put the Chivers case completely out of his mind for an hour or two, whereas as a younger man he would have found that impossible. He took the boys to the shed and unearthed the small watering cans which had been specially purchased for them. Then they filled them from the outside tap and he watched the earnest faces, the small tongues delicately traversing the lips, as they poured the water with slow care over plants which did not need it.

But the greatest treat was still to come. His grandchildren's urgent small hands tugged his larger ones impatiently towards the small square at the end of the vegetable plot which had been designated theirs at the beginning of the season. Six-year-old George was allowed first to admire, then to select and extract one of the lettuces which he had sown in a tiny row nine weeks earlier. Then, with much impatient advice from George and a modicum of assistance from his grandfather's hand-fork, young Harry extracted six of 'his' brilliant red radishes, which had developed so marvellously since he was last here.

Christine received these trophies in suitably wide-eyed wonder in the kitchen. She explained how they would be added to the salad which she and Caroline were preparing for tea. Half an hour later, the infant faces were filled with that childish delight which has no parallel, as the adults assured them that they had never tasted lettuce and radishes of such surpassing excellence.

Lambert had enjoyed the old days, when he and his son-in-law Martin had washed the dishes together after the meal and enjoyed a little innocent male bonding. Now he urged the other three adults out into the garden to supervise the children and enjoy the sunshine, whilst he stacked the dishwasher methodically but automatically. It was this undemanding process which allowed his thoughts to turn back again to the events of the day and what they had added to the Chivers case.

It was the aural as well as the visual memory, the recall of a small, agonized face saying, 'I'd everything at stake, DS Hook,' which set his mind racing towards a conclusion. Bert Hook picked him up twenty minutes after his phone call.

TWENTY-FOUR

Their route took them through Highnam. They stopped for a few minutes near the place where Darren Chivers had died nine days earlier, whilst Lambert explained his thinking to a sceptical Hook.

Then the car eased slowly, almost reluctantly forward, as he drove with excessive care through the city of Gloucester and out towards the suburb he did not want to reach. To kindly Bert Hook, the weather on this warm summer evening seemed unsuitably, almost mockingly, benign. The sun was setting behind them over the Welsh hills; it bathed this part of the city in a soft, seemingly benevolent, light. There was scarcely a breath of wind and the few white clouds were high and unmoving, so that the wide expanse of the Severn carried scarcely a ripple when they crossed it. There were few cars about, so that in places the landscape looked almost as it might have done centuries ago, when masons were raising the mighty elevations of the cathedral which still dominated the modern skyline.

They never reached the vicarage which was their intended destination. Karen Lynch was helping an elderly man in shirt sleeves and braces to tidy up a neglected grave beside the low stone wall of the churchyard. She looked up as Hook pulled up alongside her.

'Working late,' Bert Hook said to her, cursing himself for the cliché, uneasy as he had never been before in a situation like this.

'I like to keep busy,' said Karen Lynch. 'We'll go into the church,' she said, looking up at the Gothic arch of the entrance and the steeple against the blue of the sky above them. 'It's time that it was locked up for the night, anyway.' And they knew in that moment that she realized that it was over for her.

She walked five yards ahead of them, holding herself erect, taking care to limp only slightly, which she knew she could do if she shortened her step a little. She did not look over her shoulder to make sure they were following, nor speak to them again.

They were conscious as they followed her of the old man standing very still above the grave she had worked on with him, his gnarled hands clasped around the top of his spade.

Karen led them into the cool dimness of the church and locked the door behind them with steady hands. She said as if it were the conclusion of some arcane religious ritual, 'We shan't be disturbed now.' She did not hesitate, but marched slowly down the central aisle of the church, the one where she had walked two years ago to be married to Peter Lynch. John Lambert followed dutifully behind her, sliding into the front pew of the church alongside her as if this was exactly what he had expected. Bert Hook moved with soft policeman's tread up the side aisle, taking his place on the bench on the other side of her, as if it was perfectly natural that she should be flanked thus by the two large men who had come here to end this.

She was calling the shots, arranging the moves for this final act of the drama like some confident, experienced stage director, and they were content that she should do so. She looked straight ahead, at the altar and the carnations she had set there on the previous day, not at the instruments of justice on either side of her. 'How did you know?'

Lambert said quietly, 'You were the one with most to lose. You insisted on that yourself.'

'I don't know any of the other suspects.'

'No. Well, all of them had a lot at stake. Any one of them might have acted desperately. But they were acting as black-mail victims usually do in the early stages. They were paying up, meeting his demands, and hoping against hope that he would keep his word and not come back to them.'

'That's what happens, isn't it? You hope you can buy him off.'

'It never works. Blackmailers always come back for more.'

'I suppose so. But I wasn't able to test that out. I didn't have the money to meet even his first demand. He wanted five hundred and I couldn't raise that.'

'Yes. When you told us about the five hundred yesterday, you said that you hadn't been able to scratch together more than two hundred. We've heard a lot of lies and half-truths from a variety of people in the last week, but I think both if us believed that.'

'I told Darren I could never raise the money when he first came to me. I don't think he believed me. He thought I was still the old Karen from that other world, the woman who would have lied and thieved and done whatever was neces-sary to get his money. He didn't believe I'd changed. He didn't believe in all of this.' She didn't take her eyes off the altar, but they knew that she meant much more than this physical symbol, that her phrase comprehended her new husband and each minute of the working and domestic life she spent with him.

Bert Hook spoke for the first time, sounding more like a supporter than an opponent in her ears. 'So we had to ask ourselves what the consequences of failing to raise the money would be for you, Karen.'

'I expect you did, yes.' She turned and looked at him for the first time. 'I never looked at it from your point of view.'

Hook smiled, knowing her resistance was over, helping her along as willingly as if she had been an inexperienced fourteen-year-old. 'Of course you didn't, Karen. You had problems of your own. But you chose the wrong solution, didn't you?'

'I couldn't see any solution at all.'

'But murdering someone wasn't the answer was it? Even when that someone was a blackmailer.'

'I didn't murder anyone, DS Hook.' She spoke with a surprising, unreal calmness, even allowing herself a smile that a friendly man like this could think such things of her.

Hook frowned, then quietly insisted, 'You killed him Karen, on that Friday night in Highnam. There's no getting away from that.'

'And I wouldn't want to get away from it, DS Hook. That's what happened all right.' She looked back at the altar, at the brass rails she had cleaned so recently. It seemed months, not days ago, now. 'It's all finished, this, isn't it?'

'I think you'd better tell us exactly what happened, don't you?'

'Yes. Yes, that would be the best idea. I somehow felt you knew it all, but that can't be so, can it?'

'You arranged to meet him in Highnam, didn't you? Arranged to meet him where it would be quiet, so that you could get rid of him.'

'No, it wasn't like that at all. You make it sound as though I set out to kill him, and I didn't do that.'

'Tell us how it was then, Karen. Tell us how that meeting was set up.'

'Darren contacted me again when I was leaving St Mary's Hostel, a week after he'd told me he wanted five hundred pounds from me. I told him that I hadn't got the money, that I didn't see how I'd ever get it. He said that I'd have it by Friday night, or he'd turn up at the church at the weekend and let them know about the real Karen, the Karen Burton he'd known in the old days. He said I'd get the money somehow – I think he remembered that other Karen, who'd have done anything for her next fix, and thought I'd thieve for it.'

'So you agreed to meet him on that Friday night.'

'Yes. It was he who suggested Highnam, and I realized

that blackmailers want quiet spots for meetings just as much as their victims do. I couldn't see how I was ever going to go there with the money, but I went because I couldn't bear the thought of his coming here. I changed into jeans and put my trainers and my cycling gloves on and rode out there on my bike.'

'And what happened in Highnam?'

She had no hesitation. Describing the scene she had relived so many times in the hours of darkness was a relief, not an ordeal. 'I told him that I hadn't got the money, that I didn't see how I could ever get it. Darren wasn't like I remembered him in the old days.' She was silent for a moment, recalling the nightmare world of addiction she thought she had left behind her, which Chivers had brought back to her so vividly. 'He was truculent, enjoying the feeling of power over me that his knowledge gave him, enjoying insulting me, rubbing my face in the dirt.'

'And you lost your temper with him.'

'No. It wasn't anything like that. If anything, he lost his temper with me. He told me I'd have to thieve to pay him off. That there must be money somewhere around the church that I could get my hands on. I told him that I didn't do that sort of thing any more, that I couldn't do it any more. He said I'd been prepared to fuck for the next fix in the old days and that he was sure the ladies of the parish would like to know all about that. I'm not sure how much I believed it, but I said that I didn't really think he would do that. I said it would ruin my life, but it wouldn't bring him any money.'

'And how did he react to that?'

'He pulled out this pistol and said that it showed he meant business. He seemed very proud of being armed. I don't think Darren had ever had a weapon like that before. I said that I didn't believe he'd ever use it on me, that killing people wasn't his line. I think I believed that. I certainly tried to sound as if I did.'

'And what did Chivers do?'

'He told me not to push him. He held the muzzle of the pistol against the side of my head and told me not to push him.' She moved her hand slowly up to the spot on her temple, touching it gently with the tips of her fingers. 'I couldn't

stand that. It was something that had never happened to me
before. I could only feel the steel against my head and I
panicked.'

She fell silent, as if the recollection of that horror had
suspended speech in her, so that Hook had to prompt her
gently again. 'What happened when you panicked, Karen?'

She stared at the altar and the high Victorian stained-
glass window behind it. You could see the colours and the
design more clearly now in this soft evening light than when
the morning sun poured through it so dazzlingly, she thought
inconsequentially. 'I know I twisted round and flung up both
my hands to get hold of that pistol. I remember wrestling
with him, dragging the muzzle away from my head, putting
all my strength into pointing it away from me. Then it went
off.'

'You pulled the trigger?'

'I don't know. I can only remember my hands on his as I
screamed at him and wrenched the pistol away from my head.
But it doesn't matter, does it? I killed him, didn't I?'

The men on each side of her knew that it mattered very
much indeed, that murder had already been replaced by
manslaughter, that in due course a lawyer would no doubt
plead self-defence to a sympathetic court. But this was not
their business. Lambert spoke again. Like the high priest
concluding some solemn religious ritual, he quietly
pronounced the formula of arrest, whilst the three of them
listened to this ceremonial epilogue to the story.

She unlocked the door of the church and stepped outside,
looking up at its high elevations, feeling the incongruous
warmth and brightness of the evening sun on her back. She
was a prisoner now, but she was still controlling the steps in
this bizarre and tragic pavane, so that the big men on either
side of her stopped with her and waited patiently for the next
move. 'It's over, isn't it?' she said quietly.

'The agony and the deceit are over,' said Bert Hook, feeling
like a father-confessor. He had liked this woman from the
start; he now felt a ridiculous and totally unseemly sort of
love for her. 'But your life here isn't. Chief Superintendent
Lambert and I aren't lawyers, but it's my belief you'll be back
here, carrying on the work you've begun. Probably much
sooner than you think.' He was glad that he didn't hear the

warning cough he'd expected from John Lambert. He sensed instead an unspoken approval from that grave, reserved figure on the other side of their prisoner.

She glanced at Hook sharply, then turned away from the church. The old man who had been working on the grave was preparing to go now, his work concluded for the day and his spade over his shoulder. He watched the trio curiously as they moved away from the church gate and towards the car which would take her to the police station and formal charges. She paused by the door of the car and said, 'Can I have two minutes with Peter?'

They all knew it was irregular, but Lambert didn't waste time voicing the thought. 'Does he know?'

Karen Lynch shook her head. 'He knows something is wrong for me, but I haven't told him. I don't know how much he's guessed. It's the first secret I've ever had from him.'

On that simple, banal thought, her control should have broken and the tears should have gushed, but her face remained like stone.

Lambert said, 'We'll have to come into the house with you, but you can have your two minutes alone.'

They sat in the front room with its cheap furniture and its conventional prints. It was warm with the full blaze of the western sun. Lambert went and opened a window and the two men stood gazing at the deserted street outside, hearing the low, continuous murmur of voices from the rear of the house.

They gave her five minutes, not two. But just when they were considering how to interrupt the pair, they appeared together in the doorway, their arms around each other's waists, their faces unashamedly flowing with tears. Peter Lynch said, 'She's coming back, isn't she? I've told her she's coming back.'

'She'll be back,' said John Lambert gruffly. Then, as they prised her away from him at the front door, he found himself adding, 'I expect she'll be back quite soon.'

They drove past that more massive and impressive religious edifice, the Cathedral of Gloucester, where Robert Beckford was no doubt going about his Sunday evening business. No words were spoken, but Bert Hook found himself hoping that this ancient, unchanging assertion of

Christian faith would be some sort of comfort to the woman who sat so quietly beside Lambert in the back of the vehicle.

But it was the image of the Reverend Peter Lynch, standing erect but now solitary in the doorway of his vicarage, which would remain with the three people in that police car through the night.